What Others Are Saying about
Diana Wallis Taylor and *Lydia*...

"*Lydia, Woman of Philippi* is a biblically inspired story that, although set centuries ago, is a timeless and engaging fictional read filled with intellect, courage, and faith that will resonate with today's readers. With rich detail and historical accuracy, author Diana Wallis Taylor places readers right in the middle of this moving tale. As a single mother who, just like Lydia, faced one unknown after another, I cheered for Lydia as she persevered along each step of her influential journey, making such an impact that even today we view her as an inspiring heroine and a brave woman of God."

—Roxane Battle
Author, *Pockets of Joy: Deciding to Be Happy, Choosing to Be Free*

"*Lydia* is a compelling biblical novel that paints the backstory of Philippi's seller of purple in rich cultural and occupational detail, engaging the reader both spiritually and emotionally."

—Eleanor Gustafson
Author, *The Stones: A Novel of the Life of King David*

"Biblically and historically accurate, Diana Wallis Taylor brings us yet another poignant and adventurous tale, this time in the picturesque novel *Lydia*. Readers will find themselves temporarily transported to another place and time—and permanently changed as they walk beside this young widow whose faith guides her through every test life throws her way...and transforms her into a beautiful woman of God."

—Loree Lough
Bestselling author of 115 award-winning books

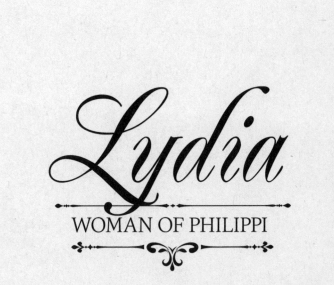

Lydia

WOMAN OF PHILIPPI

Diana Wallis Taylor

Lydia

WOMAN OF PHILIPPI

WHITAKER
HOUSE

Publisher's Note:
This novel is a work of historical fiction and is based on the biblical record. References to real people, events, organizations, and places are used in a fictional context. Any resemblance to actual living persons is entirely coincidental.

Bible quotations from Psalm 56, Psalm 118, and Isaiah are taken from the *New King James Version*, © 1979, 1980, 1982 by Thomas Nelson, Inc. Used by permission. All rights reserved. Bible quotations from Psalm 19, Psalm 23, Psalm 66, and Psalm 113 are taken from *The Complete Jewish Bible*, © 1998 by David H. Stern. Published by Jewish New Testament Publications, Inc. Used by permission. All rights reserved.

LYDIA, WOMAN OF PHILIPPI

Diana Wallis Taylor
www.dianawallistaylor.com

ISBN: 978-1-62911-896-3
eBook ISBN: 978-1-62911-897-0
Printed in the United States of America
© 2017 by Diana Wallis Taylor

Whitaker House
1030 Hunt Valley Circle
New Kensington, PA 15068
www.whitakerhouse.com

Library of Congress Cataloging-in-Publication Data (Pending)

1 2 3 4 5 6 7 8 9 10 11 ⨃ 24 23 22 21 20 19 18 17

To bold women everywhere who are willing to step out in the face of all odds and serve our risen Lord. And to my daughter, Karen, who herself persevered in difficult times and whose insights have greatly helped me in my writing through the years.

1

The day after her fourteenth birthday, Lydia sat in the inner garden of her family's villa on the outskirts of Thyatira, watching Yorgos the gardener work among the herbs. She looked around at the stone gods placed by her father in between the pillars and sighed. While her father was Roman, her mother, Sophia, a Jewess, had unobtrusively brought Lydia into her own faith. Even as a child, Lydia had wondered how anyone could worship a god made of stone who could not speak or see.

The morning sun warmed her as she quietly committed her day to Adonai, the Jewish God she had taken for her own. She recognized His peaceful presence from the synagogue where her mother was able to take her when her father was out of town. His word, read from the ancient scrolls, lifted her heart, and the words to the sixteenth psalm read on the last Sabbath ran through her mind again.

I know the Lord is always with me.
I will not be shaken, for he is right beside me.

Her reverie was interrupted by an angry voice from inside the villa. It sounded like another tantrum from her ten-year-old brother, Cassius. Instinctively, she rose and entered the main room of the villa. Cassius stood with his feet planted in front of their mother, his chin lifted in defiance.

"It is foolish to follow a god one cannot see. I am going to be a soldier like Tyrimnos and have a horse. Tyrimnos is the god of soldiers." He glared, daring his mother to disagree with him.

Seeing the anguish on Sophia's face, Lydia wanted to shake her brother for causing their gentle mother such grief. Cassius's temper tantrums often got him his way. If their mother tried to discipline him, he prevailed on his father, Atticus, who seldom sided with Sophia where his son was concerned.

Lydia drew back into the shadow of a pillar. Sometimes she resented Cassius. She had been the only child for four years before her brother was born, indulged by her father. But now, with a son to carry on his name and business, her father was beside himself with pride, and spoiled Cassius outrageously. Her mother's gentle remonstrations were ignored.

Cassius was terribly self-centered, Lydia decided. Not even six months ago, her father had proudly taken his son to the dye works to show him the family business that gave them their wealth. Cassius had balked, complaining loudly about the smell of the vats, and made such a scene his father quickly brought him home. Lydia overheard her father relate the incident to her mother, but his conclusion was that Cassius was just too young. "Surely," he had said, "my son will react differently when he is older."

This morning after breakfast, Cassius and her father had gone to the temple of the ancient sun-god, Tyrimnos. When they returned, her brother talked nonstop about the impressive statue of the god sitting on his horse while holding a double-headed battle-ax. Now this outburst.

Sophia listened, but her gentle voice was firm. "We will speak of this at another time, my son."

A pleased smile crept across Cassius's face. He had gotten away with his bluster again.

When he turned and swaggered from the room, Lydia went to her mother and put her arms around her. Reverting to the tender

Jewish term for her mother she used only when they were alone, she murmured, "Ima, I'm so sorry. He has hurt you."

"No daughter, he has hurt himself. I cannot change him, though I have tried. He will follow your father's Roman gods, though your father gives them only token worship. I have taught both of you of Adonai, from the time you were very small, but his Roman tutor, Sophos, holds sway over his mind."

"Cassius always does what he wants. Papa doesn't see it."

Lydia looked up into her mother's face and saw her eyes mist with tears. "I will not forsake our God, Ima. He hears my prayers. I feel His presence when I am praying."

A smile slowly spread across Sophia's face, softening the sadness in her eyes. "You are a blessing to me, Lydia. Yes, He hears your prayers and has a purpose for your life. I have always felt that."

Warmth filled Lydia at her mother's words.

They went out into the outer garden and sat on one of the stone benches. The warm spring sunshine flooded the plethora of flowers in every hue and shade. Butterflies in small bright flashes of color flitted from blossom to blossom. They sat quietly for a moment, listening to a bird trill his heart out from a tree nearby.

"Ima, now that I am fourteen, my father will be choosing a husband for me, will he not?"

Sophia turned to her and smiled. "Is that what occupies your mind these days?"

Lydia knew that, now she was of age to be betrothed, it was her father's duty to choose a husband for her. She let her mind dwell on a young man by the name of Stephen who smiled at her in the synagogue and even stopped to speak to her on occasion. When her mother noted this one Sabbath, Lydia blushed. She didn't tell her mother how much the young man was in her thoughts.

"My friend Nita is betrothed, but she has not met her husband-to-be. He is from a part of their family in Laodicea."

"I'm sure your father will choose someone from here in Thyatira."

"You were able to choose your husband, Ima."

"Those were unusual circumstances, Lydia. Your father's father, Thanos, was a prominent citizen and my father worked for him, selling the beautiful purple fabrics."

"But when my father came with my grandfather to the shop that day, you met him."

"True. But I was rarely in the shop. I stayed in the background. Thanos did not know I kept the books for my father. After my mother died, Papa needed the help, so I quietly did the bookkeeping. People only knew me as Ezra's daughter.

"That day there were no customers in the shop and I came out from the back room to ask my father about something. I heard a sound and turned to find Thanos and your father standing there. Atticus was staring at me." Sophia's voice was wistful. "He was tall...and handsome...it was as if a storm struck both of us. Love was something I was told came after marriage."

"I'm sure he found you very beautiful, Ima."

Sophia smiled. "His open admiration made my father uncomfortable. Perhaps he sensed trouble even then. After that day, Atticus's pursuit of me was relentless." She shook her head, remembering. "My father wanted me to marry someone of our faith, and Thanos did not want his son to marry a Jewess."

"That is what is so wonderful, Ima. You and my father were able to marry in spite of the reluctance of your father and his father. I don't remember the rest. How did my father win over Grandfather Ezra?"

There was a deep sigh from Sophia. "Papa was angry that I would even consider a Gentile. Yet he depended on Thanos for his living. He knew his decision could cost him his livelihood, but still he stubbornly refused Atticus. Then your father began to study Judaism and professed to believe in the Jewish God. He seemed so sincere that my father, somewhat mollified, believed Atticus had embraced Judaism." Sophia lowered her voice. "Atticus did not tell his father what he was doing."

"So Grandfather Ezra gave his consent."

"Yes, I was so miserable at his decision to deny Atticus, he could not stand my unhappiness. He finally agreed."

"But my father never speaks of your faith."

"There was no need. He'd gotten what he wanted and abandoned all pretext of studying Judaism."

Lydia shook her head. "Grandfather Ezra must have been upset."

"Oh my, yes. Your grandfather was furious at being duped. He would have nothing to do with us. It took your birth to bring about some reconciliation. Your grandfather loved you, and in turn, Cassius, when each of you were born. You were the delights of his life."

Lydia thought of her Grandfather Ezra. Although he died when she was seven, she remembered his smile when she came to visit, a smile that crinkled his eyes. And his story-telling. When they went to see him, he gave them kosher candy he kept on hand for her and Cassius and always insisted that her mother make the special candy apples for the holiday of Sukkot, the Jewish Feast of Tabernacles that came in the fall.

The face of Stephen came to mind again. "I wonder, if I wanted to choose someone my father did not approve of, would he consider the marriage?"

Sophia shook her head. "Your father loves you dearly, Lydia, and he has indulged you on many things as his only daughter, but on that matter, I doubt that he would bend. He likes things to go as he plans."

Stephen was Jewish. If his father came to their home to ask for her, her father would refuse him. She shook her head. A daydream was one thing, reality another. She liked Stephen but he had not indicated in any way that he wanted to choose her. Stephen was Orthodox and Stephen's father would choose a girl from a proper Orthodox family for him. Still, she had her dreams. Once she had dreamt that she and Stephen were standing under a canopy. She pushed the troublesome thoughts away.

Her mother was looking at the garden, and Lydia interrupted her thoughts again. "Ima, your father gave his consent, but how did my father get Grandfather Thanos to agree to the marriage?"

Sophia contemplated the question. "I suppose it doesn't matter now that I tell you; it's been many years." She looked Lydia full in the face.

"Your father threatened to go into the army instead of taking over the dye business if he could not marry me. He was the only son and heir and his father was furious. When Atticus held his ground, Thanos finally gave in and reluctantly gave his consent."

Lydia laughed. "I didn't know that part, Ima." Then realization came. "It is like Cassius. You can see the same thing happening. Is that what makes you sad sometimes?"

"Your brother's tutor has built the army up as glorious occupation." She waved a hand. "Cassius sees himself in uniform riding into battle. Like your father, he is the only son. He must realize his duty lies with the family, since your father has no one else."

"Perhaps my brother could serve his term in the army when he is old enough and then take over the business."

Sophia turned to watch a small bird hop along the wall and then soar off into the blue sky.

"Cassius will probably serve his time in the army when he reaches maturity, but I fear there is more holding him back from taking interest in the business, and your father does not see it."

Lydia considered her father. She loved him deeply and with abandon. Yet her father could be as willful as Cassius. He, too, had grown up as an only son and while he had finally assumed the dye business from his father, she wasn't at all sure that would be the case with her brother.

They sat there in silence for a while. Lydia knew her parent's marriage was extremely difficult for her mother at times, but Lydia had seen her father look at her mother when she was busy sewing. It was a look of love.

"I pray my father will choose someone I can be happy with," Lydia suddenly blurted.

"So it *is* marriage that occupies your mind these days." Her mother's voice was teasing. Then, more seriously, "I'm sure your father will choose wisely for his only daughter. But enough of this now." Sophia rose and turned toward the doorway. "Let us see how Iola is doing on the weaving. You must continue your lessons on the loom."

Lydia frowned. "Iola is always so cross. It is hard to pay attention when she instructs me."

Sophia raised her eyebrows. "You are the daughter of the mistress of the household and she is a servant. You must show her that you will not allow her attitude. However, I will speak to her."

Lydia reluctantly followed her mother to the weaving room. Iola sat at the loom, her face dour and lips pressed together as she moved the shuttle back and forth.

"Iola, my daughter tells me that you are not happy teaching her the skills of weaving."

The woman looked up, her eyes open in surprise. "I do not mind teaching her, Domina."

"Then can you explain your attitude?"

The older woman bowed her head. "It is the pain."

"The pain?"

"My head. The headaches seem to come so swiftly and I can hardly bear them. Perhaps it causes me to sound cross."

Her mother was instantly alert, for Sophia ministered to the needs of her slaves and was known for her healing skills.

"How long have you had these headaches, Iola?"

"For the last year, Domina. They come and go."

Lydia studied the slave woman's hands, fingers bent and wrinkled with age, and wondered how old Iola was.

"You need to be alert and precise as you insert the colors, Iola. If your head is hurting you cannot be your best and the fabric shall suffer. I am removing you from the weaving room and will assign you to the kitchen. You can help Delia there. I will consider what herbs may be helpful to you for your headache."

Relief flooded Iola's face. "Thank you Domina. I do not deserve your kindness."

Sophia put a hand on the shoulder of her servant. "In the eyes of God, we are all deserving of kindness."

Iola started to speak but closed her lips. It was not for a servant to speak to her mistress about spiritual things. The staff was well aware of the conflict of religions in the master's home.

When Iola left for the kitchen, Sophia sat down at the large loom and patted the bench beside her. Lydia, instantly repentant for her hasty judgment of the slave, silently asked Adonai to forgive her. Then she sat down and watched, fascinated, as her mother skillfully sent the shuttle through the warp and woof, pushing the thread tight against the fabric that was being woven.

After a few moments, Sophia moved over and indicated the loom. "Now you show me what you have learned."

They worked together for over an hour before stopping to have lunch. "You have done well, child. I am pleased. We must begin making more things for your wedding chest."

Her wedding chest. Lydia had happily anticipated this event one day in the future, but now a shadow crossed her mind. When would her father choose her husband, and who would it be?

Lydia and her mother sat alone at the table, for Cassius was with his tutor and sometimes took meals with him. Lydia dipped her bread in wine diluted with water and ate some figs and a piece of goat cheese. A small platter of poached fish sat in the center of the table and Lydia reached for some. Her father was seldom present at lunch, for he was usually at the dye works and took his midday meal there with the workers. He would join his family at dinner and Lydia looked forward to that all day. She wondered if her mother was ever lonely. Atticus kept his family in seclusion. Sophia went to the baths but seldom to other homes for social activities. Only very close friends came occasionally for dinner. Her father's comments led her to believe he was jealous of Sophia's beauty and did not wish to parade her before other men. Still, her mother never complained.

Sophia bore her beliefs and taught her daughter to do the same. Atticus would not permit Hanukkah to be celebrated in the house, nor would he agree to a Passover Seder. But as long as Sophia's religion was not visible to her guests, she was allowed to practice what she believed.

When Atticus was out of the city or otherwise occupied, Lydia was happy to go with her mother to the synagogue. She listened with her ears and her heart as the Scriptures were read from beautifully decorated scrolls handwritten by scribes many years before. She took part in the prayers. She loved the scroll of Isaiah and each time it was read, she felt the words spoke to her.

Behold, God is my salvation, I will trust and not be afraid.
For YAH the LORD, is my strength and song.
He has also become my salvation.

When evening came, Cassius, as usual, dominated the dinner conversation with what he had been studying with his tutor and begging his father petulantly for one wish or another. Lydia bided her time. When Cassius finally went to join his tutor, Lydia and Sophia had Atticus to themselves. Lydia sat at his feet while

Sophia worked on embroidery. He told them about his day—who had come in to buy fabric, and what he had learned at the forum. Sophia was often more aware of the news of the day than he for the women gossiped liberally at the baths and their slaves knew even more than the owners concerning what went on in the city.

This evening Atticus made a casual announcement. "Sophia, you must prepare our table for guests tomorrow evening."

She looked up. "As you wish, my lord. Who are the guests to be?"

"My friend, Claudius, brings his wife, Nona, and his son, Plinius."

Lydia sighed inwardly. Plinius. He had come with his parents many times before and she found him insufferable—vain and self-centered. Though Plinius was older, he and her brother were much alike. While some would call Plinius handsome with his tall, muscular physique and auburn, curly hair, his mouth turned down more than up. His eyes were like dark pools, brooding under heavy brows.

Sophia must have sensed something more to the coming evening. "And there is a reason for this visit, my husband?"

Atticus waved a hand expansively to encompass his wife and daughter. "I have agreed to a betrothal between Plinius and Lydia." He smiled indulgently down at his daughter.

"Plinius, Pater?"

"We have known the family for years. Now that you are of age, Claudius has agreed it would be a good match and to unite our families. He is a childhood friend—are you not pleased, Lydia?" He frowned at her, waiting for her response.

She took a deep breath and glanced at her mother. "We are not the best of friends, Pater."

He waved a hand. "Nonsense. You always got along well."

How could she tell him of the mean pranks Plinius, who was four years older, had played on her? She bowed her head, holding back the tears he wouldn't understand.

He patted her on the shoulder. "Friendship has little to do with marriage. You have been an obedient daughter; you shall be an obedient wife. It is settled."

He was not going to listen to any protests. Lydia knew her father would select her husband for her...but Plinius? For a moment the face of Stephen came to mind. She willed it away and gave an involuntary shudder. Tonight she must pray fervently. She realized that her only hope in the intervening year before the wedding was that Plinius would die of a plague, but immediately felt guilty for the thought.

2

*L*ydia's hopes for Plinius were not realized. He remained strong and healthy. The next time her father was out of town, Lydia went to the synagogue with her mother and found herself walking next to Stephen. A shadow crossed his face.

"I hear you are to be congratulated on your betrothal."

Word had spread already? She nodded. Knowing her response or attitude could cause gossip, she forced a smile on her face. "Thank you, Stephen. He is the son of family friends. I have known him most of my life. He is a fine choice." She hoped she sounded properly enthusiastic.

His perusal of her face seemed to see right through her. "Yes, a family friend. I wish you well in your marriage, Lydia."

There was something in the way he said it. Was he a friend of Plinius? Did he know what Plinius was really like? Was he mocking her? She smiled brightly and moved away to join her mother in the women's section. That day she wondered, because of their rather subdued demeanors, if the people who congratulated her also knew the real Plinius. Was it only her father who was oblivious? She fought back the tears that threatened to spill from her eyes and concentrated on the words of the rabbi who was reading the Scripture for the day from the fifty-sixth psalm:

Whenever I am afraid,

I will trust in You.
In God (I will praise His word),
In God I have put my trust;
I will not fear.
What can flesh do to me?

Her hope was in her God. He had always given her strength and she called on Him now in her spirit to strengthen her for what lay ahead. Only He could lift the weight of sorrow that beset her.

As the year passed, she continued to prepare for her wedding with a heaviness of heart that did not lift, no matter how hard she struggled. She was careful, even with friends, to speak well of Plinius. He was to be her husband and her father was so pleased with the match. When Plinius came with his parents, she was as gracious as she was able and modestly kept her eyes down. She entrusted her private anguish to her God.

She spent time on the loom, weaving the linen fabric for her clothing. Her mother stepped up efforts to make sure she was proficient on the loom and able to weave the fine cotton that was the fabric of the family clothing. Several tunics were woven of various colors for her bridal wardrobe. On impulse one day, she took out the lute she had learned to play but had put away in a small chest in frustration over her inability to play perfectly. Now, as her fingers moved over the strings, she found comfort in the soft, musical sounds.

Each day Lydia was also expected to carefully observe as her mother directed the cook and helpers in the kitchen. She memorized the herbs her mother used in various dishes and helped make the bread each morning under her mother's watchful eye. Even if she had a servant in her new home to do the work, she needed to know the ingredients and consistency of the dough. The year was the culmination of learning the skills her mother employed in running a home and overseeing the servants.

As the day of the wedding approached, Sophia took Lydia aside. "Which of your two handmaids would you like to take with you?"

Lydia thought a moment. "Jael. She's closer to my age."

"Azubah is more experienced, Lydia."

"Still, I would like to take Jael."

"Very well. It is your choice. At least she is trainable. I'm sure Claudius has already installed other servants in your new home."

Lydia nodded. She would be mistress of her home, but the servants would be strangers. *I wonder what sort of servants he has chosen?*

Lydia had finally confessed her feelings about Plinius at a time when she and her mother were alone with no servants nearby to listen.

"I saw your face, and knew, Lydia. I'd suspected that he was not as charming as he seems."

"Is there nothing I can do?"

Sophia sighed. "They are your father's best friends. He is so delighted with the match they have been planning since you and Plinius were small. He would be angry at the thought of offending them. You have no choice, child. He has the right to choose your husband."

A tear slipped down Lydia's face.

"You and Father chose each other."

Sophia put a finger under Lydia's chin and tipped up her face. "Perhaps Plinius has changed as he has grown. You must look on the bright side and trust our God."

<hr>

The morning she dreaded dawned clear and sunny. She awakened, sighed heavily, and stared at the ceiling. Absentmindedly, she fingered the iron ring on the third finger of her left hand. Her feelings did not matter. She would have to do her best to be a good wife to him. The dowry had been agreed to and gifts exchanged and Plinius had given her a perfunctory kiss.

Closing her eyes again, she prayed silently. *Lord, give me courage to get through this day and be an obedient bride.*

Her thoughts were broken as Azubah and Jael entered with Sophia behind them. Her mother was carrying Lydia's wedding clothes, a *tunica recta*, of soft white wool. Lydia fingered the fine fabric and smiled. "It's beautiful."

Jael held the traditional belt of wool that would go around Lydia's waist and be tied in the knot of Hercules, to be untied by Plinius on her wedding night.

With the soft tunic slipped over her head, Lydia sat down at her dressing table. Their preparations would take all morning. Jael began to dress her hair in the ceremonial style required of a Roman bride. When her hair was done, a flame-colored veil was draped over the arrangement. Then, on top of the veil, Sophia placed a wreath Lydia had woven herself from flowers in their garden.

"You make a lovely bride, mistress," Azubah gushed.

Sophia slipped the traditional wool belt around Lydia's waist and secured the knot. While Lydia preferred to ignore the Roman customs, her mother knew that for her father's sake, they must observe them. The Roman guests would expect the traditional ceremonies, as would Plinius and his parents.

Because her father was not in her room to observe, Lydia did not dedicate her childhood locket, her *bulla*, to the *lares*, the gods of their household, as most Roman brides did. She had been to weddings of friends and watched them perform this act. Out of respect for her friends, she remained silent, not wishing to impose her views as a God-fearer nor embarrass her father.

Now, on her wedding day, Sophia put one of her own silver pendants in the shape of a flower around Lydia's neck and gave her two small silver earrings to complete her bridal outfit.

Outwardly, Lydia was ready to face her bridegroom. She took a deep breath and sent a silent prayer heavenward to quiet her mind and compose herself.

As they started down the stairs, Lydia was struck by a beautiful fragrance. She looked around at the house, decorated with garlands of flowers, tree boughs in bloom, and colorful tapestries. The servants had been busy.

Lydia walked slowly toward Plinius as her mother joined Lydia's father. Claudius and Nona, the parents of Plinius, beamed their approval. The atrium was filled with guests including her Uncle Lucadius and Aunt Blandina. It was one of the rare times her aunt and uncle had traveled from their home in Laodicea to Thyatira. She glanced up at her uncle, his face long and thin with a prominent nose. He was not a handsome man, but her aunt was no beauty herself. Overly well-proportioned, she had a look of permanent disapproval on her face.

The guests crowded around the perimeter of the large room, smiling and murmuring.

"A lovely bride...."

"Such a handsome couple...."

As she finally reached the other side of the room, Lydia glanced up into the face of her bridegroom. He looked her over without tenderness, his eyes appraising her in a bold way that sent a chill up her back. She bravely gave him her hand, and together they faced the priest. They each recited their vows and made the expected offering of cake to the Roman god, Jupiter. As she ate her piece of cake, Lydia could not look at Plinius. A flock of butterflies had been turned loose in her stomach, and she struggled to appear calm. When it came time to sacrifice a young goat to appease the gods, it was all Lydia could do to retain her composure. Her stomach churned at the bloody sight and it was only with great effort that she did not run from the scene.

The wedding ceremony completed, Lydia and Plinius turned to accept the congratulations of their guests.

"Come," Atticus cried out, magnanimously waving a hand, "join me in the dining room and refresh yourselves." Small gifts had been placed earlier at each place setting for the guests.

Lydia glanced at her mother, knowing Sophia had more guests on this day than she had ever entertained before. But Sophia smiled calmly as though it were every day she fed a crowd of fifty. Lydia knew her mother had worked for days with the cook to prepare a meal worthy of her daughter's wedding and one that would please her husband. Bowls of dark juicy grapes, plums, and pears added color to the table along with dishes of vegetables: cucumbers and cabbage cooked with lentils and garlic. The succulent chicken was roasted with herbs until it nearly fell off the bone.

Knowing her husband's favorites, Sophia had the cook include roasted pork, which Atticus loved, and a rare delicacy, steamed oysters. When they were served, Lydia caught her mother's eye and nodded. She and her mother followed the Jewish dietary rules, which did not allow pork or shellfish. As unobtrusively as possible, the two women declined those dishes. As the servant offered the pork, Lydia gave a slight shake of her head but happened to glance at Plinius.

"You do not care for pork, Lydia?"

A jolt of fear coursed through her at the disdain on his face. Would he forbid her to follow the Jewish dietary laws as she had from her childhood? She shook her head but was saved from responding by the guest on the other side of Plinius who sought his attention.

Plinius lifted his cup for a servant to refill with wine. By the end of the meal, he'd partaken freely as the guests made toast after toast. Finally, as his father stood up, he rose as well, a little unsteadily, and joined Lydia for the bridal procession to the home his father had obtained for them.

Sophia, following a custom meant to demonstrate her reluctance to part with a daughter, put her arms around Lydia as if to keep her from her bridegroom. Plinius jerked Lydia away, a little more roughly than custom called for.

Plinius went ahead to the villa that would be their home to receive her while his two younger brothers, Hortus and Karpos, walked on each side of Lydia holding her hands. Her brother Cassius followed with the wedding torch made of wound hawthorne branches. Plinius threw nuts, sweetmeats, and sesame cakes to the eager crowd who shouted out bawdy comments and sang rude songs as he passed. Lydia held her head high and walked respectfully with her young brothers-in-law, her parents following along with the guests. Her heart beat wildly as she anticipated what was to come at the wedding couch and steeled herself to face what she must. She'd had three coins. One had gone to Plinius, one was tossed at the crossroads, the third, which she kept, was to be offered to the *lares* of their new household.

When she reached their home, she wound the doorposts with bands of wool and anointed the door with oil and fat from two small containers, handed to her by her mother, as emblems of plenty. Her attendants lifted her over the threshold so she would not trip and bring bad luck to the marriage. As they set her down quickly, she faced her new husband. He met her with another torch and a cup of water as a token of the life they were to live together. Lydia watched his face as he hurried through the duties expected of him, his words slurred.

Lydia kindled the hearth with the torch he offered her and then went to the doorway and tossed the torch to the waiting crowd, who shouted good wishes and then began to disperse.

Plinius closed the door firmly and turned to Lydia, his eyes glittering. Her heart pounded as he untied the knot of Hercules and tossed it aside. He swept her up and deposited her rather unceremoniously on the wedding couch. The veil and wreath of flowers slipped to the floor. He took her swiftly with no endearments or apologies for the pain as he claimed his rights as her husband.

3

*L*ydia walked slowly, the weight of her pregnancy causing her to pause from time to time. Plinius wanted a son and his attitude showed that she could produce no other gender to please him. He had joined the Roman army to serve his required time and relished all the action, preferring the company of other soldiers to his wife. He was seldom home, and she had no doubt, knowing his eye for women, that he found ample female company during the long months away from her.

This afternoon Plinius was due home, but her time to give birth was so close she hoped he would not press himself on her. At the sound of horses outside the villa, Lydia reluctantly made her way to the atrium to dutifully greet her husband.

Plinius strode in the doorway looking tanned and strong in the uniform of a Roman tribune. His father's wealth had purchased the rank for him and he walked with the hint of a swagger.

"Well, I see you have not dropped the child as yet. I was hoping you would have a son to greet me."

She bowed her head slightly. "My time is soon, my lord. The child could be born any day."

He handed his cloak and helmet to a servant and unbuckled his sword. "That would be convenient. I return in ten days."

Convenient? A retort burned on her tongue but she forced herself to remain silent and submissive. Plinius was not pleasant when he was angry.

He did not offer her his arm as they went to the dining room and she moved slowly behind him, sinking down on her cushioned chair as he sprawled languidly on his dining couch.

He eyed the table, laden with fresh apricots and cherries, steamed artichokes with asparagus, and wild grouse. She felt an inward sigh of relief as he nodded appreciatively and reached for some meat from the platter. After two cups of wine, he eyed her curiously. "You are not as appealing when you are so misshapen, Lydia. I trust after my son is born you will regain your former curves."

Tears stung Lydia's eyes, but she would not give him the satisfaction of showing weakness. She merely nodded and ate quietly.

They endured a strained silence for almost a half an hour as she watched Plinius consume cup after cup of wine. Wary of his temper when he had drunk too much, she shrank inwardly. Just then, the pains began.

Arching her back, she cried out for her maidservant. "Jael!"

Plinius jumped up, his face registering alarm. "Take my wife to her chamber. I don't need to view this."

Jael hurried into the dining room with another servant and between the two of them they half-walked, half-carried Lydia to her bed.

Sophia was sent for and came quickly. Pain rolled through Lydia for hours as her mother took turns with the servants, wiping perspiration from her forehead and dipping cloths in cool water to lay across her brow. Athena, the midwife, came and checked her from time to time, urging her to push as hard as she could. Finally, when Lydia felt she could no longer bear the pain, the child slipped from her body.

"Mistress, you have a daughter," Jael said softly. The midwife cleaned up the baby and wrapped it in a linen cloth. Sophia took the child and gently placed her in Lydia's arms. "She is small but very beautiful. What will you call her?"

Lydia was momentarily filled with joy. A girl. A girl she could teach weaving and other skills. A girl would remain with her and not go off to school as a boy would. Then reality sobered her thoughts.

Plinius wanted a son. Lydia knew he would not be pleased. She considered how he might react. What would he do? Fear ran through her. Would he force her to get rid of the child?

Plinius was called into the room and as Sophia and the two maidservants stepped back, he stared down at the baby in obvious disgust. "I should have known you would produce a girl."

"Would you deny the child?" she held her breath.

A smile played about his lips as he saw her fear. He rubbed his chin with his thumb and forefinger as if to debate the idea.

"A daughter might be useful for an alliance I have in mind. You may keep the child."

"Thank you, my lord. You are generous." Her heart thumped against her chest until she was sure he could hear it.

"What shall we name her, my husband?"

He shrugged. "Name her what you wish. It matters little to me. How soon can you take up your duties as a wife?"

Lydia stared at him wide-eyed. She turned her head to her mother, silently imploring her to help her.

Sophia drew herself up, balancing firmness with submission. "Plinius, she has given birth. It will take a few weeks to heal."

"Do not overstep your boundaries, Sophia," he murmured and the tone of his voice caused Sophia to take a step back.

He glanced down at Lydia who felt herself shrink into the bed. "You have ten days," he said coldly, "and the next child had better be a son." With a scowl he strode from the room.

Lydia looked after him, tears spilling from her eyes. Then, gazing down at her small daughter, she lifted her chin bravely. "We will name her Marianne."

Sophia put her arms around her daughter. "Our God will give you strength, Lydia. Trust Him."

Athena ministered to Lydia's body with her herbs and poultices, and had her get up to move around the room as soon as she could stand. The fear of Plinius's temper drove Lydia to do her best to recover quickly.

She hadn't seen Plinius since the day Marianne was born. He finally appeared on the eighth day. With both sets of parents present, Marianne was officially named. Plinius appeared bored through the entire ceremony. This time, noting the frowns on the face of his parents, she realized they were aware all was not as it should be.

Claudius took his son aside during the celebration, and Lydia noted that Claudius spoke sternly to him. She didn't know what was said, but dreaded the response of her husband. Plinius did not like to be told what to do.

"I don't want another child so soon," Lydia finally confessed on the ninth day when Athena came to see how she was doing.

Athena took a small packet of powder from her bag. No one else was in the room, the servants having been sent to the kitchen for Lydia's lunch.

"Mix this with some water, my lady. After you have been with your husband, drink the liquid as soon as possible." She gave Lydia a meaningful look.

Lydia nodded in understanding. "Thank you."

When the midwife was gone, Lydia prepared the liquid in a small pottery jar, hid it behind a plant in her room, and waited. As the evening shadows grew long, Plinius was true to his word and came to her. When he had done what he came to do, roughly and without a tender word, he fell at last into a sound slumber. Lydia rose, pain jarring her body, and approached the plant. She took the small jar from its hiding place. As she prepared to swallow the liquid, she hesitated. Was this right? Would God be angry with her? If she had another child, would it not be His will? She lowered the jar and contemplated it a moment, then reluctantly poured the contents in a flowerpot and hid the jar behind the leaves. She lowered herself to a small bench by the window and stared out at the night for a long time, letting the tears she'd held back slide down her cheeks. She loved the psalms of the great King David, and now words from the fifty-sixth psalm came to her mind.

You…put my tears in Your bottle; are they not in your book?
When I cry out to you, then my enemies will turn back;
This I know, because God is for me…in God I have put my trust.
I will not be afraid. What can man do to me?

Her life was in the hands of her God and she would trust Him.

When pain and weariness drove her to the bed, she curled up in a ball as far from Plinius as she could and fell into an exhausted sleep. When she awakened in the morning, to her relief, Plinius had left.

Jael came early, bringing Marianne with her. Her small daughter had been crying for her breakfast. As Lydia took the baby and pressed the small mouth to her, she cringed at the pain that swept through her body. The midwife had told her that nursing drew her womb back and she had thought she was prepared for it. She looked down at the small hand that was pushing against her tender skin and was overwhelmed with love for her child. If Adonai decreed another child, she would accept it. Children would help fill the emptiness that sat like a lead weight on her chest.

4

Marianne was a happy child and, with Lydia's coaching, tolerated the occasional visits by her father. Plinius had little time for his daughter and let Lydia know in every way possible how displeased he was with her lack of ability to bear him a son.

With Plinius absent most of the time, Lydia was free to instruct her daughter in her own faith. She and her mother took Marianne to the synagogue to hear the Holy Scriptures and listen to the cantor sing the words from the psalms. They looked up at the stars at night and at the flowers in the daytime. They sat in the garden and listened to the birdcalls, as Lydia told her child of the God of the heavens who created it all.

"Ima," Marianne asked when she was five, "Why do we have those little people standing in the walls?"

"They are the Roman gods of your father, Marianne. We do not pray to them because they are made of stone and wood and cannot hear our prayers or answer us. We keep them there because your father likes them and we must respect his wishes."

The little girl studied the figures carefully. "I like Adonai better, Ima," she said, then nodded her head for emphasis and took her mother's hand. Lydia's heart sang.

———————

At sixteen, Lydia's brother Cassius became a man in the eyes of the Roman world. He laid his *bulla*, made of two gold pieces on a chain and placed around his neck as a baby, before the *lares* of the household. Removing the crimson-bordered tunic of his boyhood, he put on the pure white toga of a man. Though they were not in Rome, Atticus insisted that his entire household, including the slaves, join in the procession to the Temple of Apollo, in lieu of the Roman Forum. There a small sacrifice was made to the god and a scribe added the name of Cassius to the list of Roman citizens. A banquet followed and Atticus once again prevailed on Sophia to entertain a large number of guests.

Lydia observed her brother's arrogance as he accepted the congratulations of their guests. At the table he spoke animatedly to his former tutor, a retired army captain. It was no secret in their household that Cassius intended to join the army when he reached the age of manhood, to the dismay of his father.

She had listened to her brother and father argue this last year many times as her father tried to engage his son's interest in the dye business that furnished their income. Cassius instead saw himself as Tyrimnos, the figure of the Roman god of battle he worshipped.

When Lydia looked back at her mother, she caught a brief moment of sorrow on Sophia's face. When Sophia saw her daughter watching her, she smiled and quickly resumed the role of a gracious hostess, seeing to her guests.

Both Sophia and Lydia were keenly aware of the motive that lay behind the bold proposal Cassius put forth at the dinner table only a few days before.

"Pater, if you will pay for my rank, it would make things easier for me in the army. It's only for four years. I can learn the dye business after my service."

On that occasion, having gone to her parents' home for dinner, Lydia listened to her brother and saw what her father would not see. It was another lie, to get what he wanted. Cassius had no intention of taking on the dye works. How could she tell her father she'd overheard him talking to his servant and referring to their father's occupation as a "smelly business"?

Lydia helped see to their guests, but she was aware of her mother's obvious relief when the last of them returned to their villas.

⸻

Over the years of her marriage, during the long absences of her husband, Lydia often went to her parents' villa for dinner. Her parents doted on their granddaughter and Lydia was lonely.

This night there were no other guests and toward the end of the meal, Sophia turned to Lydia and, in a quiet voice, said, "Plinius has been gone several months." Her eyes searched her daughter's face. "Have you heard from him?"

Her father, who had refused to accept the fact that he had made a poor choice for his daughter's marriage, impatiently flung one hand in the air. "He is serving in the army, he cannot write all the time. Perhaps he needs greater incentive to visit home."

Lydia sighed. Whenever she came, there were hints that she should have another child, to keep Marianne company. Each time Plinius had been home, her parents' expectant faces told her they were eager for news that she was with child again.

Marianne had been born nine months after Lydia's wedding and in the years since, she often wondered why she had not conceived again. For a while, Plinius came to her bed frequently, determined to leave her with child before he left on his next campaign. He would return each time only to sneer at her in disappointment when he discovered there was still no child expected.

Lydia wondered how she could keep avoiding the issue. She was tired of the pretense. This time she boldly faced her father and told the truth. "It takes two people to create a child. After waiting so long for me to give him a son, Plinius has not come to my bed in a long time."

Sophia gasped and Atticus was taken aback. He opened his mouth and closed it again.

It was Sophia who spoke first. "Why have you not told us this sooner?"

"What was there to say? My husband spends his time with other women and, when he comes home, sleeps in his own room. We share an occasional meal, but in silence. Then he is gone again."

"This is unacceptable," Atticus snorted, then leaned forward and peered at her intently. "What have you done to offend him?"

"It takes little to offend Plinius, Pater. He wed me at his parent's insistence. He has spoken of divorce more than once since I have not provided him with an heir, but does not go through with it. I don't think he wants to be married again. A wife at home, even in name only, appears to be convenient."

Atticus shook his head slowly. "You've known each other since you were children. It seemed a good match to his parents and to us."

"I knew what Plinius was like, Pater. He was cruel to me... pulling my hair, playing tricks. He once put a worm down the back of my tunic. He would pinch me just to hear me cry out and then assume an innocent face when an adult appeared."

"Why did you not speak of these things?"

She sighed. "I was only a child, and he was the son of your best friend. Would you have listened to me? I hoped perhaps Plinius had changed in the years since we were children."

Sophia reached out a hand and put it on Lydia's arm. "You have been brave, daughter. I know you have run your household well and the servants speak respectfully of you."

At Lydia's raised eyebrow, Sophia smiled. "Much is learned from servants, Lydia."

Atticus frowned. "Are Claudius and Nola aware of this situation?"

Lydia thought it best not to mention the cutting remarks from her mother-in-law over her obvious inability to provide an heir for Plinius.

"I see little of them. They too have been anxious for their son to produce an heir. I have disappointed them."

Her father lifted his chin and she saw a flash of anger in his eyes. "It is the will of the gods, how can a mere mortal combat that?" He squinted at her. "Have you made the proper sacrifices to Venus? After all, she is the goddess of the hearth and children."

Lydia glanced at her mother. She didn't wish to lie. Finally, she bowed her head and said with all humility, "I have prayed very hard, Father. Adonai has not granted my prayer."

With a snort of disgust, Atticus turned on Sophia. "It is my fault. I have been weak and have allowed your foreign religion in my home. You do not worship the proper gods, only this Jewish God. That is why this has happened." He pounded a fist in his palm. "No more! You will follow the customs of Rome. I do not want to hear the name of this Jewish God spoken in this house again. Is that clear?"

He had blustered like this before, and as Sophia bowed her head, Lydia wondered if she was praying. Her father accepted his wife's silence as submission. He sat back, a distressed expression on his face, and reached for his cup of wine. Lydia pursed her lips. Once again, her father had seen fit to assert his authority.

They had spoken of these matters enough. She turned to her father and, feigning interest, asked, "Have you had word from Cassius?"

Atticus brightened. "He returns home at the end of this year. Hopefully he has had enough of the army and is ready to settle down and help me in the dye works. The business will go to him when I am gone. It's time he did his duty by me."

"Has he given any indication he is willing to take on the business at last, Pater?"

His shoulders slumped and he glanced at Sophia. "He says the smell of the dye vats give him a headache."

Seeing the sadness on his face, Lydia smiled at him. "I have a surprise. Marianne has prepared a song for you."

It seemed a welcome distraction and Atticus settled himself, peering expectantly at the doorway as Marianne appeared.

Now nearly ten, Marianne was slender like Lydia with tawny golden hair that curled on her shoulders. Her eyes, almost indigo blue, along with her fair skin, foreshadowed the beauty she would become in a few short years. As she observed her daughter, Lydia thought with dread of the day Plinius would arrange a marriage for her.

Marianne's voice was clear and sweet as she sang and Lydia noted the pleased looks on the faces of her parents.

As Lydia prepared to return home, Marianne went to say goodbye to her grandfather on the far side of the atrium. Sophia took advantage of the moment to take Lydia aside.

"Daughter, if there is any way you can persuade Plinius to come to you again, you must try. If he is killed or dies, you have no heir and will be forced to leave the villa to one of his brothers. That is Roman law. I pray you will not find yourself in this position. I am mistress of our villa, but if your father dies, Cassius will be *paterfamilias* and I must depend on my son to permit me to stay. If you could bear a son it would be years before you would face this situation."

Lydia put a hand on Sophia's arm. "I do understand, but there is nothing I can do to force this, Ima." She sighed. "Nevertheless, the next time Plinius comes I promise to make every effort to entice him to be a husband to me."

Sophia nodded and glancing back at her husband, murmured, "I will pray and you must pray also. It may be that our God will have mercy on you and grant you a son."

On the way home in her father's carriage, Lydia glanced over at her daughter who was occupied with looking out the window at the city. Lydia leaned back and considered her mother's words. Her prayers for a son in the years following Marianne's birth had gone unanswered. Plinius often railed at her for her incompetence and uselessness, stalking away in disgust. How many times had she gone into the garden and cried bitterly? How could she remain married to such a man?

5

At the baths the following week, the women whispered together and an undercurrent of fear echoed through the marble rooms. The Roman army was fighting a difficult war over control of Armenia, a client state of Rome from the reign of Caesar Augustus. The Parthians had installed their own king, Tiridates. When Nero became emperor, the Parthians staged a series of revolts in their own country, and the Roman, Tigranes VI, replaced Tiridates. The men returning to their families from this campaign were confident of their control of Armenia.

But the battle call went out again, and the emperor even called up some retired veterans to lead Roman troops. When the men had gone, the faces of the women in the town reflected their fear.

Drusa, married to Hortus, took Lydia aside. "Do you not worry for Plinius? You appear so calm. My father had word that in the battle of Rhandeia, our troops are bearing heavy losses. Was not Plinius in that battle?"

Lydia would not speak of the situation in her home. She spoke only in glowing terms of her husband when the other women were around. No negative comments would find their way back to her father-in-law. There was no use straining their relationship any further than it already was.

"I pray every day for Plinius. I'm sure he will give a good account for himself in battle."

Drusa sighed. "You are very brave. If Hortus were in the army I would die of fright."

Lydia resisted the urge to comment. Hortus was exempted from the army for poor eyesight. Drusa, with her round face and eyes too close together, was not much in the way of a beauty. Lydia felt the girl was just happy to be married. To her credit, she had produced a son for her husband. Her tongue, which prattled on, sometimes incessantly, made Lydia feel sorry for Hortus, in spite of his handicap.

As Lydia stepped out of the warm, soothing pool, Jael met her with a towel. A few minutes later she was stretched out on a table enjoying a massage.

The network among slaves was well-known. Lydia knew they seemed to have the news almost before their master or mistress and Jael was no exception. Lydia asked, "What have you heard about the war in Armenia?"

There was a pause. "It goes badly, mistress. Many soldiers killed on both sides."

Lydia dutifully prayed for Plinius, that he would come to know the God she served, yet as hard as she prayed, she found herself struggling with indifference as to how her husband was faring. Was she past caring whether he was in the middle of the battle?

That evening, her parents joined her for dinner and, steering the conversation to an area of interest to her father, Lydia inquired of the war.

Her father picked up a juicy piece of chicken and popped it into his mouth, then broke a small loaf of bread and dipped it in a garlic sauce. "The troops are in good hands. Gnaeus Domitius Corbulo has been appointed as supreme command of the campaign."

"Is he not the one who distinguished himself in Germania, Father?"

"True, he has been the governor of Asia until now. Troops from Syria including four legions and several units of auxiliaries have been transferred to his command. If anyone can turn the battle in our favor, it is Corbulo."

Most fathers did not share talk of soldiers and war with their daughters, but it pleased Atticus to discuss various subjects with her. He enjoyed her quick mind and intelligent questions.

"Do you fear for Cassius, Father?"

"I have made offerings to the gods daily. I can only hope he will return to us."

"There is much conflicting news about the city, Father. Now we are victorious, now attacking and burning the Armenian capital, Artaxata, now withdrawing."

Later, Lydia prayed for her brother Cassius for her parent's sake, but found herself half-wishing that Plinius would not return. Her subsequent guilt drove her to her knees to ask the God's forgiveness and pledge once again to be an obedient wife—should her husband return.

———————————

Lydia was in the garden showing Marianne some fine embroidery stitches when she heard the voice of her maidservant, Jael, calling to her.

"Domina! Come quickly."

Lydia could hear the fear in Jael's voice as the girl rushed toward her.

Marianne looked up, her eyes wide with apprehension. "Ima, is something wrong?"

"We must find out. Come with me."

They hurried to the atrium where Atticus stood waiting, his face drawn and haggard.

As she faced her father, he put a hand on her shoulder, and glanced apprehensively at his young granddaughter. "You must be brave, daughter. I do not bring good news."

She led him to a nearby couch and he sank down heavily on it. "Father, what is wrong?"

He shook his head slowly. "Plinius is dead."

"He was killed in battle?"

Marianne's small voice spoke behind her. "My father is dead?" The girl had a tender heart and in spite of his lack of attention, he was her father and she loved him. Lydia put an arm around her daughter as tears rolled down Marianne's cheeks.

Atticus glanced at his granddaughter and with a slight nod of his head indicated that Marianne should leave them.

"Marianne, would you go to the kitchen and tell the servants to prepare refreshments for your grandfather?"

The girl nodded in obedience and, wiping her eyes on her tunic sleeve, left the atrium. Atticus took Lydia's hand. "It is worse than you know. They were in a heavy battle and he thought he heard the sound for retreat. He pulled his unit back and they ran from the scene. It was a mistake and the commander was furious. He had Plinius decimated along with a tenth of his battalion."

"Decimated?"

"Killed by his own comrades for cowardice."

Lydia's hand moved to her mouth. *Cowardice?* Poor Plinius. It was a sad ending for his life. Then another thought crept into her consciousness. "What will become of Marianne and me, Father?"

"Hortus is married and already has a villa, but his brother, Karpos, marries soon…and will require your villa for himself and his bride," he answered.

It had been Lydia's home for almost thirteen years and the only home Marianne had known. Yet Lydia could not fight Roman law. She had not produced a son and heir. She would have to leave.

Her father answered her unspoken question. "I've come to bring you and Marianne home."

Lydia glanced around her at the villa. With the exception of Marianne, there were no good memories to leave behind. She thought of the unhappy years she spent there. "I will gather our things," she said calmly.

6

In the months that followed in her parents' villa, Lydia began to find peace in her spirit. The servants spoiled Marianne and there was no dread of a husband coming home. To her chagrin, however, the subject of marriage seemed to occupy her father's thoughts. He felt she should marry again and had inquired diligently for a suitable husband for her.

Lydia was quietly adamant. "I do not wish to marry again, Pater. I am nearing thirty and have only produced one child and no sons. I am not a good prospect for anyone wanting children."

Her father had not been successful in securing a second marriage for Lydia and had waved his hands in frustration as the most recent foray into eligible suitors proved unfruitful.

"What will you do if something happens to me, Lydia? Your brother will have the villa and where will you and Marianne go? She is twelve, old enough to be betrothed. I should be looking for her, not her mother."

"She has two more years. She is young still. Besides, I have something of great importance to ask you."

He paused in his pacing and stared at her. "What is that?"

"Teach me the dye business so that I can be independent and provide for myself and, if need be, my mother."

He gave a snort of disbelief. "The Dyers' Guild would not accept a woman, Lydia. It is a preposterous idea. Besides, Cassius has promised to eventually learn the business."

She put a hand on his arm. "Pater, he has avoided the issue all his life. He doesn't wish to carry on the business. He likes the army and made that clear the last time he was here. The entire household heard your quarrel and his words."

Atticus opened his mouth to speak and then closed it again, his shoulders slumping in defeat. He shrugged and sank down on a chair. Finally, he looked up at her, his eyes sorrowful.

Knowing Cassius had not contacted his family in a year, her father had few arguments.

"Cassius made his decision. I cannot sway him. He is ungrateful for the comforts and luxuries our business has provided for him."

She stood quietly before him, waiting, watching the changing emotions cross her father's face as he contemplated her request.

"You truly wish to learn the dye business? You would not find it distasteful?"

Excitement filled her, but she spoke carefully. "I love the process and the beautiful colors of the fabrics. I would work hard to make you proud of me."

He stared at the floor so long she became impatient. "Pater?"

He stood slowly and put one hand on her shoulder. "Those are brave words, daughter. I will give you six months and see how it goes. If you do well, the business will come to you. If you change your mind, or do not prove worthy, it will go to my brother, Lucadius. We will start tomorrow. Be ready to accompany me after breakfast."

She reached up and kissed him on the cheek. "You won't be sorry, Pater."

He shook his head slowly. "I'm already sorry, but I have no choice. Now go away and let me be, I have some arrangements to make."

She left him and hurried to the weaving room to apprise her mother and daughter of the momentous news.

Sophia stared at her, her eyes wide. "Your father is going to teach you the dye business?

But that is not work for a woman."

"As I reminded father, I am a matron, Ima, nearly thirty. I do not wish to marry again and someone must take over the business one day."

"But Cassius...."

"We both know that is a futile path. He does not wish to take on our father's trade."

"What about Lucadius? Would he take over your father's dye business?"

"I doubt it. He likes being a merchant and dealing in trade and shipping in Laodicea. Consider, Ima—what would happen if my father should die?"

Lydia watched her mother as Sophia sighed and nodded.

"When will you start?"

"Tomorrow morning. I will accompany Father to the dye works after breakfast."

Sophia came and touched Lydia's face with a soft hand. "You are brave, my daughter, and have endured much." She tilted her head to one side. "I believe your father will be surprised."

7

*L*ydia was up at dawn, choosing a simple off-white tunic and a leather girdle. She looked out the window at the pink and gold sky of the rising sun. *Let me be successful, Lord. Help me to learn all I can and not disappoint my pater.* She felt strength in her spirit and drew courage in trusting her God's plan for her.

Jael came and dressed her hair in a simple style—this time she was not dressing for dinner, she was dressing for work. The thought warmed her.

After a hurried breakfast of cheese, bread, and *mustum,* her preferred beverage of grape juice sweetened with honey, she rode with her father in the open cart through the city to the dye works. As they passed through the heart of the industrial area, she smelled the aroma of fresh bread baking in the clay ovens and listened to the merchants hawking rugs of brilliant colors. On one street, leather goods, sandals, and traveling pouches were for sale. Another street displayed the wares of the pottery makers, with bowls, cups, and large platters. Then, glancing down one street, she glimpsed the slave market with men and women from northern Africa, Syria, and other conquered territories standing on blocks to be inspected by ready buyers. She cringed. No one deserved to be displayed in that way. The thought came to her that her handmaid was a slave, but she brushed it away. It was too hard to realize that Jael had been auctioned off like that when Atticus bought her.

They approached the sea where large blocks of water had been cordoned off, according to the rights of the different dye makers. No one wanted to build on the waterfront where the sea shells were harvested, due to the odor.

Her father, who had been mostly silent on the trip, turned to her. "I have spoken with the Guild. Since you are a woman, I have arranged for you to be excused from the meetings. They would not, ah, be helpful to you."

"I would be happy to attend the meetings, Pater."

He coughed. "There are certain, ah, ceremonies that would not be wise for you to participate in. Let us not discuss this further. That is my decision."

Lydia glanced sideways at her father but remained silent. What took place at these Guild meetings that he did not want to have her participate in? She was curious, but knew her father. When he made a decision, it was best to obey.

They reached the workshop by the sea and the slave who drove the horse-drawn cart was sent back to the villa. He would return for them at the appointed time.

Lydia controlled her excitement at the thought of learning her father's business and concentrated on being observant. The workshop was divided into three sections; in one, there was a well that gave them a water supply. A workbench ran along one wall. The second room contained almost fourteen big vats of dye. The third room, closest to the sea, was the largest. There, the spiny shellfish from the sea, called murex, were brought in to extract the purple dye, so popular for the stripes on the togas of senators and the upper class, as well as the emperor himself. The red dye was used for the stripes on the sons of prominent citizens.

Lydia almost had to hold her nose when they entered the room with the large vats of plants. *Cassius did have a point about the strong odor*, she admitted to herself. Her father pointed out the contents of the different vats: alkanet, whose root imparted a red dye, archil from seaweed for a different color of purple, madder root for a deeper red dye, safflower, producing a yellow dye, and woad, which produced a deep blue color, popular with the noble ladies of Thyatira. Lydia realized that the strongest odor came from the woad plants.

Slaves were busy tending the large vats, assessing the depth of color. In an open area, other workers were hanging dyed fabrics on long poles to dry.

As her father began to explain how the dyes were extracted and how the fabrics were dyed, Lydia listened carefully. Her father did not introduce her to each worker, but let them know she was his daughter and was to be treated with respect. An older man approached.

"Master, you have honored us with a visit from your daughter. How can I be of assistance?"

Atticus turned to Lydia. "This is Kebu. He is the overseer for the dye works. He is irreplaceable and knows the business better than I do." The last was said with a smile.

Lydia nodded to him. The man appeared to be Egyptian. His dark eyes twinkled at her. His head was completely bald. Kebu bowed in acknowledgement, and Lydia sensed a strong bond between this man and her father. She knew then that she would try hard to please Kebu, for she sensed he would be very important to her in the future.

Kebu waved a hand in invitation and for several hours she followed the overseer and her father from stage to stage in the processing of the murex, collected from the ocean, gleaning the spiny shellfish from the sea, beating them with iron bars to break the shells. The slimy pile was then left in the sun several hours to let the color mature. One of the lower slaves had to wade into the pile of now-stinking shellfish to sop up the ooze and dry it out. Those who had this distasteful job had purple legs from the dye. Lydia determined that the murex produced the truest purple and wondered whether perhaps it would be wise for the business to concentrate on the purple dye. Certainly it would produce the most wealth for her family due to the thousands of murex that had to be gathered for just one *toga pieta*. But she kept her thoughts to herself.

After she had become somewhat familiar with the basic process, her father prepared to leave the dye works. Kebu bowed again, smiling but contemplating her silently beneath heavy brows.

Her father answered his unspoken question. "My daughter and I will return tomorrow. She is willing to learn the business and you must teach her all you know."

"Yes, master, that will be my pleasure."

They walked into the city and she covered her head with a scarf against the sun. Her father took her to the street of the dye merchants, to his shop where the fabrics were sold. His clients, he explained, were the Roman matrons and slaves who purchased for their household or master. The shop had to be far from the dye works since they would not like the smell. Soft benches with cushions were placed for the Roman matrons and soft draperies covered the stone walls. Lydia watched as a woman examined a bolt of purple cloth. When she had chosen what she needed for her son and husband, she looked with pleasure at the other dyed fabrics in their inviting shades.

A man was helping the matron and Lydia's father waited quietly in the background. Lydia thought the bargaining would go on forever, but the shop manager was shrewd and strove for a good price. When the woman finally left with her purchases, he then turned to Atticus and Lydia.

"Master, this is your daughter?"

"Indeed. Lydia, this is Sargon. He manages the shop for me and chooses the fabrics that come from the dye works."

Sargon appeared to be in his fifties. His skin was bronzed and his beard came to a point down from his chin. A gold earring graced one ear.

"Sargon, I'm teaching my daughter the business, from the dye works to the dyeing and sale of the cloth."

Sargon lifted his eyebrows briefly and a frown crossed his face, but he smiled. "You are blessed above all men to have such a daughter who is interested in what you do, Master."

Lydia wondered if Sargon knew of her brother's reluctance to have anything to do with the dye works for he seemed only momentarily surprised she was learning the business.

She was shown the various fabrics that were folded and placed on open shelves. As she gazed at the beautiful colors, she was aware now of the work that went into the exquisite material. A new appreciation for her father's business touched her heart.

She came home exhausted but jubilant. It was something she could do and it would provide income one day when her father was gone, to provide for her needs and, if her mother was still living, a household for them.

Lydia took time to see what Marianne had been doing that day and inspect her daughter's sewing before bathing herself and dressing for dinner. Marianne was full of questions and Lydia told her all that she had seen. Sophia was more concerned with the faint, unpleasant odor that clung to Lydia when she returned.

"You will have to discard your clothing each day, daughter. How will you handle that?"

"I will not always be close to the dye works. That was only so I could understand what happens there and how the dye is made. A slave, Kebu, manages that part of it quite well. Father says I may be more involved in selling the fabrics."

Sophia only shook her head.

That evening, alone in her room, Lydia thanked Adonai for opening this door for her. The only dark thought was of her uncle.

He had little to do with the dye business but had definite views on women. He would be horrified to learn she was being taught what he considered a man's business. She sighed. Fortunately it was something she did not have to face…yet.

8

As the months passed, it became routine for Lydia to accompany her father after breakfast. They spent time reviewing the dye process; time in the shop; and much time studying the figures and the process of accounting. As factor, Sargon handled all the bookkeeping at the shop and seemed pleased by her quick grasp of the accounts.

The most favorable season for taking the murex was just after the rising of the Dog Star, before spring. Lydia watched the slaves draw the nets from the sea filled with murex. The shells were crushed and Lydia was again amazed at the number of murex that had to be gathered and crushed for such a small amount of dye. Around twenty ounces of salt was added to the thick liquid and it was allowed to steep for three days. Then large cauldrons were prepared for boiling the dye. The dye liquor was skimmed from time to time and with it some flesh that clung to the veins of the murex. A clean fleece was plunged into the boiling dye from time to time to check the color. It was left in the dye five hours and then carded and thrown in again until the dye reached the desired hue of purple.

The process fascinated Lydia. Even though she sometimes had to draw her mantle over her nose due to the smell coming from the vats, she steeled herself to understand fully everything she needed to know. She understood now the process by which the dyes reached their best color and how the fabrics were prepared and dipped to just the right shade and then hung on long drying poles to be later folded and taken to the shop for sale. She knew how much the overseers were paid and learned the best prices of the various bolts of cloth. She observed Sargon carefully from behind a screen as he skillfully handled each transaction. Lydia contemplated how best to deal with this in the future, but soon realized she would not be participating in actual sales. Her father had two capable men to oversee those areas of the business.

One afternoon, when a rather disagreeable matron left, having nearly worn Sargon out by changing her mind numerous times, Lydia stepped out from behind the screen.

"You are the epitome of patience, Sargon. How do you do it?"

"Ah, mistress, the women like to be flattered and cajoled. They know I will give them the best price and that we have the finest fabrics on the street. It is to our advantage to treat each customer with the respect they deserve."

"Then you are a very wise man. You have helped me understand so much."

"You have learned well, mistress, yet you must remain in the background of the shop. The matrons will not allow a woman to wait upon them."

She sighed heavily. "I do understand that, Sargon, but what do I do if my father dies and I am in charge?"

"The gods would say, 'wait until you must cross that bridge.'" He inclined his head. "I will serve you, mistress, as I have served your father. Have no fear."

Lydia felt relief flood her face and relax her shoulders.

"Thank you, Sargon. I am counting on that."

Atticus was nearing fifty-five, but worked as hard as a man half his age. When he developed chest pains one day, he tried to continue to work, but eventually had to be carried home in great distress. As he lay in his bed, the physician tried bleeding him with leeches, but it didn't help. Perspiration dotted his forehead and Sophia and Lydia took turns tending to his needs. Marianne knelt close to her mother, her tear-streaked face a picture of woe. When he struggled to speak, they all leaned forward.

"Daughter, I must speak with you...alone."

Sophia gave her a puzzled look but led Marianne out of the room. When they were alone, Lydia waited.

Barely able to whisper the words without pain, Atticus looked up at her. "I have made arrangements. I will give...Cassius one more chance to take over my business. I do not know what he will do, but you and your mother...will be provided for. The papers... signed. My lawyer here will contact you in the event of my... death. Quintus Licinius. You have met him." He closed his eyes, exhausted by the effort. She remembered the man who was her father's lawyer-agent in Thyatira. Just as she thought he was asleep and got up to leave, Atticus opened his eyes again and reached out to grasp her arm. "There is more. I have a business also in Philippi. Sargon will contact my agent there. There are funds...."

His hand let go of her arm and dropped to his side and his eyes closed again. When she was sure he was asleep, Lydia slipped out to find her mother and daughter. They huddled together outside his room, consumed with worry.

An urgent message had been sent to Cassius to return as quickly as possible. Even then, it was almost six days before he was able to get to the villa, having ridden night and day with another soldier as companion.

Tossing his helmet, sword, and cape to a servant, he strode into the room behind Lydia who had met him in the atrium to apprise him of his father's condition.

"Pater, how do you feel?" It was a compassionate Cassius who knelt by his father's bedside.

Though surprised at his concerned attitude, Sophia and Lydia remained in the background, letting him speak to his father alone.

"Cassius, my son. You have come." Atticus's words were labored and he spoke in short breaths.

"Yes, Pater, my commander gave me leave to return home immediately."

"Will…you remain here now, my son? I need you…take over the dye works. Only son…family trade…tell me you will do this."

Cassius bowed his head and, as he frowned, Lydia saw a glimpse of the old Cassius in the turn of his mouth. She knew what her father wanted to hear, and so did Cassius.

"Let us speak of this when you are well, Pater."

Atticus looked at his son a long moment and then seemed to shrink back into himself. He heard, as did Lydia and her mother, what Cassius was really saying.

Her father's eyes were dark pools of sorrow as he looked at Lydia. "Come, daughter, draw near to me." His voice was stronger.

She obeyed and waited quietly for him to speak again.

"My son will not follow me in my trade. I know that now." He put up a hand when Cassius sought weakly to protest. "You have made it clear. I have been forced to train your sister in all the facets of the business and selling of the cloth in the shop. When I am gone she will take my place."

Cassius looked at his sister in disbelief. "A woman, running the dye works? It is not women's work. I will sell the business first."

Atticus rose up as much as he was able, his eyes flashing at his son. "You will do no such thing. I have already written the agreement and sealed it with my seal. Our lawyer is aware of my wishes and it cannot be undone. If you had agreed to take my place as was your duty, I would have changed it. You have chosen the army and that is your decision. This is mine!" He fell back, exhausted by the effort his words had taken.

Cassius glared at Lydia as if letting her know he would fight her on this when their father was gone. She regarded him calmly, aware her father's decision could not be undone by any effort of her brother. He could not change Roman law.

In spite of the turbulent emotions that ran rampant across his face, Cassius kept a vigil by his father's bedside, leaving only to rest as his mother and Lydia tended to the dying man.

Two days later, the crisis came. Atticus cried out and pressed his hands to his chest, his eyes glazed with pain. When his hands dropped to his sides, Sophia held one and Lydia the other while Cassius stood at the foot of the bed staring down at his father.

"My...beautiful Sophia...my children...I go to my fathers, farewell...." He gave one last gasp and was gone.

Sophia and Lydia wept on his chest while Marianne leaned against Lydia's side, her sobs coming in small gasps. Cassius remained at the foot of the bed, his face drawn and pinched as he bowed his head. Then he suddenly turned and strode out of the room. The servants entered to help Sophia wash and prepare the body, then dress Atticus in his finest clothes. When he was ready, Cassius returned and placed a coin under his father's tongue as payment to Charon, the figure who rowed the dead across the rivers of the underworld. Atticus had belonged to a funeral society, a *Collegia*, and thus, fortunately for Sophia, his burial costs were paid for. While it was the custom for patrician families to allow the dead to remain for viewing eight days, Atticus was not a noble or of any high rank. They waited only until her uncle Lucadius and Blandina arrived.

Lydia's aunt murmured about not receiving the notice in time and how difficult the trip had been. She eyed Sophia as if it was all her fault.

Atticus's cremation took place that night. Some of his prized possessions were added to the bier to attend him in the underworld. His ashes were then placed in an urn to be taken to the *Pomerium*, the burial vaults outside the city.

After all the traditions and rites had been observed, Cassius, Lucadius, and Blandina sat with Lydia and Sophia at dinner. Cassius had been quiet the last few days and earlier, when Sophia walked down the corridor with Lydia to the weaving room, her face told of her inner anguish. "I know not what your brother will do now, Lydia. He is angry at what your father has done. The villa is his by law and only he can decide if we will stay or go."

Lydia put a hand on her mother's arm. "We will be all right whatever his decision, Mater. Father has arranged it all."

Sophia's eyebrows raised, but Lydia put a finger on her lips and shook her head. Now was not the time to speak of it. They entered the dining room for the evening meal. Lydia's heart seemed to be in her throat; something was going to happen, but she did not know when.

Now, as the first dish of fish was served, Lucadius turned to Cassius. "How will you handle the business now? Will you leave the army?"

Cassius almost smirked. "Ask my illustrious sister. Our father has left the business to her."

Blandina gasped and Lucadius could not hide his shock. "A woman running the dye business? Preposterous. What was your father thinking? You must forbid this. Lydia needs to marry and be under the authority of a husband."

"No matter. I had planned on selling it, but Father chose to give Lydia the shop and dye works. It is out of my hands. I return to the army. Now that I have attained the rank of centurion, I prefer the army to riding herd on my father's trade. A smelly occupation

Lydia has taken on. She is welcome to it, if she can handle it." He laughed mirthlessly. "I give her a few months and she'll be ready to sell."

Her uncle turned to Lydia with a tone of disgust. "What do you know about running such a business? The Guilds will not allow a woman to take part."

Lydia took a deep breath and sent a silent prayer to God to give her courage. She lifted her chin and looked her uncle in the eye.

"I have been learning the business daily for the last six months, Uncle. I know how it is run and how the dying is done. I will work behind the scenes, keeping the books and overseeing both. My father has capable managers who have been a great help to me, both at the dye works and the shop. I shall rely on them to continue to do what they have done for my father."

Blandina huffed as she and Lucadius turned to Cassius for his response.

Cassius leaned back, eyeing his sister. His face was hard. "Because I shall return to the army, I will assign two servants to care for the villa until my return. As you wish to remain independent of my authority, I suggest you and my niece find another dwelling." When Sophia began to protest, he added, "Mater, if you wish to side with my sister, you may go also." He spread a hand magnanimously. "I am not without compassion in the event of my father's death. I will give all of you two months." His smile was anything but pleasant.

9

Sophia gazed steadily at her son, but kept her voice submissive. "You have the right to the villa by law, my son.
We will do as you ask."

Lydia bowed her head in agreement, but inside she seethed. He
would be gone, what need did he have to cause them to leave the villa?
At least two months gave her time to make arrangements. She had
visited her father's solicitor and was amazed at what her father had
done. She would share with her mother when the time was right, but
Cassius must not know what her father had planned. Their lawyer,
Quintus, had been surprised by her father's wishes, but made sure all
was in order according to Roman law. He also told her he would contact the other lawyer-agent in Philippi and notify him of her father's
death. When he had a reply, he would let her know.

Her mind whirling with things to do, Lydia merely nodded
in obedience to her brother's command. "We will do as you say,
Cassius."

Lucadius regarded Marianne. "My dear Cassius, have you considered that your niece is of marriageable age? Do you wish me to
seek an alliance for her when you return to the army?"

Marianne, nearly fifteen, remained silent at the table. At her
great-uncle's pronouncement, her eyes widened and she glanced up
at her mother with fear in her eyes.

Cassius stroked his chin. "An excellent suggestion, Uncle. I had an alliance in mind but the family declined. You may see to it in my absence."

———————————

Her brother bid a terse farewell to his mother and sister, and after a closed conference with his uncle, left to return to the army. Lydia felt her uncle would be giving Cassius a report on her handling of the business, as well as whether she, her mother, and Marianne vacated the villa.

Lydia had done her best to be agreeable to Cassius, feeling that it was the last time she would see or speak to him. She sensed he was sure, along with her uncle, that she wouldn't last long running the business and would be anxious to sell in a few months. Barring her from the villa would make her path even more difficult.

Lydia consoled Sophia who not only grieved for the loss of her husband, but over her son and his unkindness. The women prayed together with Marianne that Lucadius would find an acceptable match. Lydia didn't want her only child to be exposed to what she herself had endured under the hand of Plinius.

Lucadius lost no time in searching among the elite of the city for prospective suitors. Several of the young men were already betrothed and he was losing hope of accomplishing his mission when a slave arrived at the villa with a parchment.

Lucadius beamed with delight. "It seems we have been contacted by one of the Roman magistrates indicating he is willing to discuss a possible union between his son and Marianne. Sergio Marcorius. Do you know of this man's reputation in the city?" He turned to Sophia.

Sophia smiled. "I have heard of him, my Lord, and it has been favorable."

Sensing his problem reaching a solution, Lucadius invited Sergio and his son to the villa to discuss the matter.

When Sophia was alone with Lydia, she almost clapped her hands with joy. "I have seen Sergio Marcorius in the synagogue. He is Roman but he is a God-fearer. May Adonai be praised for His goodness for He has answered our prayers."

Sergio, in his sixties, was tall with piercing blue eyes and hair that was nearly white. He walked slowly and deliberately as he entered the atrium of the villa.

His son, Marcellus, appeared in his mid-twenties and Lydia wondered why he was yet unmarried. Most Roman young men were betrothed by the time they were eighteen.

Lydia had Marianne's hair dressed with small silver pins, and the girl wore a blue toga with soft silver sandals and a silver belt. When Lydia, Sophia, and Marianne arrived to join her uncle and aunt and their guests for dinner, Marianne paused for the briefest moment as her eyes met those of Marcellus.

The fact that the young man was more than pleasing to look upon was not lost on Sophia or Lydia.

When refreshments were called for, to Lydia's chagrin, Sergio let it be known that he and his family were God-fearers and followed the Jewish God, Adonai, rather than the Roman gods.

Lucadius looked down his Roman nose at the prospective suitor, feeling he would not be at all acceptable to his nephew.

"The girl's father was a Roman who honored the Roman gods, sir. Your religion would be a hindrance to the girl following the wishes of her *paterfamilias*." He teetered on the verge of dismissing them, yet they were his only prospects and he wished to return home as soon as possible.

Both Lydia and her mother had noted that when Marianne and Marcellus had gazed upon one another, something sparked between them. Lydia felt in her heart that Marcellus was the one.

As Lydia crossed the room to serve their guests a cup of wine, she murmured softly to Sergio, "Marianne also follows Adonai."

He nodded and Lydia realized they had known this when they proposed the marriage. Now she watched her uncle as indecision hardened his features.

Lucadius turned to Sophia, aware since his brother's marriage that she was a Jewess. "This would be acceptable to your husband?"

"Atticus is gone, and Marianne is a God-fearer herself. What does it matter now?"

"The girl follows this Jewish God?" He gave a snort of contempt.

"She does, as does Lydia."

"I should have suspected," he shrugged somewhat disdainfully, "but as you say, what does it matter now. I promised Cassius I would find a husband for his niece and I have done so. The sooner this matter is concluded the sooner I can return to my home."

Lydia suspected that Blandina had been wearing him out with complaints. She went off constantly about the food, the speed at which the servants met her needs, and the difficulty of being away from her own large villa for an extended time. Blandina had little regard for her niece's dilemma. She, at least, had produced sons and heirs.

Sophia bowed her head and said softly. "It is a good family and well thought of in the city."

He sighed heavily and waved a hand. "Then it is done. I shall inform Cassius of the matter." Then he paused. "Perhaps it is best not to mention the boy's religion."

"Perhaps it is wise, Lucadius. You have done your duty."

Lydia caught her mother's eye and smiled. It was indeed done, thanks to the hand of Adonai. Marianne would be happy.

Then a thought occurred to Lydia. Marianne's husband-to-be was a God-fearer and his father was not only a God-fearer, but also a prominent Roman citizen. Would her uncle forbid a rabbi to officiate at the wedding? Who would officiate? She sighed. Jehovah had brought the two young people together. It was in His hands.

Before Sergio and Marcellus left, it was determined that a date one month hence was an auspicious day for a wedding. Times had changed since Lydia's own marriage, when a one-year bethrothal was required. Now, Lydia half-wondered whether the wedding of her daughter should be even sooner. Blandina and Lucadius were demanding guests. Knowing that Sophia and Lydia had to leave in two months' time only increased Blandina's contempt for them. But Lydia bore the woman's attitude with grace.

One day, on the assumption she was going into the city to shop, Lydia unobtrusively traveled to the dye works and conferred with Kebu. He welcomed her and vowed to serve her as he had served the father.

"I will rely on that, Kebu," she smiled.

She then called on Sargon, waiting until a customer had gone to speak privately with him.

"I am sorrowful, Domina, for the death of your father. He was a good master, and kind."

"Thank you, Sargon. It is a great loss. As I'm sure you know, my father left the business to me. I will need your help." She told him of her brother's edict and, as she related her brother's words, a scowl came over Sargon's face. It was obvious he did not hold her brother in high regard.

"You do not deserve such unkindness, Domina. Where will you go?"

She glanced around, making sure they were still alone. "This was my father's plan, Sargon," and she told him of the villa in Philippi.

"I will miss speaking with you, Sargon; I will come again before we leave. There is a wedding to plan for my daughter, and then my mother and I must travel to Philippi. I know you are in contact with my father's agent there and I shall introduce myself when we have settled in the new villa."

"Aieee, so far away, Domina. What of the shop here?"

"I'm not sure as yet. I will let you know of my arrangements."

He looked at her earnestly. "The God you believe in is strong, Domina. I believe He will help you in all you have to do."

"I'm sure He will, Sargon." She tried to sound positive, yet left the shop uncertain and worried. She could not just leave it in the hands of Kebu and Sargon. They needed an overseer and she didn't know who that would be. She needed to pray earnestly for a solution.

10

*B*landina's maidservant was carrying bundles to the atrium.

"You are leaving, Aunt?" Lydia asked as Blandina swept into the room.

"We have chosen not to stay for the wedding," she announced. "It will not be the ceremony we are used to and we don't wish to appear to condone it."

When Sophia joined them, Blandina shot her a look of contempt. "No doubt your adherence to this strange religion hastened your husband to his grave."

A cutting response sprang instantly to Lydia's lips, but she held her peace. "It was good of you to travel so far for the burial of my father. I'm sorry you were not able to be here before he died."

Lucadius came down the hall and the frown that seldom left his face had deepened.

Sophia smiled. "Thank you, Lucadius, for arranging the matter of Marianne's wedding on Cassius's behalf."

Blandina pursed her lips and turned toward Lydia. "Had you provided your husband with a son, you would not be in this desperate position. Where will you go?"

Lydia glanced at her mother. "We are making arrangements."

Lucadius glared at his niece. "This whole idea of you running your father's business is ill-conceived. Surely he was not in his right mind before he died. As your brother has indicated, you will tire of this business soon. It will prove too much for you."

Lydia remained calm. Their condescending words only made her more determined. At the sound of her uncle's *carpentum* pulling in front of the villa, Sophia and Lydia walked their guests to the door.

Ever gracious in spite of her sister-in-law's unkind words, Sophia wished them a safe journey. When the two trying relatives had entered their carriage, she firmly closed the door of the atrium.

Lydia caught her mother's eye and the two of them laughed. Sophia just shook her head.

"I for one am delighted they didn't stay. They would have made the wedding seem like a funeral." She took Lydia's arm. "Come, we have planning to do, and not much time to do it."

That afternoon, as they sat together in the garden after a busy morning of wedding planning, Sophia shook her head. "What are we to do, Lydia? The days move swiftly. Where are we to go?"

"We will prepare for Marianne's wedding, Ima. Then we will pack our things. I have a plan. Father sensed that Cassius might do something like this, and he made preparations. There is a small villa in Philippi that Pater used when he traveled there for business. It has been put in my name. It will be our new home."

A note of panic crept into Sophia's voice. "Philippi? What will we do there? How will we live?"

Lydia smiled at her mother. "Remember, Pater left the dye works to me. I have capable people running it here. Pater told me he had another fabric shop in Philippi, and he hired a trustworthy man with experience to serve as factor and manage the business for him. I will continue to sell the purple cloth, even as my father did."

"But what about the business here? Who will take care of things?"

"Sargon will continue to do what he has been doing as will Kebu at the dye works. Perhaps our lawyer, Quintus, will have a suggestion for overseer, or Sargon. "

Sophia' eyes widened. "You never cease to surprise me, daughter. You have planned well, but I had no idea that your father would do this for you."

"He knew Cassius better than we thought, Ima. We will find other Jews and God-fearers in Philippi too. I'm sure of it."

"Then let us see to Marianne's wedding. When she is safely married, we will quietly plan for Philippi."

Lydia hugged her mother. "No one need know our plans other than that we are leaving."

"True, but we must decide which servants will go with us and who to leave behind to manage the villa for Cassius."

"We will both consider that, Ima. In the meantime let us search for cloth for Marianne's wedding dress."

Two days after Lydia's aunt and uncle had gone, a parchment arrived from Philippi. It was from Magnus Titelius, her father's lawyer-agent in Philippi.

To the esteemed daughter of Atticus Vasillis.

It is with regret that I inform you of the state of your father's business here in Philippi. Upon learning of your father's death and that his daughter would be coming to oversee the business, your manager, Porthos Decelus, closed the shop, took the recent funds he had not yet turned over to me, and fled the city. The shop now sits vacant. I would endeavor to discourage you from coming under the circumstances. It may be difficult to find a replacement. I await your decision.

Your servant,
Magnus Titelius

11

*L*ydia read and reread the letter, her heart racing. Avoiding her mother, she had the small traveling cart brought to the door and hurried into the city to talk with Sargon. She did not know where else to go.

Thankfully, there were no customers when she stepped out of the cart and entered the shop.

"You are upset, madam. Please seat yourself and rest a moment. How can I be of help to you?"

Encouraged by the kindness and concern on his face, she found her voice. "Sargon, there is a great problem. The manager in Philippi has run away and left the shop unattended. The agent there tells me the man also stole what funds he had not yet turned over to the agent. What am I to do? I do not know how to secure another manager and I must keep my ownership of the shop a secret."

He gave her a reassuring smile. "Have no fear, madam. I also heard the news and I have contacts in the trade. It may be that I have someone who could be of help to you. I will make inquiries discreetly and send you word in Philippi."

Her eyes widened. "Oh, Sargon. I would be most grateful."

"Your father has placed a large burden on your shoulders, yet I believe that with the strength of this God you believe in, you shall be successful."

"May you be blessed for your service and loyalty. I do not know what I would do without you, Sargon."

He smiled benignly. "May you never have to find out."

Feeling peace seep into her spirit, she stepped up into the cart and, as Yorgos drove her home, she prayed silently that Adonai would bring her the one she needed in Philippi.

* * *

Sergio and Marcellus came to dinner and Marcellus presented Marianne with the gift of a beautiful ruby ring. He slipped it on the third finger of her left hand, sealing their betrothal. Lydia and Sergio discussed the ceremony itself.

"Since we are God-fearers, madam, it would appear best to have a rabbi perform the ceremony. I have no objection to using the canopy."

Lydia nodded. "I agree that we cannot have a Roman ceremony or give any credence to the Roman gods. I appreciate that you are agreeable to a different kind of wedding."

They decided that a rabbi Sergio knew, who understood the dilemma, would perform the marriage ceremony. The couple would exchange vows and a contract would be signed according to Roman and Jewish law that provided for Marianne should anything happen to Marcellus. Unlike the custom, however, it was specifically stated that, should Marianne not produce a male heir, the villa would remain her home. Lydia had discussed the omission of this Roman custom with Sergio and he agreed. Lydia was thus assured that Marianne would not be put out of her home as she herself had been.

Sergio rubbed his chin. "Let us keep the ceremony private, with just our families. I will invite guests later to a reception to celebrate the marriage."

Lydia was relieved that it had been worked out so easily. "As you wish," she agreed.

"It is our God who must bless this union of my son and your daughter." He smiled. "I suspect it is our God who brought the two of them together."

"They do appear to be happy with each other, sir. It is an answer to prayer. I'm sure my uncle had a different union in mind."

He rubbed his chin. "That brings me to a question. Your brother is *paterfamilias* but he has gone back to the army. Your uncle has also gone. Is there anyone else who might raise an objection to the marriage?"

Lydia shook her head. "No one."

"Then as a Roman citizen, you may sign the document of marriage. A villa is being prepared for them." He paused, and his eyes were kind as he searched her face. "You and your mother have a place to go? I heard of your brother's edict."

"You are most kind, sir…."

"As we are to be related, it would please me to have you call me Sergio."

"Then you must call me Lydia."

"Agreed. Now, as I was saying…where are you going when you leave the villa?"

She sighed. "Now that my uncle and brother are gone, I can tell you. My father has a villa in Philippi, which he has placed in my name. He also has another fabric shop there. He traveled there from time to time to make sure all was running smoothly. A factor by the name of Porthos ran the shop as Sargon does here, receiving and selling our fabrics for my father. A lawyer-agent, Magnus Titelius, handles the business affairs while he is gone. Magnus puts the funds from the shop in the bank in Philippi."

She omitted the morning's worrisome news.

He raised his eyebrows and nodded. "That sounds good. However, who will manage the business here when you go to Philippi?"

She shook her head. "I'm not sure."

"Then may I offer the services of myself and my son? As I said, we are family. We are not unfamiliar with the trade and can oversee things here and ship the fabrics to Philippi along with an agreed amount of funds to make sure you are comfortable there."

Lydia could hardly contain her joy. Adonai had once again gone before them and taken care of her need. She trusted the characters of Sergio and Marcellus. Her business would be in capable and honest hands.

"Thank you, Sergio. I would certainly be grateful for your help."

His face softened. "Forgive me, Lydia, but you are a very attractive woman. How is it that you did not marry again after the death of your husband?"

She looked at him a moment. He was a handsome man for his age. And he was eligible as a widower. It would be an advantageous marriage for the right woman. She also knew that he still grieved for his wife who had died five years before.

"Perhaps for the same reasons you have not married again, Sergio. Sometimes one marriage is enough." She would not elaborate on the state of her own marriage. *Let him assume what he will,* she thought.

"Ah, you are an astute woman. I believe you will do well in your new venture."

A servant brought them wine and they toasted their partnership.

She stood and smiled at him. "Let us find my daughter and your son. No doubt they are unaware we have even been gone."

With a chuckle, he followed her to the garden.

12

*M*arianne was beautiful in her white tunic. Her face glowed with love and excitement. Lydia clasped a golden girdle around her waist and gave her a pair of gold earrings to wear as a gift. She then helped her daughter with the soft blue mantle and placed a wreath of flowers on her head.

"My daughter, you make a lovely bride." Lydia beamed at her.

"Oh Ima, I am so happy. I loved Marcellus from the moment I saw him at the synagogue, but I didn't know what Uncle Cassius would do. I overheard him talking to Uncle Lucadius about an alliance and I was afraid. I thought he would marry me off to some old man."

"Adonai has watched over you and protected you, Marianne. Marcellus is the husband He chose for you."

Sophia stood in the doorway. "Is my granddaughter ready? The rabbi awaits our bride."

With her mother on one side and her grandmother on the other, Marianne walked to her wedding. They entered the garden of the villa where Sergio, Marcellus, and a few close friends of the family waited.

In a simple ceremony, Marianne walked around the *chuppah* seven times and then stood by Marcellus as the Rabbi married them. Marcellus slipped a simple gold band on her left hand and, to end the ceremony, broke a glass that had been wrapped in a napkin with his foot. Marcellus had signed the *ketubah*, or marriage contract, just before the ceremony. Now Marianne signed it too, and it was witnessed by Sergio and Lydia.

Lydia, watching the amended ceremony, was pleased that her daughter and new son-in-law were combining the Jewish wedding with some of the aspects of the Roman customs. She was grateful that they were not going to be sacrificing to Roman gods.

After the ceremony, everyone went to the home of Sergio and Marcellus for the wedding feast. Lydia was surprised at the number of Roman citizens who arrived. Sergio was obviously well-regarded in the city.

Sergio's dining room, the *triclinium*, was large enough to seat all of his guests. Men reclined on couches and women sat on padded chairs. Slaves hurried around with basins, washing the feet of the guests who had removed their sandals in the atrium.

Small pronged spoons called *cochlear* were placed at each setting for snails. Platters were piled with shrimp, slices of duck, steamed mackerel, and several different kinds of olives. Loaves of fresh bread were placed beside a fish dipping sauce. Platters of grapes, figs, pears, and apples gave color to the table along with a variety of cheeses. Lydia noticed a platter of pork, and realized it was a token for Sergio's Roman guests, who preferred it to duck or chicken. A salad was provided with kale, cabbage, chard, carrots, leeks, and radishes. Another slave held a mixture of steamed vegetables, asparagus, parsnips, green beans and broccoli, and went around offering it to guests. Other slaves waited with basins of water and linen cloths for guests to wash their fingers between courses. Sergio had also provided fine linen napkins for his guests, though, as was custom, some brought their own.

It was a wedding feast fit for a king. Marcellus was Sergio's only child and he had spared no expense. Wine was poured freely into each guest's goblet.

Finally, it was time for Marcellus to walk his bride to their new villa. It was a joyous crowd that called out good wishes as well as bawdy comments as they walked through the city. Lydia was concerned about her mother's stamina, but Sophia smiled as she walked and did not show any fatigue.

Marcellus and Marianne embraced their parents and with a wave to the crowd, entered their villa and shut the door. Marcellus had triumphantly walked his bride to the villa his father had bought for them, and from the tender looks he gave Marianne, Lydia felt assured that her daughter's wedding night would not be the nightmare her own had been. Marcellus would be a gentle husband.

No torch was thrown to the crowd, and no rituals to the gods were performed, but most of the guests didn't seem to notice. Some had consumed a little too much wine to be aware that the Roman rituals were not carried out. With more comments and laughter, the guests dispersed and returned to their homes. Yorgos met them with the small cart, and Lydia and her mother were more than happy to not have to walk to their own villa.

As they rode along, Lydia's euphoria over the wedding seemed to dissipate as she realized that now they must turn their attention to leaving their home. The future held so many unknowns. She glanced at her mother and was startled to see the sorrow on Sophia's face. Was she thinking the same thing? They quietly wrapped their arms around each other.

13

The day after Marianne's wedding, Lydia and her mother sat in the cool of the central garden of the villa.

Lydia was still amazed. "I confess I was puzzled as to how the wedding would go, but Adonai answered our prayers. When Uncle chose not to stay for the wedding, I was so relieved."

"Sergio anticipated your uncle's reluctance to take part in the marriage of God-fearers." Sophia chuckled. "He and your aunt could not leave fast enough."

That brought a smile.

The two women sat in companionable silence for a while, but finally, Sophia rose. "We have only two weeks before we leave here. There is much to do. We will leave Iola to tend the household as she is too old to move to another city, but without a family to tend to, the house should not be hard for her. We can leave Yorgos. He has been with us many years and has taken care of the gardens. At his age he also would not be comfortable leaving. With Cassius gone they can be trusted to take care of the villa. I will take my servant Chara and our cook, Delia. She will have little to do with the family gone. Will you take Jael?"

Lydia nodded. "That sounds like a good plan. Yes, I will take Jael. She has been a friend as well as a servant over these long, lonely years."

Sophia paused for a moment at the mention of the word *friend* in regard to a servant, but did not comment.

Her mother's brows knit together in thought. "I wonder if we would be allowed the furnishings from our own rooms. Cassius did not specify what we could take, but it would probably be best if we did not take any furnishings from the main house."

Lydia put a hand on her mother's arm. "The villa in Philippi is small, but Pater said it is furnished. We can travel lightly with just our clothes and personal items. Besides, it will make it easier since we have to travel by ship from Troas."

Sophia looked away for a moment and her eyes were moist. "It has been my home for thirty years. I chose some of the furnishings with your father's indulgence. It will be hard to walk away. I know Cassius was retaliating and felt we had no place to go." She sighed. "I am sorry for the son I raised yet thankful that your father made a way for us."

"Pater loved you. He would not let you go out into the streets. I have not seen the villa in Philippi but he described it to me. It is not as large as this one, and has a smaller inner garden, but there are olive trees and some fruit trees. Papa told me his caretaker there, Hektor, has been with him many years. I am sure we will be comfortable there, Ima."

"You are sure the business will support us?"

"Yes, along with the business here and the fabric shop in Philippi. Sargon will continue to handle the fabrics here and Kebu will still oversee the dyes."

"But who will oversee them?"

"Adonai has taken care of that too. The business is now family-owned and Sergio has agreed, along with Marcellus, to make sure things run smoothly here. Kudu will show Marcellus how the dye works are run and he, along with his father, will work with Sargon and oversee shipping the fabrics to Philippi for me."

Her mother's eyes widened. "And will you sell the fabrics in Philippi, daughter?"

Lydia hesitated. She would not burden her mother with the news of the problems in Philippi. She had enough to be concerned with.

"Papa said there was a factor already running the shop for him." She did not need to tell Sophia the man had run away with some of their badly needed funds.

"I sent my father's lawyer-agent, Magnus Titelius, a notice that we would be coming. We will have to speak with him when we arrive. Sargon knows him. It is all we can do."

Sophia shook her head. "It will not be easy, I'm sure. We can only pray and know that Adonai goes before us."

The women parted to their own rooms to begin to pack the things they would take. Lydia was thankful they still had her father's ornate traveling wagon with elaborate carvings in the wooden sides. Cassius had not thought about how his mother and sister would travel and fortunately did not forbid them the use of it as he hurried away back to the army.

⸺ ⸻ ✦ ⸻ ⸺

Iola and Yorgos wept as they helped place the women's things in the wagon. At least it was enclosed and they would not be in the sun. Then Iola embraced Delia, Jael, and Chara in turn. The slaves had worked together for many years.

Iola turned a sad face to Sophia. "Mistress, you have been kind to me, and I will miss you. The house will be lonely with just Yorgos and me. I should go with you."

Sophia put a hand on Iola's shoulder. "You have been a faithful servant, Iola, but the journey and a new home would be too much for you. Here you can spend your last years in peace. Cassius will rarely be home."

She turned to the faithful gardener. "You, also, will have a place to spend your final years, Yorgos. Now you can still be among the plants you love."

He bowed his head. "Thank you, Mistress, you are too good to us. May the God you follow watch over and protect you."

When the last of their personal goods had been loaded, Lydia looked back at the home she had been born in.

Marianne and Marcellus came with his father to see them off and Marianne wept on Lydia's shoulder. "When shall I see you again, Ima?"

"We are in the hands of Adonai, Marianne. He will direct our paths. In time, you must come and visit us in Philippi."

She turned to Marcellus. "I am grateful to you for your help with the fabrics and the business here in Thyatira. I will expect the first shipment in a month, after we are settled." She embraced her son-in-law and nodded to Sergio.

He stepped forward and addressed Sophia. "I am sorry for the reason for your journey, but know our God goes with you and will direct your path. May He bless you in your new home. Do not fear for the business here. Marcellus and I will make sure all goes well."

Sophia could only nod her thanks. Words seemed inadequate for all he had done for them.

Yorgos helped Sophia and Lydia into the carriage and then Delia, Jael, and Chara climbed in across from them.

Sergio, learning of their situation, had offered a slave named Macedon, meaning "large one," to drive the *carpentum*. He was nearly seven feet tall, and, seeing his size, Lydia knew he could more than handle driving the long journey to Troas and back to the villa. He carried papers from Sergio authorizing his travel should he be stopped on the way home alone.

Macedon flicked his whip and the two huge mules pulling the *carpentum* moved away at a brisk trot. Lydia leaned out the window and waved until they rounded a bend in the road and her daughter was out of sight. She settled back, adjusting to the gentle rocking of the coach. She felt a thrum of excitement. Finally, they were on their way.

14

Macedon drove them steadily to the first inn, halfway to Pergamum. He let Sophia know he would sleep with the wagon, feeling responsible for guarding their goods. Lydia and her mother shared a double bed in a small room that smelled as if it had not been cleaned in years. Sophia rented the only other room in the inn for their three servants and later learned it was even worse. Yet, weary from the long hours in the carriage, they were quickly asleep.

At dawn Jael and Chara helped their mistresses freshen themselves as best they could. The innkeeper offered simple bread and goat cheese for their breakfast. He had no fruit. Lydia and her mother looked at the cheese with its touch of mold and at the not-quite-fresh bread and decided to forgo his meager fare since Delia had prepared food. They hurried their three servants out to the coach. Lydia hoped the next stop would be an improvement on this one.

In the carriage, Delia opened the basket she had prepared at the villa, with cheese, dried apples, pears, and several loaves of bread. The women ate little, hoping to make the contents last as long as possible, yet Lydia realized she would need to buy fresh supplies along the way.

As they entered a small village, the women smelled warm meat cooking.

"Macedon, stop the carriage." Lydia called out. She and her mother approached the vendor's stall. Lydia purchased warm lamb wrapped in a piece of flatbread for each of them.

The inn at Pergamum was a little better and the women ate the simple breakfast offered. At each stop, Sophia made sure food was taken to Macedon, and he rewarded her with grateful smiles. While he spoke little, he gave them the assurance that he was watching out for them. Anyone approaching the carriage received a scowl and, due to his size, few even approached.

Macedon helped the women into the carriage and they were on their way. It was another hundred miles from Pergamum to the port and it would be necessary to stop in a small village for the night. Lydia was beginning to feel ill with the rocking of the carriage, and each time they stopped, she stepped out, grateful to stretch her legs.

The next village where they stopped did not have an inn, but they were referred to the home of a family that had a large extra room and sometimes took in travelers.

"A room, Domina?" The woman was obviously flustered. "For all of you?" Observing the clothing that Lydia and her mother wore, the wife clasped her hands and looked back at her husband. He shrugged and nodded. "We will be happy to grant you lodging, Domina."

When Sophia held out their payment, the husband quickly took the coins, his eyes wide. "We will do our best, Domina," he murmured.

The three servants were given rugs for sleeping on the floor above the animals while Lydia and her mother slept on a bed of straw that was covered with a rug. They wrapped their cloaks about them for warmth.

Lydia smiled at her mother. "Well, it is not your room in our villa, but I for one am exhausted and will sleep well!"

Sophia agreed. "It is far better than that first inn where we stayed!"

They slept soundly, awakened only by the crowing of a rooster in the shelter below.

The family gave them fresh cheese and grapes to eat along with warm bread just out of the oven and diluted wine. It was the best food the women had tasted in days and they let their beaming hostess know.

In the afternoon, Lydia sensed a change in the air and inhaled the fresh smell of the sea. They were approaching the port of Troas. As they passed through a forest of sturdy oaks, Lydia gazed at them in wonder. *How old they must be to grow so tall!* she thought.

As they entered the city, peasants stopped to stare, eyebrows raised with curiosity as they watched the ornate carriage go by. As they entered the agora, their ears were accosted by the cacophony of the marketplace; bleating goats awaiting sale or butchering and chickens in wicker cages squawking their displeasure. The strong smell of fish filled the air as they passed the seafood merchants. Vendors called out to them, holding up their wares, and loudly attempting to drown out the other merchants to catch their attention. As the carriage continued to roll by, one merchant shook his fist in frustration, but Macedon did not stop. They passed a magnificent temple, a gymnasium, and, to Lydia's delight, a building advertising public baths.

Sophia called out to their driver. "Stop at the baths, Macedon. We need to refresh ourselves before boarding the ship."

The big man nodded and obediently pulled up under the shade of a copse of trees. Jael and Chara gathered fresh clothes from the trunks and, while Macedon settled himself by the carriage to wait, the five women headed for the baths.

Lydia glanced back at their guardian. He appeared to doze, but perhaps sensing her gaze, opened one eye. She smiled to herself. Macedon would not be caught unawares.

After soaking in the warm water of the baths and enjoying a rubdown by their maidservants, Lydia and Sophia were refreshed. They had shed the dust of their long journey from Thyatira. Now they faced a journey by sea and must next seek passage on a ship heading for Neapolis. She sent Jael ahead to place the soiled clothes in one of the trunks. Just then Lydia heard Jael cry out, and the women hurried outside the building to see two men obviously bent on harming her. One man had grasped her hair and was trying to kiss her while the other grabbed her arm in an effort to drag her away toward a heavy stand of trees.

Suddenly, there was a primal bellow and a huge dark hand lifted one of the men straight up into the air. The other man, seeing Macedon's angry face and huge size, attempted to run away but the big slave's left hand caught his tunic. Macedon knocked the heads of the attackers together and dropped them in the street like two bags of wheat. They scrambled to their feet and stumbled away, moving as fast as their addled brains allowed. Macedon stood with his hands on his hips, a satisfied smile on his face.

Lydia rushed to Jael's side to comfort her weeping servant. "It is all right. Our guardian has taken care of them." She turned to the big man. "Thank you, Macedon. What would we have done without you?"

He bowed his head. "I was charged with your safe-keeping, Domina."

Sophia looked after the departing men. "We must be on alert at all times. None of us are safe alone. From now on, we will stay together." She turned to Jael and the other servants. "Let us return to the coach." The women complied gladly.

As they approached the docks, Lydia sent up a quick prayer for guidance. God had protected them so far, surely He would help them find a ship. She and her mother entered a small building that seemed to be where one purchased passage. Lydia took a deep breath and addressed the man behind the counter.

"Is this where we obtain passage on one of the ships traveling to Philippi?"

The man looked them over and raised one eyebrow. "You are traveling alone?"

"No, this is my mother, and we have three servants with us. We will need passage for five."

He contemplated them for a moment. "There is a ship going to Neapolis that stops briefly in Samothrace. You will have to find someone to take you to Philippi from the docks. It is over ten miles from the harbor. You have no man traveling with you?" He frowned. "It is not safe for women traveling alone."

Remembering the incident outside the baths, Lydia spoke up bravely. "We will be all right, for Adonai goes with us."

The man snorted. "Jews!" He waved them toward the harbor. "You will have to see the captain of the ship. He will decide if he can give you passage." He turned his back on them in dismissal.

Lydia bit down the words she was tempted to say at his rudeness, and, taking her mother by the arm, joined their three servants and headed for the docks. There was a fine sailing ship rocking gently at anchor and the women stopped at the side of the gangplank just in time to avoid being run over by two sailors with bare chests, merchandise on their shoulders, boarding the ship.

Lydia called up to a sailor on the deck. "May we speak to the captain?"

He looked them over a moment and then left the railing and disappeared for a few moments. A large man, obviously in charge, looked down at them.

"I am Captain Stamos. What is it you want?"

Lydia had thought of what she needed to say without telling a lie. "My father has died and I am taking my mother home to Philippi. We need passage on your ship."

"How many of you are there?"

"Five of us, sir. It is most urgent."

"This man accompanies you?" He nodded at Macedon.

Sophia spoke up. "The slave belongs to my daughter's household and must return to Thyatira with the coach. My son is a centurion in the Roman army. His duties made it impossible for him to accompany us."

At the mention that her son was in the Roman army, the captain stroked his beard and studied them. "I have one cabin. It was going to be used by the owner of the ship, but his wife is ill and he was not able to travel. It would have to accommodate all five of you. The voyage will take five days."

Lydia sighed with relief. "We will take it. What is your passage fee?"

When they had agreed on a sum and Sophia had paid him from her dwindling funds, Lydia nodded to Macedon and he began to unload their trunks, carrying them with ease up the gangplank to the cabin. After five trips, all was on board.

Sophia stood looking up at their protector. "Thank you, Macedon, for all you have done for us. May our God watch over you as you return to Sergio with our gratitude."

"May your journey be a safe one, Mistress." He nodded his huge head and returned to the coach.

Lydia watched him walk away. "I pray he will be able to return safely, Mater. He will be alone."

Sophia nodded. "Yes, but Adonai will watch over him on his journey."

There were two built-in bunks in the cabin and Lydia determined that they were just wide enough for two women. Delia eyed the room apprehensively, perhaps noting the same thing.

"We will take turns. When four are sleeping the other will keep watch. Since we have no man protecting us we will have to be alert at all times and stay together." Sophia eyed the servants. "No woman is to venture alone around the ship. Is that understood?" They nodded. It was all they could do. Chara looked around. "Shall I take the first watch, Domina? I am not tired." She glanced at Jael and Delia.

Sophia shook her head. "We will wait until the ship sets sail, Chara." Anxious to get a breath of fresh air, the five women ventured up on deck, being careful to stay back by the wheelhouse and out of the way of the sailors preparing the ship to leave the harbor. Lydia found herself fascinated as sailors climbed the rigging to loosen sails and others scrambled about the ship to the first mate's barked orders. He glared once at the women but they were successfully endeavoring to stay out of the way and he dismissed them with a shake of his head.

Sails unfurled, like a great lady leaving her court, the ship turned her prow toward the opening of the harbor and glided toward the open sea. As the ship rocked back and forth with the swells of the sea, it wasn't long before all five women were at the rail, disposing of the food they had recently eaten.

15

After a brief stop at Samothrace to unload and load cargo, the ship set sail again for Neapolis, where they would disembark for the journey inland to Philippi. Lydia found the captain a stern but kind man who spoke to them at times about their journey. To her relief, Lydia learned that he had given orders that the women were not to be bothered by the crew. Hopefully it would be smooth sailing to Neapolis.

To Lydia's relief, the mild weather held. Lydia began to enjoy the venture of her first time on a sailing ship, but sighed as she saw her mother standing at the rail, looking back the direction they had come. It had been hard for her to leave her home. Lydia went and put an arm around Sophia and they stood there joined in quiet understanding. Jael, Delia, and Chara fared better as the days went by, but all the women shared the anticipation of walking on dry land again.

Lydia enjoyed watching the sea birds that followed the ship, evidently hoping for any scraps the cook or the sailors would throw overboard. The women ate from Delia's basket that had been refurbished in the last marketplace.

"I am thankful we don't have to partake of the ship's food," Chara murmured. "I heard two of the sailors saying it was barely edible."

Sophia raised an eyebrow. Lydia glanced her way also. When did Chara hear this? They were supposed to stay together. Jael quickly spoke up. "I was with her, Domina, when we heard the men say so."

She gave them a stern look, but said nothing.

As the ship entered the harbor at Neapolis, Lydia breathed a sigh of relief. They had made it this far. She looked out from the rails of the ship to the port, teeming with slaves carrying bundles, baskets, crates, and large pottery jars. It was as busy as Troas had been, and, while they had reached their first destination, there was still the matter of finding transport to take them to Philippi.

Captain Stamos had been courteous to them, and it seemed that he was their best chance of finding a wagon and driver.

Lydia approached him, waiting politely for him to recognize her.

"Madam?"

"Sir, we are in need of another wagon to transport us and our goods to Philippi. Do you know of someone who could take us?"

Captain Stamos frowned and stroked his beard a moment. "Yes, I know of someone. I will send one of my men to fetch him. He will charge you well, but he is dependable. His name is Vitas."

The captain had his men unload their goods and pile them on the dock as the women stood by, checking to make sure all was intact. Sophia appeared tired and Lydia had her sit down on one of the chests while she looked around for the man Captain Stamos had sent for.

A rough-looking man approached them and eyed the women and their luggage. His face was hard and calculating.

"Perhaps I can be of help to you. I have an establishment not far from here. You can refresh yourselves." He almost leered at Lydia. "Are you here to seek work of some kind?"

Lydia was shocked. Did he take them for the loose women who were found at the temples?

Sophia rose to her full height. "We are not in need of your assistance. We are returning to our home and have already secured transport." At her firm tone, the man stepped back. He shrugged and, after a last glance at Lydia, strolled away.

They sat on their baggage as the sun seemed to get hotter by the moment. Where was the man the captain had sent for?

Finally, a tall man, possibly Greek, strode rapidly toward them. His tunic did not hide his muscular build and a shock of blond hair framed an angular face and piercing brown eyes. He stopped and looked over the women, apparently not happy with what he saw.

Lydia felt they must appear like wilted flowers in the heat.

"You are the women going to Philippi?"

Lydia stepped forward. "Yes, are you Vitas?" She was surprised at the strange shock she felt when those dark eyes met hers.

His handsome face appeared disdainful. "There is no man traveling with you? What is your business in Philippi?"

From the tone of his question, Lydia became incensed. "If you do not wish to take us, that is your decision. We will find someone else. My mother is weary, as we all are from the voyage, and we wish to get home."

A slight smile tugged at his mouth. "Ah, you live in Philippi." It was not a question. He nodded toward a wagon nearby. "My name is Nikolas. Vitas is a friend of mine and is occupied elsewhere. He has agreed to loan me his wagon since I am also traveling that way."

Lydia, irritated at his attitude, was tempted to refuse his services. Yet, glancing back at her mother fanning herself in the hot sun, Lydia capitulated. "We will accept your service. What is your fee?"

He looked around at the five of them and, appraising Sophia and Lydia's clothing as belonging to the upper class, named a figure that caused Lydia to stare at him wide-eyed.

"Surely you can name a more reasonable sum. Would you take advantage of a grieving woman and daughter who have lost their husband and father?"

He blinked, then sighed. "My apologies. I did not know your circumstances. I am not a monster. I will cut the fee in half."

With their baggage loaded into the wagon, the three slaves perched on top as best they could, while Lydia and her mother were forced to share the seat with Nikolas. Putting an arm around her mother, Lydia gritted her teeth.

16

As the wagon rumbled along the road, Lydia fanned herself with her hand. She tried to picture the villa as her father described it to her and anticipation rose in her heart. She yearned for a place where she and her mother could be safe. She understood that Philippi was originally a settlement for veteran Roman soldiers who wanted to retire with some land. As a Roman colony, it had self-governance and freedom from paying tribute to the Emperor but all the rights and customs of those who lived in Italy, including Roman dress, language, coinage and holidays. As her father had told her about the city, Lydia could almost visualize it.

"People in the city are divided into citizens and peregrinus, or strangers. We are not from Italy, so you would be the latter. You have learned Latin, which is the language of the city. There are magistrates called praetors who regulate the government affairs."

"And the villa is free and clear to me, Pater? No one can claim it?"

He patted her hand. "No one." He was quiet a moment and closed his eyes. She leaned forward, fearing the worst, but he opened his eyes again.

"You will like the villa, daughter. It is not as large as this one, or the one you lived in as a wife, but you and your mother will be comfortable there."

She hung her head. "How can I be sure the villa will be needed, Pater? Surely Cassius will be busy with the army and away most of the time."

"Perhaps I know your brother better than you think I do. He can be vindictive, daughter. I pray he will make the right decision, but there is no guarantee of what he intends to do."

Her mind churned with more questions. There was so much she wanted, needed to know. "How will I carry on the business in Philippi, Pater?"

"Introduce yourself to my lawyer-agent, Magnus Titelius, and then my factor, Porthos. He will advise you. I sent a message advising him that you might be coming but have not heard back as yet." He looked away a moment. "I pray all is well."

He winced as the pain returned, and was silent again. When he had gathered himself, he nodded. "You may also wish to speak with Sargon. He has contacts in the city and may have heard news from Porthos by now."

"I will speak to him very soon, Pater."

He had reached out with his waning strength and placed a hand on hers. They had remained that way for a long moment as the shadows began to creep along the walls of the garden outside.

Two days later her father had died.

* * *

Now, as they traveled, Lydia realized Nikolas was speaking to her. Since he was not a slave he obviously didn't feel he must acquiesce to her silence.

"Have you lived in Philippi long?" he asked.

Lydia glanced at her mother and shook her head. "Not long." She reached into her bag and pulled out the parchment that gave the directions to the villa. "Do you know where this is?"

He glanced at the map. "I can find it. Do you not know the way?"

Heat warmed Lydia's face. The man was impertinent and asked too many questions.

"This was for our driver, whoever he was."

That slight smile appeared at the corners of his mouth again. He seemed to take delight in upsetting her.

"Do you work in Philippi, or are you just available to drive weary women in a borrowed wagon?" She was aware her voice had taken on a sarcastic tone.

"I came here seeking employment. There is a promising opportunity here."

When he did not elaborate, they rode again in silence. Lydia tried to keep her thigh from brushing his, but it was difficult as the wagon jostled them together. She found his leg hard and firm, and the touch sent a strange sensation through her. She swallowed and looked away at the fields as they passed. Perhaps she would trade places with her mother at the next stop.

The three women in the back of the cart murmured among themselves and finally Delia spoke up, addressing her mistress. "Domina, there is a stand of trees. May we stop for a few moments?" She looked anxiously at Sophia.

Sophia understood. "Nikolas, please stop the wagon. We have personal matters to attend to."

He pulled up the reins and the mules halted. Nikolas jumped down and came around to hand her mother and Lydia down from the wagon. The three slaves helped each other. Lydia waited by the wagon with Jael as Chara and Delia followed their mistress into the copse of trees. When they returned a few minutes later, Lydia and Jael took their turn.

Nikolas strolled off into another nearby copse of trees and returned as Lydia and Jael approached the wagon. He stood quietly, his eyes on Lydia, and his open appraisal made her uneasy. She nodded to her mother to go up ahead of her and, while Sophia lifted an eyebrow in question, she took the middle of the seat. As

Nikolas handed Lydia up, she noticed him holding back a smile. The man was insufferable. The sooner they reached the villa and sent him on his way, the better.

They approached the city and the *Via Egnatia*, the main street, but Nikolas turned the mules onto a side road and continued for a short distance. Glancing at the parchment, he then turned again onto a narrow drive that led to an attractive, white-washed building sitting amid a grove of trees. Tall white columns graced the entrance to the front door and the steps had been covered in beautiful patterned tiles. As Nikolas brought the wagon to a stop, Lydia realized it was *their* villa. They were home.

Sophia stepped down from the wagon and stood gazing at it. "This is beautiful, Lydia. A very peaceful location."

A man emerged from the house. He was dark-skinned, perhaps Syrian, and the smile on his face was genuine. He bowed to Sophia and Lydia, and then, with deference, addressed Lydia.

"I am Hektor, Domina. Your father wrote me of your coming. All is in readiness for you and your mother."

Lydia liked him. If her father had placed him there, he was trustworthy. The tension lifted from her shoulders.

Lydia noted that Nikolas listened to this conversation with interest. Now he knew it was their first time here. Lydia ignored him. To his credit, Nikolas said nothing and simply helped Hektor carry their baggage into the villa. Lydia stepped into her new home for the first time. The entry was not grand, but she appreciated the variety of beautiful birds portrayed in the mosaics of the floor. The last of their belongings were deposited in the entry and Lydia thanked Nikolas for his help. She opened her small bag and paid him the sum he'd requested and then stood back, waiting.

"I will return the wagon to my friend, and come back in a week. Perhaps you will be well-settled by then."

Lydia's eyes widened. Come back to the villa? The man was brazen. "Please see to your wagon. I wish you a safe journey back to

Neapolis." She was sure he heard what she didn't say—*and please stay there.*

He only smiled, bowed to Lydia and her mother, and returned to the wagon. When he had gone, Sophia tipped her head at Lydia.

"He is a man who does what he wants, is he not? I sense he disturbed you."

Lydia huffed. "Let us not speak of him again. He was rude and insufferable. I am glad he has gone on his way." She put her arm through Sophia's. "Let us explore our new home."

Hektor, who had been standing nearby, stepped forward. "It will be my delight to show it to you, Domina."

Sophia turned to Jael, Delia, and Chara. "Come with us. You will need to know the villa since you are to serve here."

From the entry, Hektor led them to the center of the villa where a fountain fed a small pool. The tinkling of the water had a soothing sound, and seeing the stone bench nearby, Lydia felt it would be a wonderful resting place for her mother and herself.

They entered the kitchen off the center atrium and Delia's practiced eye took in the cooking area, the table for baking, and a small spout fed by a cistern over the stone sink for water. The women marveled at the innovation. There was a clay oven, and just outside the kitchen Lydia noticed a small garden for vegetables and herbs. Delia would be in her element and Lydia smiled to herself as she noted Delia's satisfied look.

On each side of the atrium Hektor pointed out bedrooms. The smaller one, furnished simply with a bed, a table with an oil lamp, and a rug, seemed obviously to belong to Hektor. The other room near the kitchen seemed larger. Lydia was amazed that it already held three beds. Their maidservants would share that room. How had Hektor known?

Hektor led them up a flight of stone steps with alcoves in the wall that held Roman household gods. Lydia glanced at them and then turned to the servant. "We will remove these, Hektor, as soon as possible."

He raised his eyebrows. "All of them, Domina?"

"All of them," Sophia added firmly.

He nodded his head. "As you wish, Domina." He then opened the door to a small room.

"A place you all will wish to be aware of."

Hektor pointed to a pipe that extended from the wall. "It is fed by another cistern outside the wall that collects rainwater." A stone alcove with a drain hole occupied one corner. In the other corner sat a clay chamber pot.

Lydia wrinkled her nose. It was not like the Roman baths.

Sophia raised her eyebrows and shrugged. "It will do."

Down the short hallway doors opened to two more bedrooms, furnished simply, and to Lydia, almost bare, but obviously for the former master and mistress of the villa. Lydia heard a soft sigh from her mother. It was far different from the room Sophia had shared with Lydia's father for so many years.

"We will find some things in Philippi to add to our rooms, Ima," she said quickly. "They are of a pleasant size."

Sophia chose one room. "I will take this one, Chara." Her servant nodded. Lydia entered the other room and Jael glanced around as if mentally noting where her mistress's things would go. Then the two servants hurried downstairs to begin fetching the baggage left in the atrium.

Her mother gave Lydia a wan smile but squared her shoulders. "Let us explore the garden and see what fruit is available."

Hektor beamed. "This way, Domina."

Arm in arm, Lydia and her mother followed him down the stairs and out a side door.

They passed two ancient olive trees, which Lydia guessed might have been growing there long before the villa. Further on, Hektor pointed out a pomegranate tree, two pear trees, two apple trees, and a sycamore-fig tree. There was a small grape arbor, and beyond that more fruit trees. Their orchard seemed small, but Lydia was amazed it had even that much fruit. At least it would adequately meet the needs of her family. The fig tree still held fruit and Hektor picked two, then handed one to each of them.

"Perhaps you would wish to sample?" He waited, eyebrows raised, as Lydia and her mother bit into the ripe fruit. They were the best figs Lydia had ever tasted, and she told Hektor as much, to his pleasure.

When they returned to the house, Lydia escorted her mother upstairs. Jael and Chara had been busy unpacking clothing and other possessions and putting them away.

Lydia realized her mother was weary from the long trip and encouraged her to lie down and rest for a while. Leaving Sophia in Chara's capable hands, Lydia wandered back down to the garden and sat on a stone bench, surveying her new domain. As soon as they were settled, she needed to go into Philippi and locate her father's lawyer-agent who handled the funds for the shop. Perhaps he would know what her first step should be. Sargon would contact her as soon as he had word of someone to assist her. She knew there was communication between slaves and not a word must get out of her owning the business. She sighed. Sargon would have to be discreet indeed.

"Domina?" She turned to see Hektor nearby. He presented her with a cup of cool wine and some bread. "Perhaps you would care for some refreshment?"

She looked at his lined face, his dark eyes filled with concern, and gave him a grateful smile. "Thank you, Hektor, it is most needed."

He beamed. "It is hard to make such a change, Domina. Your father wanted to be sure all was in readiness for you, in the event of his...his passing. He was good to me and always treated me well. I will miss him, Domina."

"My father planned well, Hektor. I do not know what we would have done if we had not had the villa to come to."

Hektor nodded and appeared to start to say something, but remained silent.

"You have a question?"

"If you will forgive me asking, Domina, but the household gods? You wish to remove them?"

"Yes, my mother is Jewish and I am a God-fearer." She sighed. "Not all our servants share our view, as yet."

He thought for a moment. "I have wondered about the Jewish God. Some of the travelers entering our city have spoken of Him and there is talk among the servants."

"If you wish to know more, we would be glad to share Him with you. Is there a Jewish synagogue in the city?"

His brow furrowed. "No, not to my knowledge."

"Oh, I was hoping there would be one."

He brightened. "I have heard that some of those who wish to pray meet down by the Gangites River on the seventh day of the week. They call it the Sabbath. I would be happy to show you the way whenever you wish."

"Thank you, Hektor."

Lydia was pleased. She would tell her mother that soon they could look into going there. With a lighter heart, she went to the kitchen to see what Delia was preparing for their dinner and what they needed to purchase in Philippi.

Delia had taken charge of the kitchen and inspected the herb garden. "It is a good kitchen, mistress," she ventured, "but perhaps there are supplies we will need...." She looked expectantly at Lydia.

"We will go very soon, perhaps in two days. You and my mother will then be able to go to the agora and purchase what you need."

Lydia wanted to put off telling her mother about the state of the shop as long as possible in the hopes she would have a manager...soon.

"I'm sure my mother will have some suggestions when she comes down for our evening meal." There was a pot of something on the small clay stove and Lydia realized she was hungry.

"It smells delicious."

"I found some carrots and beans in the garden, as well as some cabbage. I've made a stew for your dinner. We still have some bread from the last marketplace to finish up until I can bake our own. There are also nuts in the storage room and fresh figs from the orchard."

Lydia nodded. "The bread oven is adequate, Delia?"

"Yes, Domina."

Lydia nodded, then turned and went upstairs. Perhaps her mother had awakened from her nap. The afternoon shadows were already crossing the yard and soon it would be sunset.

Chara was brushing Sophia's hair as Lydia entered the room. "You feel more rested, Ima?"

Sophia turned and smiled. "Yes, and I find I am hungry. Has Delia found anything for our supper?"

"She is resourceful as usual. Dinner smells enticing."

When Chara had arranged Sophia's hair in a simple style, mother and daughter went down the stairs.

The stew proved indeed delicious and Lydia found herself dipping several pieces of bread in the bowl. Another platter held figs from the orchard, sliced melon, and almonds. After the meal, Lydia and Sophia went out to the garden to enjoy the slightly cooler air and watched the sun, like a fiery orb, sink slowly out of sight. Some light still lingered and they sat on the stone bench, enjoying the peace.

Lydia's mind still turned with the problem of the shop. "Tomorrow I will speak with Magnus Titelius, Papa's agent. We will discuss the shop and our arrangement."

Sophia patted her hand. "I'm sure it will go well. Your father would not choose a man who is unreliable."

Lydia remained silent. The factor had certainly shown himself to be unreliable even though the agent and her father's other employees had been with him for years and respected him. She determined not to say anything that would cause her mother concern. The business *had* to succeed. She kept her voice light. "I am confident the agent will make sure everything goes well. It is just a new venture for me."

Sophia turned to her. "Adonai has led us thus far, and He has a plan. We must pray and wait for it to unfold. As much as you have learned from your father about the dyes and the fabrics, I'm sure you will make a success of it."

Remembering what Hektor had told her, Lydia quickly turned the conversation in a more favorable direction. "Hektor told me that some God-fearers meet down by the Gangites River on the Sabbath. He will take us there when we are settled."

Sophia frowned. "There is no synagogue in Philippi?"

"Evidently not, but perhaps in time."

"Well, at least there is a place to meet other people of our faith. I will look forward to going there." She took Lydia's hand. "Let us pray, daughter. Adonai has seen us safely to our new home, and He knows our needs."

As they bowed their heads to give their cares into the hands of the Lord they trusted, Lydia still could not help but worry over what awaited them in Philippi.

17

The next morning Lydia awoke and glanced toward the open window. The sun was up and the heat of the coming day was already making itself known. The garden was peaceful except for the clucking of the chickens not far away and the plaintive bleating of the goat who was looking for his breakfast. She looked around her new room, suddenly remembering where she was. She was tempted to lie back and stay in bed a little longer, but the thought suddenly occurred to her that Hektor was going to take her into Philippi to see her father's lawyer-agent…and see the state of her father's shop.

Her feet had no sooner touched the floor than Jael entered. Her servant seemed to have a sixth sense of when her mistress was awake.

"You slept well, Domina?"

"Yes, but this is a significant day."

"You are worried about what you will find?"

Lydia gave her a bleak smile. "You read my mind sometimes, Jael."

Jael nodded. "Will your mother go with you?"

"She and Delia wish to purchase supplies, but perhaps it will be possible tomorrow. She is still tired from the journey and the

sorrow of losing my father." She looked up as Jael was arranging her hair. "She needs something to occupy herself."

"And you will be busy with the shop, Domina? Perhaps little time for the villa?"

Lydia cocked her head. "Ah, I see where you are going with this. Perhaps it would be best if Mater took charge of the villa, since I will be in Philippi most days."

Jael helped her put on a plain linen tunic and tied a leather belt around her waist. Lydia slipped into her sandals and sat down at her dressing table as Jael began to brush her hair.

"Something simple this morning, Domina?"

"Yes. I need to look like I'm…in authority."

Lydia left her room just as her mother was leaving hers. "You slept well?"

Sophia nodded. "I look forward to seeing the city after you have matters at the shop settled. Today Delia and I will make a list of things we need."

Lydia glanced at Jael and back to her mother. "I've been think-ing, Ima, that since I will be busy with the shop, would you consider taking charge of the villa? You ran our home so well in Thyatira, and I will have much to do in Philippi."

"But this is your home, Lydia. Your father gave it to you. I should not be mistress here."

"It is our villa, not just mine. Pater knew we would be sharing it. It would be one less thing I have to worry about."

Sophia searched her daughter's face a moment, then bright-ened. "Then that is what I will do."

Lydia took her arm, "Good. Now that we've settled that matter, let us have some breakfast. I must leave within the hour and it is already getting warm."

She knew Delia and Chara had been worried about their mis-tress, and when Lydia came down the stairs, she saw Jael give an

almost imperceptible nod to the other two women. Their smiles told her of their relief.

———————•———•———•———————

Hektor brought around a small carriage. It was not the *carpentum* she had traveled in to the seaport of Troas, but it would at least hold four. Noting the single mule, Lydia wondered how many other surprises this villa held. At least she did not have to walk into the city.

Lydia settled herself and waited until Jael climbed up next to her. Her maidservant and Hektor would have to be her chaperones. As they started for the city, Lydia mused. Was the villa her father's way of making up for all the years he had favored Cassius? While he had said little to her, she knew he was impressed with her diligence in learning the dye business. His attitude had changed and he had certainly provided for their every need here in Philippi. She gazed at the scenery and the buildings of the city but couldn't yet look forward to exploring the various streets and stalls of the agora with her mother. She was too nervous about finding a factor to manage the shop.

Sargon had told her there were other merchants who sold the purple fabrics, and her father had also mentioned that there was a Dyers' Guild in the city but it would be better if she kept a low profile and let her manager handle the shop. She tried to control her anxiety for it would not bode well to let the lawyer see how nervous she was. They needed to work together.

Lydia described to Hektor the building her father had described to her, and Hektor, nodding, eventually pulled up in front of a large, pretentious edifice. Its marble columns seemed to proclaim affluence. Taking a deep breath, Lydia entered the building with Jael close behind.

A Roman soldier was crossing the large entry and for a moment her mind went to Cassius. The man's eyes flickered over her and he was about to pass on, when she gathered her courage.

"Sir, can you direct us to the office of Magnus Titelius? He is a lawyer."

The soldier frowned a moment but nodded his head in a direction across the entry and up a flight of stairs. "I've just done business with him. He is in his office." With that, the soldier hurried on out of the building.

Lydia climbed the stairs and found herself at the doorway of a large office. One or two scribes were working diligently on various scrolls. A large, heavyset man with almost-white hair sat behind an enormous table spread with scrolls. He looked up, his eyebrows raised. "Yes?"

"Sir? I am Lydia, daughter of Atticus of Thyatira."

He studied her a moment and then nodded. "Ah, not sure you would come." She noted he was wearing a toga with the purple stripe of the upper class. It was the rich color of the fabrics sold in her father's shops. He sighed, rose, and came around the table. "So you are here. Magnus Titelius at your service, madam. I am honored to meet the daughter of my old friend, but forgive me; after my letter, I thought you would change your mind." He shook his head. "That scoundrel took a nice bag of money with him. I had no idea the direction he took, but reported him to the authorities."

He swept a hand toward an ornate chair by his desk. "Please, be seated, madam." She did so as Jael moved quietly to stand behind her chair.

"I do not think I can help you find a new manager for the shop. As soon as the other Guilds find out the new owner is a woman, there would be…ah…difficulties."

"I am familiar with the difficulties, sir. I do have someone looking for me, quietly, of course."

He stroked his ample chin. "As I mentioned in my letter, I have funds for you which I have not yet sent due to your father's death. It was an awkward situation. I was not to send them to Cassius according to your father, but to you, and I needed to know what you would do with the business."

She clasped her hands. "I appreciated your warning, but my mother and I had no choice but to come here. My brother was angry that Pater left the business to me and he couldn't sell it. We had to leave our villa."

His brows knit together. "He refused you the villa? His mother also?"

She nodded. "I think he felt that if he did, I would be forced to sell the business."

"He is *paterfamilias*." He shrugged.

"Sir, I must be absolutely sure of my ownership of the villa, for personal reasons."

"Do not fear. I have the document that proves you are the legal owner of the villa. I will keep one here and I will give you a copy to keep in your home…should it be needed."

He was referring to Cassius. Did he also feel her brother would come here and seek her out?

She waited as he turned to a cabinet behind his desk and pulled out some scrolls and a small leather bag. "This belongs to you. It should help you and your mother until you can…ah, procure someone for the shop." He perused one of the scrolls briefly and handed it to her.

"This is what you need, madam. All is in order according to Roman law."

As she received the treasured scroll, Lydia sensed the lawyer didn't have a great deal of faith that she would be able to find anyone to manage the shop. She stood and he placed the bag in her hand and handed her the other scrolls.

"Here are the accounts my servant found in the shop. It will give you some idea of how things were before your father died. I imagine it was not anything your missing factor needed or he would have taken them too."

He studied her a moment. "You are a widow. Had you given thought to marrying again? You are an attractive woman, and while not young, you are still eligible. It would solve the problem you have with the shop. Or," he said as he stroked his chin, "you could sell the business and reap a nice profit. You would be able to live comfortably for a long time."

Lydia swallowed her temper. It would do no good to antagonize the one man in Philippi whom she might need on her side.

She kept her tone friendly and submissive. "I appreciate your suggestion. The former did not seem to be an option for me, and as to the latter, I will have to see how successful I am before I face that decision."

Easing his bulk down in his chair again, he studied her. "As you choose, madam. You have a hard road ahead of you, but perhaps you will persevere. When you have been in business a year, come and see me. There are further instructions from your father, but they must wait. I wish you well. Please keep me informed of your progress." His expression became benevolent and for a moment he reminded her of her father. "I will help in any way I can, out of respect for your father." Then he returned to his desk and began to unroll one of the scrolls in front of him to peruse. She and Jael were dismissed.

Further instructions? As she boarded the *carpentum* again, she had more questions than answers. *What did her father have in mind?*

18

As the carriage approached the street of the fabric vendors, she almost missed her father's shop. Its shades were drawn and the sign advertising its wares hung at an angle. It looked like it had been closed up for some time—and abandoned.

"Are you all right, Domina?" Jael turned to her, eyes dark with concern.

Lydia stared at the building. All she could think of was that it was a good thing her mother had not come today. All her bravado melted away as she slowly climbed down from the carriage.

She turned to Hektor. "Do you know how long Porthos has been gone?"

"I am not in the city often…but according to the other merchants nearby, he left after receiving a letter. That is all I know, Domina."

A letter. Lydia suspected it was the one telling him of her father's death. With no benefactor and an uncertain future, he had taken the funds and run.

She stared at the shambles. It would take some work to make it look like a profitable business again.

Jael joined her and looked the shop over. "Domina, we can put it in order again. We can bring Delia and Chara. It would not take us long."

Lydia gave her a half-smile. "I appreciate your zeal, Jael, but even after it was in order, then what?"

A woman came up to the shop and frowned, shaking her head. When she turned and saw Lydia, she approached the two women with her lips pressed together in a thin line.

"If you are looking to buy cloth, he is gone. I don't know where he went. This shop had the finest purple cloth in the city."

Lydia smiled in a way she hoped was encouraging. "We just arrived and learned this." She took a breath and smiled at the woman. "I am given to understand that the new factor is coming but he has been delayed. The shop will be opening for customers very soon. There is a new shipment of fabrics arriving."

The woman sniffed. "How do you know this? Where is the owner?"

Lydia resisted the urge to say why she was there. "My...uh, family owns the shop."

The woman sniffed. "We'll see." And with a dubious look at Lydia, she stalked away.

Hektor inserted an ancient key in the lock and the wooden door swung open. A musty smell greeted the women as they stepped inside. Some bolts of cloth were still on the wooden shelves, dusty but intact. Jael was right, she needed someone to set the shop to rights again. She bowed her head and sent up a quick prayer for wisdom.

As she was contemplating what to do next, a male voice came from the doorway.

"I had not expected to meet you again so soon, madam. Were you looking for the factor?"

Nikolas was leaning up against the doorpost. His dark eyes studied her, his eyebrows raised in question.

"We meet again," she managed. Gathering herself up, she lifted her chin. "Why are you here?"

He glanced around the shop. "I was curious about why it closed. I was told the owner would be looking for a new factor. That is the position I intended to apply for, but he is not here."

He looked past her and, seeing only Hektor standing with the lock and key, gave her another questioning look.

She drew herself up and lifted her chin. "I own the shop now. My father left it to me."

His face registered unbelief. "*You* own the shop? You are the daughter of Atticus Vasillis?" He frowned. "I am familiar with the Vasillis family business but I understood there was a brother."

By now her temper was getting the best of her. She glanced at the anxious faces of Hektor and Jael.

"It was a blow to my father that my brother preferred the army to running what he called, 'a smelly business.' I know all the aspects of the business. My father trained me for months before he died, and willed it to me to support my mother and myself. My father's manager, Sargon, sold the fabrics and I stayed in the background of the shop in Thyatira."

"It was Sargon who sent me here."

Her eyes widened. *This* was the man Sargon knew of?

Nikolas shook his head slightly. "You may be knowledgeable, madam, but it will do no good if you have no one to deal with the customers."

She sighed, deflated. "I am quite aware of the situation." Embarrassment filled her as the words tumbled out of her mouth. Now he knew how desperate she was.

Surprisingly, his face softened. "Well, as I see it, you need a factor, and I need employment. I have never worked for a woman, but perhaps we can find an agreement?"

She had to take charge of this conversation. Lifting her chin, she spoke firmly. "You have experience?" She chided herself. Sargon wouldn't have sent him if he didn't.

A smile twitched at the corners of his mouth. "Yes, I am knowledgeable concerning the dye business. I worked for another dyer in Thyatira for several years. He envied the color of your fabrics. I am more than familiar with the shop of the Vasillis family." He studied her again. "So you really are the daughter of Atticus?"

"Yes."

"My former employers were jealous of the color of your purple, considered the finest in the city. Unfortunately, the man I worked for died and his sons took over the business. They proceeded to alienate all his customers. I saw the future of the shop and left."

"How is it that you are were here in Philippi before us?"

"A different ship, madam." He perused the shop a moment and then turned back to her. "I've known Sargon for several years. He merely told me there might be a place to work in the fabric trade in Philippi. He described the shop. He had just received word from a source that Porthos was gone and the new owner might be looking for a factor to manage the shop. Evidently he did not think it necessary to tell me who the new owner was."

"If you had known it was a woman, would you have come?"

From his hesitation, she had her answer.

Lydia's mind raced as she tried to form a plan. "If I hire you, can you get this shop cleaned up and ready for customers in three days? My son-in-law is sending a shipment of fabrics from Thyatira and they should arrive at any time."

He considered her words and for a moment seemed indecisive. Then, "Will you give me a free hand in the shop and the arrangement of the fabrics?"

She had to make a decision; there was no time to think about it. "Very well, I will trust your word. You are hired, but I shall return in a couple of days to inspect your progress."

He appeared amused. "Very well, madam, shall we settle on my wages?" He named a sum, which seemed reasonable to her.

Hektor, who had remained silent through the exchange, moved closer and with his back to Nikolas gave her an imperceptible nod.

"That is acceptable."

When he agreed, her relief was almost tangible.

They went over the shop together, discussing what needed to be done. His ideas pleased her but she merely nodded. She couldn't bring herself to give him the satisfaction of showing how much she approved.

A curtain covered the doorway to a back room. It held a bed, a small table, and a lamp. Nikolas appeared pleased. "This will do for me. I can watch over the shop and have a place to live as well as work." He glanced at her as if she would disagree with him.

"I suppose it will do."

Once again that amused smile.

"You will need new scrolls to record the shop's business. I will include the cost of these with your wages." When they stepped back into the main room, Nikolas carefully examined each of the few remaining bolts of fabric.

"They are salvageable, but I will go over each one to check for stains or tears."

"Very well." She looked around again. He had a great deal of work to do.

Jael, who had remained in the background, climbed back up on the carriage. Nikolas handed Lydia up. "I will expect you in three days, madam. If the shipment arrives before then, I will send you word."

She contemplated the situation and then lowered her voice. "Remember, no one is to know a woman owns the shop, Nikolas."

There it was again—that infuriating smirk of his!

"Madam, you can be assured, I have no intention of sharing that fact with anyone."

19

*L*ydia was still feeling her irritation when she hurried into the villa to find her mother. Sophia was sitting on the stone bench by the fountain in the center of the house. Lydia sat down next to her with a large sigh. "How was your day, Ima?"

Her mother studied her with a slight smile. "Perhaps I should ask how *your* day went. You do not seem pleased."

Lydia shared her conversation with the lawyer-agent.

"The manager left the shop in disarray and took money with him?"

"That is what I found, Mater. Fortunately he'd turned over some of the funds from the shop to the lawyer before learning of my father's death."

"You will have to find what the income was when the shop was in operation. The books should help you, unless the man Porthos was dishonest in that area also."

"True, I cannot be sure, considering what he's done. I pray the shop will be active soon and with the new shipment pending, we should do well."

"But who will sell the fabrics for you?"

Lydia then told her of Nikolas and what had transpired at the shop.

Sophia raised her eyebrows. "The man who drove us to the villa? *He* is the man Sargon sent you? I thought you cared very little for him!"

"The very same. I was desperate, not knowing where to start. I was going to come back for our servants to help me straighten up the shop. I gave Nikolas what money I had to get him started but I have a feeling he will clean up the shop himself. There is a small bed in the back room where he can sleep. I'm relieved someone is watching over the goods now."

Sophia was thoughtful. "And when do you think the shipment of fabrics from Thyatira will arrive?"

"Marcellus said he would send it two weeks or so after we left. It took us five days to get here. I would think in the next week or two it will arrive. At least someone will be there to receive it."

"And you trust this man?"

"I had no choice. Sargon seemed to approve of him or he would not have sent him, and whom else do I have? I could not advertise for a manager, for then the city would know a woman owned the shop and that would be disastrous."

"I suppose you are right. When you go back in three days, I would like to go along, not only to see what Nikolas has accomplished, but also to see the city itself. I am longing to visit the public baths."

"All is well here in the villa?"

Sophia nodded. "With Delia in the kitchen and Chara and Jael to help me, the house is in order. The evening meal is being prepared right now. Hektor seems relieved that Delia is in charge of the inside of the villa. He loves the garden and orchard and will make sure we have all the vegetables and fruits the land around the villa can produce." She smiled. "Jael seems to enjoy the chickens and the goat. Perhaps she can help Hektor with them."

Lydia looked out over their small orchard. "Hektor tells me there is an acropolis for games. The *Via Egnatia* runs through the marketplace. There is a library and of course many temples, especially a large one for the goddess, Cybele."

Sophia was thoughtful. "I pray that there is no animosity here against Jews or God-fearers. I sensed an undercurrent of something hostile in Thyatira."

———————•———————

After their dinner, Lydia retrieved some of the scrolls from the psalms she had purchased from a Jewish merchant in Thyatira. Since they had no synagogue to hear the words of Adonai now, Lydia read to her mother and the servants. The *Tehillim*, the psalms of David the shepherd king, touched her heart, and this evening she read from the Septuagint's nineteenth psalm.

The heavens declare the glory of God,
The dome of the sky speaks the work of his hands.
Every day it utters speech,
Every night it reveals knowledge.
Without speech, without a word,
Without their voices being heard,
Their line goes out through all the earth
And their words to the end of the world.
In them he places a tent for the sun,
Which comes out like a bridegroom from the bridal chamber,
With delight like an athlete to run his race.
It rises at one end of the sky,
Circles around to the other side,
And nothing escapes its heat.
The Torah of Adonai *is perfect,*
Restoring the inner person.
The instruction of Adonai *is sure,*
Making wise the thoughtless.
The precepts of Adonai *are right,*
Rejoicing the heart.

The mitzvah of ADONAI *is pure,*
Enlightening the eyes.
The fear of ADONAI *is clean,*
Enduring forever.
The rulings of ADONAI *are true,*
They are righteous all together,
More desirable than gold,
Than much fine gold,
Also sweeter than honey
Or drippings from the honeycomb.

Lydia stopped there for the evening. It was a long psalm. The women were silent for a moment. Then Jael spoke up. "Adonai is merciful is He not, Domina? He is a forgiving God?"

"Yes, Jael. He is in the heavens watching over us always. The great king, David, who wrote this psalm, trusted Him all his life. God helped David defeat the mighty giant, Goliath, a warrior who was over nine feet tall, with only a single stone from his sling. David was only a shepherd boy, but he trusted in God."

Chara said, "He has watched over you and my mistress, Domina. Did He not provide for you and see you safely to this haven?"

"He did indeed," murmured Sophia.

Jael looked toward the stairway. "Do not the Roman gods watch over us also and answer our prayers?"

Sophia responded, "The figures in the alcoves of this house were made of wood. We know that when a woodcutter cuts a tree, he takes part of the wood for his fire, to warm himself and to cook his food. But in the same way, he uses the other part of the same tree to make an idol that can not speak, hear, nor see, and sets it up to worship it. How can an idol answer prayers if it is made from a tree?"

Chara's brows knit together. "Does Adonai answer your prayers with a voice, Domina?"

Lydia smiled at her. "I hear His voice in my heart and through His Word. I know when He is speaking to me and directing me."

Delia looked earnestly at her mistress. "I have watched you, Domina. He directs your life. I believe He is a good God. I believe in Him."

Sophia reached out and laid her hand gently on Delia's arm. "That is a good thing, Delia. I am happy for you." She gazed at Jael and Chara in turn. "That is a decision each of you must make for yourselves one day. I pray Adonai will reveal Himself to you. All you need to do is to ask Him, for He is a God who loves His people."

Suddenly noting her mother's weariness, Lydia rose. "Shall we retire, Ima?"

Sophia nodded and started toward the stairs before turning to Delia. "You have checked the dough?"

Delia gave her a puzzled look. Her mistress seldom questioned her on its preparation. "It will be ready in the morning, Domina."

Sophia nodded and ascended the stairs with Chara. Lydia followed with Jael.

When Jael left her, Lydia sat for a long time on the window seat and stared out at the darkened orchard. A bird's song broke the silence, answered by its mate. A sense of melancholy washed over her, and Lydia realized how lonely she was. She had much to be thankful for in her father's provision, but would she spend her final years alone, like her mother? She thought of the psalm where the sun like a bridegroom came out of his chamber with delight. Her bridegroom had not been delighted with her. Vowing to be brave for her mother's sake, Lydia wiped away a lone tear that made its way down her cheek and listened to the sounds of the night.

She bowed her head to pray. *Oh Adonai, You know my heart and what I must do to provide for us. Give me wisdom and strength, lest I be guilty of those presumptuous sins and offend You. We are in Your care and I thank you for Your provision.*

A small breeze flowed in the window, brushing her face and she felt a gentle peace settle over her heart.

20

The third day after first finding her father's shop, Lydia prepared to return to evaluate what Nikolas had accomplished and explore the city with her mother. As she contemplated facing him again, Lydia's emotions tumbled about. What was there about this man that upset her so? She and her mother had prayed that morning that their new shop manager was all he purported himself to be. Why, then, did she feel so restless?

Passing through the busy agora with all the noise of a large marketplace, Hektor pulled up in front of the shop and Lydia was pleasantly surprised. The trash in front was gone and the stone had been washed down. The banner declaring their wares had been cleaned and hung carefully. Hektor helped Lydia and her mother down from the wagon. As they entered, a matron was looking at the few bolts of cloth that Nikolas had arranged attractively on a nearby shelf. Fabric had been hung on the walls to give the room a more elegant look.

"This is all you have?" The lady's voice was petulant and demanding. "When will you have more to choose from?"

"Ah, Domina, I see that you have a discerning eye for good fabric. That is what we are known for. We are most saddened by the loss of the previous factor and the condition in which he left the shop. The new shipment is due any day now and you will have your choice of the finest purple cloth. Your patience will be well rewarded." Nikolas gave her a most charming smile and she was visibly flustered.

"Very well, I will, ah, trust in the good reputation of your shop. I shall be back." With a coy smile she sailed past Lydia and Sophia. "You might as well wait," she murmured to them in passing, "there is little here now."

When the matron had gone, Lydia turned to Nikolas. "We came in three days, as you suggested."

Nikolas bowed slightly toward Sophia. "I trust you feel settled in your new home?"

"Yes, thank you." She glanced at the few bolts of fabric. "This shop always did well. I trust you can accomplish that again."

"Have no fear, madam, the shop is in good hands."

Lydia spoke up. Did he not remember *she* was his employer? She forced down her irritation. Years of subservience to male superiority tempered her response. "I am pleased that you have made the shop look respectable once more."

Nikolas turned those dark eyes on her and his mouth twitched at her words. Was he laughing at her? Suddenly she felt as flustered as the matron who had just left. She shook herself mentally and lifted her chin. "Have you had any other customers?"

He seemed amused by his effect on her. "Yes, madam, we have had many inquiries. I am hoping that the promised shipment from Thyatira arrives soon. I cannot just keep telling them more fabrics are coming."

"Adonai has heard our prayers. He will see our need."

"You speak of the Jewish God?" It was more a statement than a question.

"My mother is Jewish. I also follow Adonai."

His brows knit together. "I am Greek, but I have heard much about this Jewish God." He rubbed his chin. "I have sought to know more about Him. The dedication of the Jews intrigues me, and my prayers to the Greek gods, and even the Roman ones, seem to go unanswered."

Lydia was startled at this confession and vulnerability. He had seemed so sure of himself, almost arrogant.

Sophia studied him a moment, perhaps judging his sincerity. "Tomorrow is the Sabbath but there is no synagogue in Philippi. Our slave informed us that some God-fearers meet down by the river to pray. It may be that you could speak with someone there who could answer your questions."

He paused, contemplating her words. "Yes, thank you. Perhaps I will seek them out." He turned to Lydia. "Will my employer also be there?"

Lydia felt her anger rise. His impertinence had returned. "We would like to meet other Jews and God-fearers in the city," she replied simply.

Another matron entered the shop and Nikolas almost instantly assumed his role of merchant. Intent on charming possible customers, he halted the conversation by nodding to Lydia and Sophia. "Please come again in a few days. The new fabrics should be here by then." They were dismissed.

As they once again entered the carriage, Sophia put a hand on Lydia's arm. "Shall we view the city that is to be our new home?"

Lydia knew Sophia had sensed her frustration with Nikolas and as usual, in her quiet way, sought to divert it. Lydia smiled at her mother. "Yes, let us indeed see the city...and, of course, the baths."

They rode past several temples and the acropolis, used for gladiatorial contests. A rocky slope on the northern side of the road was covered with numerous inscriptions, reliefs, and carvings, evidence of cults and deities that showed the religious diversity of the city. As they approached one colonnaded street, Lydia quickly touched her mother on the shoulder. "Ima, the baths."

"Oh, Lydia, you found them! After the Sabbath, we shall come with Jael and Chara."

The sun was past its zenith, and the day was moving into afternoon. "It grows late. We should purchase our supplies and return home."

While Hektor waited, the two women perused the food merchants, purchasing some spices, fruit, and, to Sophia's delight, a pottery jar filled with honey.

"I must bring Delia here after the Sabbath. She is particular about the food for her kitchen."

Lydia laughed. "Indeed she is."

As they drove past the shop again on their way home, Nikolas suddenly stepped out and put up a hand to stop them.

"I'm glad I saw you. The ship carrying the fabric from Thyatira has docked. They will be unloading this afternoon."

Elated that the goods that meant their livelihood had arrived, Lydia glanced at her mother who nodded. "We shall wait."

The two women entered the relative cool of the shop and Nikolas brought a bench for them to sit on.

He sighed, evidence of his own relief. "We will be back in business by tomorrow." Lydia nodded, not sure how to say what was on her mind. How would they handle the funds he collected from the sales?

He evidently had been thinking of the same thing. "I will enter each sale in the books, Domina, and will come to your villa weekly to bring what is due you. If you come to the shop, you must stay out of sight in the back room." At her raised eyebrows, he hastened to add, "If you come too often to the shop, there will be talk among the merchants."

As much as she disliked his reminder, she had to admit he was right. She could not come every day or the merchants nearby would suspect a different relationship. She could not afford to jeopardize her reputation.

"I am aware of your concerns, Nikolas. I will expect you at the villa, but of course I intend to come from time to time with my mother or my servant, to inspect the shop."

"That is your prerogative, madam."

Sophia spoke up. "Nikolas, you were asking about the Jewish God. We read from the ancient Jewish scrolls every evening. Perhaps when you bring the receipts you could join us for our discussions."

Lydia silently ground her teeth. She would speak to her mother about presumptive invitations.

Just then a wagon driven by two men approached the shop. They stopped at the door, jumped down, and began to unload bundles wrapped in heavy cloth. The women watched, stepping further and further to the back of the shop. By the time all the bundles were unloaded, there seemed scarcely room for the women or Nikolas. Lydia slipped Nikolas money to pay them. She silently thanked the lawyer for the extra funds he'd saved for her.

One of the men held out a smaller bundle. "For the woman named Lydia. Do you know her? We were told if we delivered these goods, we would be paid."

Lydia stepped forward. "I am she." She looked to Nikolas, and he paid the men.

One sailor handed her the bundle. Lydia carried a letter to Marianne with her in hopes of sending it back on a ship when their goods arrived. She retrieved the scroll and handed it to one of the men. "For my son-in-law in Thyatira."

He nodded and put it in a pouch. When the two sailors had gone, taking the wagon back to the docks, Nikolas cut the leather thongs that were tightly wrapped around the bundle and opened it. Inside was a box, and he silently gave it back to Lydia.

Lydia opened the box and took out a bag of Roman coins. From the weight of it, there was enough to sustain them for several months. Lydia looked down at the pouch. Their needs here had been met abundantly. She glanced up at Nikolas, wondering again if he could be trusted and what his motives were. Would he take advantage of her newly acquired funds that she so naively opened in his presence?

A letter was also enclosed from Marcellus.

We send greetings from myself and Marianne. We have sent this first shipment and others will follow, approximately two months apart. Also, we are sending proceeds from the shop here. We will send them periodically with each shipment.

We are happy to announce that Marianne is with child, and in approximately six months we look forward to sending you news of a grandson or granddaughter. We trust you are well and arrived safely. Marianne sends her love, Marcellus.

"Ima!" Lydia exclaimed. "Marcellus has shared good news. You are to be a great-grandmother."

Sophia touched her shoulder. "May Adonai be praised!"

Nikolas interrupted. "If you will excuse me, Domina, I have a great deal of work to do. When word gets around that the fabric is here, I anticipate a deluge of matrons."

Sophia took Lydia's arm. "I am ready. Let us return home."

Nikolas was already busy opening the bundles of beautiful dyed cloth, and Lydia felt her heart rise looking at the beautiful shades of purple. From the number of bundles, she realized he would be there half the night working and arranging them on the shelves. At least the look on his face told her he was pleased with the quality of the fabric. He fingered it gently, smiling and nodding.

She and her mother were only in his way, and while Lydia longed to see the shelves filled, it was time to leave. Nikolas gave her a brief nod, his mind obviously occupied.

As they rode back to the villa, Lydia suddenly realized how weary she was. The stress of dealing with Nikolas, the anxiety of not knowing when the fabric would arrive, and in a sense, relief that she didn't have to deal with it all, had taken its toll. Perhaps Adonai had sent Nikolas to them after all.

She thought of those dark, piercing eyes once again, and wondered at the emotions they evoked. She must deal with him on a weekly basis, and more often, if he took advantage of her mother's well-meaning invitation. Suddenly the future seemed full of questions and she had no answers.

21

The next time they drove to Philippi, it was for much-needed refreshment at the baths. Jael and Chara were perched on the back of the cart to accompany them. As Hektor drove, once again Lydia was once again impressed with the city of Philippi. It had a life force that seemed to hum with the activity of its people. While she noted the many statues dedicated to Roman gods, she and her mother held hope that they would meet even more believers in the true God as time went on. The coming Sabbath they would go to the river, where, hopefully, they could meet others who followed Adonai.

As they left Neapolis, the port city where she and her mother had disembarked, they began traveling on the *Via Egnatia*, the great Roman highway her father told her about, that went through the city of Philippi ten miles away. It wound through the city and continued 490 miles across Macedonia, linking the Adriatic with the Aegean Sea. She tried to imagine someone traveling the length of that highway and wondered about the cities and towns it served.

They passed through the agora, but on this day they would forgo the shopping. Since they had arrived, Lydia had learned there were two bath houses at the end of one of the more colonnaded streets. They chose the closest one. Leaving Hektor with the carriage, the four women entered the building.

Marble mosaics filled the beautiful floors and the stuccoed walls were painted with frescoes of trees, birds, and other pastoral images. The ceiling was blue with gold stars and celestial beings. Lydia got a glimpse of a garden through one portico, with its statues and fountain. Through another portico they glimpsed a room that was obviously a library of some kind. Lydia made a note to herself to take her mother into the garden area after the baths. Perhaps they served refreshments there.

In the *apodyterium*, the women were joined by Jael and Chara, who had entered through the slave entrance. Lydia and Sophia left their clothes on shelves, and proceeded to the *frigidarium*, the cold room. With their servants holding their towels, Lydia and her mother dipped in briefly before wrapping themselves and proceeding to the *tepidarium*, the warm room. It was relaxing and they stayed there a little longer.

"The villa is lovely, Lydia. Everything there seems to meet our needs. I love the fruit trees."

"We are getting nice eggs from the chickens also, Mater."

"At least we can provide our own chicken for a meal or two."

Lydia smiled and glanced up at Jael who hovered nearby. "I don't know if we can kill one, Jael seems to be very attached to them."

Jael laughed.

"Hektor seems very dependable. I can imagine your father staying there at the villa when he went to see how the shop there was doing. He would be gone for at least two weeks and I always wondered where he went."

It was not unusual for a Roman patrician to have a mistress hidden away in another city and although Lydia wondered briefly if someone else had lived at the villa before them, neither she nor her mother would consider bringing up the subject. Wives kept silent about those things, just as she had not mentioned to her husband's family that there were other women in his life.

Moving on to the *caldarium*, the hot room, Lydia and Sophia dropped their towels again and slipped into the water slowly to adjust to the higher temperature. Lydia felt her muscles relax and her worries about the shop seemed to slip away in the soothing water.

At last they returned to the *tepidarium* where their servants, Jael and Chara, had been assigned two massage tables. Under Jael's deft fingers, Lydia sighed and almost went to sleep.

When at last they retrieved their clothes and entered the garden, Lydia handed over the necessary coins to the woman at the entrance. They were served *mulsum*, a freshly made mixture of wine and honey, along with a small platter of fresh grapes and pears.

Feeling totally refreshed, Lydia took her mother's arm as they returned to the carriage. Lydia had agreed not to visit the shop too often, and though she was tempted to stop by, she directed Hektor to the marketplace instead.

Wandering among the various stalls, Lydia bought a new pair of sandals for herself and her mother and, debating the amount of time she would have to keep it, finally bought some fresh fish for Delia to work her wonders with. She also bought some oysters. The tradesmen wrapped them well and she handed the packages to Jael to carry.

On the way home, they passed the theater and Lydia wistfully wondered if there was a way she and her mother could go that would seem proper. They had no male to accompany them and only male slaves were considered chaperones. Perhaps Nikolas? But then she chided herself. He was not her slave, nor a man of the upper Roman class; he was an employee and a Greek. It would not be appropriate. She caught her mother's eye and suspected Sophia was also thinking of the theater, but did not voice her thoughts.

They passed within sight of the shop and Lydia glanced over. Two Roman matrons were leaving with bundles in their arms and pleased looks on their faces. Nikolas was proving his worth, however taxing his arrogance.

22

The Sabbath dawned bright and clear. Lydia lay in her bed listening to the song of a bird outside her window. It was still early for Jael to arrive, so she rose, wandered over to the window, and looked out upon the small orchard. The shadows were retreating over the wall and the chickens stirred in their pen. As she gave the day over to her God, a sense of His presence swept over her being. She had experienced this only a few times in her life, once as a child when she had watched the light dance on the leaves of the sycamore tree one Sabbath, and twice more, during the darkest times of her marriage.

"What do you have for me today, Lord?"

No answer came forth, but she felt her excitement rise at the prospect of meeting other God-fearers at the river.

Hektor brought the small carriage around to the front of the villa. It was built for only four, but Lydia didn't want to leave anyone behind. Delia, Jael, and Chara squeezed together on one side with Lydia and her mother on the other. Lydia and Sophia's custom was to observe the Jewish Sabbath, and they did not allow their servants to work on that day. Although all three slaves had been with them in Sophia's household for many years, only Delia had expressed interest in the Jewish God.

When they arrived at the river, a small group of women were praying. Sophia glanced at them. "I see no Jews here. Only a group of women."

As the carriage came to a stop, the women looked up and two gave Lydia's group tentative smiles.

One of the women approached them. "Welcome. I am Marcia. Are you also God-fearers?"

Sophia smiled. "Yes, we are. We are new in Philippi and hoped to find others of our faith."

Marcia beckoned the other three women and gestured toward them as they approached. "This is Julia, my sister, and these are Euodia and Avita."

The woman called Julia noted the maidservants and Hektor. "Where are you from? We have not seen you here before."

Lydia glanced at her mother and responded. "I am Lydia and this is my mother, Sophia. We are both widows and have come from Thyatira to live in my father's villa here. He has a fabric business in the agora." She turned toward the cart. "These are our maidservants: Jael, Chara, and Delia. Hektor works for us at the villa and drives the carriage."

The women looked at each other. "Did you say you have a business here in Philippi?" Marcia asked.

"It was my father's. We sell the Tyrolian purple cloth. Since my father's death, a factor and lawyer-agent run the business for us."

Julia suddenly brightened. "That must be the shop that has just re-opened in the agora. It has the most beautiful fabrics. We are not Roman and have no need of the purple, but I stopped in one day to view the cloth. It is said to be the best of all the purple cloth sellers."

Sophia answered, "I'm glad the shop is doing well. We have not been there other than to see it when we came. I am still in mourning for my husband."

There was a murmur of sympathy from the group.

"Did your husband die here in Philippi?" This from Avita, who had mostly remained quiet.

Marcia gave her a disapproving glance and turned back to Sophia. "Forgive my sister, she can be too curious at times."

"I understand. It's all right," Sophia answered. "My husband died in Thyatira. We have come to Philippi to start a new life. We were told we would find other God-fearers here."

Lydia had been quiet, listening to the exchange. "We interrupted your time of prayer. Please continue."

The group glanced at each other and then Marcia beckoned them. "Come, join us and let us thank the Most High God for bringing you to our small gathering."

Lydia felt her heart fill with joy as she and her mother joined in a sweet time of fellowship and deep prayer.

Marcia, who seemed to be the leader of the group, pulled a small scroll from a cloth bag she carried and began to read. Lydia recognized the twenty-third psalm of David. It was one of her favorites.

ADONAI is my shepherd; I lack nothing
He has me lie down in grassy pastures
He leads me by quiet water,
He restores my inner person.
He guides me in the right paths,
For the sake of his own name.
Even if I pass through death-dark ravines,
I will fear no disaster; for you are with me;
Your rod and staff reassure me.
You prepare a table for me,
Even as my enemies watch;

You anoint my head with oil
From an overflowing cup.
Goodness and peace will pursue me
Every day of my life;
And I will live in the house of ADONAI
For years and years to come.

As Lydia listened to the intonation of the familiar words, she thought of the many ways Adonai had watched over her as a child, through a disastrous marriage to Plinius, during the heart-wrenching death of her father, and in the move to Philippi. Always He had gone before her to prepare the way. She felt a sense of belonging, that here was the place Adonai wanted her to be. She didn't know His plan for her, but she knew that at each turn in the road, He had been there.

The group closed with a song, another psalm.

Shout to God, all the earth!
Sing the glory of his name, make his praise glorious.
Tell God, "How awesome are your deeds!
At your great power, your enemies cringe.
All the earth bows down to you, sings praises to you, sings praises
to your name."

Lydia smiled at the women. "Thank you for including us in your worship time." She and Sophia embraced each of them.

Marcia took Lydia's hand. "Do come and join us again the next Sabbath. We are hoping to find a better place to meet, but God will show us when it is time."

After agreeing come again the following week, Lydia and her household returned home. Her heart was full and, like a warm cloak, she sensed the presence of Adonai.

You are dear to Me, daughter. Trust Me for what is to come.

What was to come? What did He have in store for her?

23

When Nikolas delivered the first proceeds from the week's sales, he reluctantly agreed to stay at Sophia's urging as Lydia read from the psalms. She chose the one hundred and thirteenth psalm, and as she read she struggled to concentrate, knowing his eyes were intent on her.

... ADONAI is high above all nations,
His glory above the heavens.
Who is like ADONAI our God, seated in the heights,
Humbling himself to look on heaven and on earth.

She paused and Nikolas quickly asked, "He is truly high above the heavens, but how is one to know Him? He is elusive, like a spirit."

Lydia glanced at her mother and Sophia nodded. "Nikolas, if God could come down to earth as another man and we could understand Him, would He still be God?"

Nikolas frowned and finally shook his head. "No, He cannot be one of us, for He is all-powerful. Yet He seems elusive. How can He understand the lives we live here on earth if He is so far above us?

Sophia persisted. "Think of the next part of the psalm." Lydia read the next portion aloud.

To the upright he shines like a light in the dark,
Merciful, compassionate, and righteous.

Little by little they discussed the rest of the psalm and its meaning. Nikolas asked many questions, and Lydia realized he was not just being polite but was truly seeking answers.

Suddenly he rose. "I must return to the shop. I will think on these things."

With a nod to Lydia and Sophia, he was gone.

Lydia watched him mount the mule he had purchased with his first earnings.

"Do you think he will become a God-fearer, Ima?"

Sophia had come to stand beside her. "I believe Adonai has His hand on Nikolas. Yes, I believe he will come in time. His heart is hungry."

Nikolas faithfully brought the earnings from the shop to her villa each week. Sometimes he stayed to listen to the Scriptures and sometimes he found excuses for returning to the city. For a while Lydia wondered whether he returned so quickly to see a woman, and the thought always came with a pang of jealousy. She packed away the feeling. He was nothing more to her than an employee, and a trying one at that.

Lydia gazed out of her window at the garden early one morning. It was the third Sabbath she and her mother and servants would go to the river to meet with the other God-fearers. Lydia considered inviting their new friends to the villa, but was reluctant, feeling that perhaps it was too soon.

She turned from the window as Jael entered.

Since she was never up before her servant came in the morning, Lydia smiled at the startled look on Jael's face.

"Is it not a beautiful morning, Jael?"

"Yes, Domina, it is that." Jael would not comment on any actions of her mistress, so she merely nodded and opened the cupboard to retrieve Lydia's clothes for the day.

Lydia felt a twinge of guilt that she had stayed in bed so many mornings until Jael came to get her ready for the day. She dressed quickly, anxious to be on their way to the river.

Once again the five of them traveled to the river. This morning, a happy anticipation filled her heart. Adonai had spoken to her heart in the night.

Be ready.

What did it mean? Be ready for the direction He was leading her? She didn't understand, but prayed to be open for whatever the day held.

Be ready.

She had learned to listen to the voice of Adonai. As her mother climbed out of the carriage, Lydia nodded to her servants to follow.

When they reached the river, Lydia looked around. Her friends were nowhere to be seen. There were times when she longed to hear the cantor's voice in the synagogue back in Thyatira, to hear the precious Scriptures read from the Torah. For a moment a wave of homesickness swept over her, thinking of all the changes in her life these last six months.

Nearby the chirping of a few sparrows added a note of cheer to the morning as she watched the river rushing by the embankment. She sighed and hoped the others would come as they usually did. In the meantime, she and her mother could at least pray. They sat on a wooden bench by the river. Their servants sat on a bench nearby. A soft breeze brushed Lydia's cheek. Maybe her dream was just wishful thinking, but she couldn't seem to shake the feeling of anticipation.

Eventually Avita, Euodia, and Marcia arrived along with Julia. Grateful that she and her servants were not alone to worship, Lydia greeted them warmly.

They gathered in their usual circle and Marcia led in prayer.

"Lord God of the heavens and the earth, we worship You today. We come under the canopy of heaven to praise Your holy name. We thank You for bringing us to a place of safety and meeting our most pressing needs...."

The sound of footsteps interrupted her.

Marcia paused and looked intently ahead. They all turned to observe a group of men approaching. Wary of strangers who might disrupt their worship, Lydia watched with apprehension.

From their facial features, three of the men appeared to be Jews but the fourth was a Gentile, she thought perhaps Greek. Had they come to pray? One man, who seemed to be the leader of the group, strode purposefully toward them. He was short with a strange rolling gait, his eyes overshadowed by bushy brows that marched across his forehead. He studied the group for a moment and then, to Lydia's surprise, came straight to her.

"Greetings in the name of the Lord. My name is Paul and these are my friends, Silas, Timothy, and Luke. Forgive us for interrupting your prayers. We are looking for God-fearers and heard that some came here to pray."

Lydia raised her eyebrows. He was certainly bold. She was tempted to give him a brief answer and gather her servants to leave, but the intensity of his gaze held her where she was. "I am a God-fearer, sir, as are these others. We have come here to pray, as there is no synagogue in the city."

The man beamed. "I knew the Lord led us here for a reason. Tell me, have you heard of Jesus, the Christ?"

Jael put a hand on her mistress's arm, and Lydia wondered if they should engage these men in further conversation. Surprising herself, she responded. "We do not know of this Jesus."

Paul nodded to his companions as if to affirm something and then turned back to her. "We are servants of the Most High God, and His Son, Jesus. May we share with you why we have come?"

Delia suddenly spoke up. "Domina, there is talk among the slaves and servants about this Jesus. He was a healer and did many miracles while He was alive."

Lydia frowned and looked at Paul. "You wish to tell us about a dead man?"

Paul didn't seem taken aback by her straight-forward question. "He died, but He rose again and is alive forevermore. He has made a way for all who believe in Him to have everlasting life, here on earth and one day in heaven."

As his companions sat on a nearby bench, Paul began. "Are you familiar with the Scriptures concerning the Messiah?"

Marcia and Lydia exchanged glances before Lydia answered. "I have been familiar with the Torah since I was a child." She nodded toward Sophia. "My mother is Jewish."

"Wonderful. Esteemed lady, I am a Jew. At one time I was called Saul, raised at the feet of Gamaliel, one of the great rabbis of our time. I was a zealous young man, steeped in the Scriptures and following the Torah to the letter. Then I heard of these followers of The Way, as they were called. They were men and women who had placed their faith in Jesus of Nazareth as their Messiah. I thought it blasphemy and dangerous to our religion. In the name of our leaders, I persecuted all I could find and arrested the believers I found there. I was even responsible for the deaths of some."

Lydia gasped. *What sort of a man was this?* "By what authority would you do such a thing?"

Paul did not appear to be offended. "Our people are ruled by Caesar, that is true, but we Jews are accountable to the leaders of our people. As such, the temple police carry out the orders of the High Priest against anyone who breaks the commandments of the Torah."

Lydia thought a moment. Yes, she had forgotten that. What he said was true. She nodded for him to continue.

"I was on my way to Damascus with temple guards, carrying letters from our leaders. I was authorized to find and arrest any of the believers I found there. As we approached the city, a bright light shone all around us. I fell to the ground and heard a voice saying to me, 'Saul! Saul! Why are you persecuting Me?'

"'Who are You, Lord?' I asked. And the voice replied, 'I am Jesus, the One you are persecuting. Now get up and go into the city, and you will be told what to do.'

"My men were speechless. They heard the sound of a voice but saw no one. I picked myself up off the ground but when I opened my eyes, I was blind."

Lydia frowned at this man's incredible story and glanced at her companions, who also appeared puzzled. "You were blind? How is it that you can now see?"

"My companions led me into the city to a house where I could stay. I remained there for three days, neither eating nor drinking. I spent the hours in prayer trying to understand what had happened to me, beseeching God to have mercy on me for what I had done."

"Then I saw in a vision a man named Ananias, a follower of The Way, coming to the house where I was staying. Indeed, the man did come to see me, for God had sent him there. Because of my reputation for persecuting the believers, he was hesitant, but obeyed the voice of the Lord. He laid hands on me and prayed in the name of Jesus for me to regain my sight. It was as if scales fell from my eyes and I could see again. I was baptized in a nearby *mikvah* and received the blessing of the Holy Spirit."

Sophia spoke up. "That is truly a remarkable tale. I have never heard of a blind man who was given back his sight. Tell me more about this Jesus. Who was He?"

Paul answered. "As God-fearers, you are no doubt familiar with the words of the prophet Isaiah, who tells us that a virgin shall conceive and bear a son, and He shall be called the Son of the Most High, and of His kingdom there shall be no end. God came to a virgin in Nazareth and gave her the blessed gift of bearing His Son, conceived by the Holy Spirit. Since the seed of Adam comes from the Father, as our Redeemer, and the Messiah we have long awaited, Jesus could not have an earthly father for then He would carry the sin of Adam."

Lydia nodded, and looked around at her mother and the rest of the women.

Paul continued. "Jesus grew to manhood in the small village of Nazareth...."

Sophia spoke up. "How could He be the Messiah if He was born in Nazareth? The prophet Micah tells us He was to be born in Bethlehem, the city of David."

"Ah, but He was, dear lady. At the time of His birth, Caesar Augustus sent out word that there was to be a census. Every head of household was to return to the city of his clan to be registered along with his family. Joseph, the earthly father of Jesus, was required to go to Bethlehem along with his wife, Mary, who was great with child."

Lydia interrupted, growing more curious in spite of herself. "Did they know about His powers when He was a child?"

"No, my lady. It was not until He was thirty, the age for a rabbi to begin his work, that He began His ministry. His mission was to share with our people that the Messiah was here, among them. In the power of His Father, God, He began working many miracles, healing those who were sick, lepers, the lame, and opening the eyes of the blind. There are thousands of witnesses to these miracles all over Judea. He came to His own people and to our shame, most of us knew Him not. Our leaders, jealous of His powers and fearing rebellion against Rome by His followers, put Him to death on a cross."

Lydia caught her breath. "They crucified Him? But that is the Roman punishment for thieves and murderers."

"He was neither, my lady, yet He was sacrificed for all who believe in Him. No longer is there the need for a sacrifice of a lamb for a sin offering on the Day of Atonement. Jesus was God's lamb, and His blood was shed to cover our sins for all time."

Lydia spoke up, still feeling skeptical, "How do you know this is true if He is dead?"

Paul smiled, and his face shone as if an inner light made his eyes glow. "He is alive forevermore. Three days after they placed Him in a tomb, God raised Him from the dead. Several women followers first, including His mother, Mary, then His disciples and hundreds of other believers saw Him alive. We have heard this from many people. The same day He was resurrected, many graves were opened and those resurrected ones came into the city of Jerusalem and were seen. There are those alive today who can attest to this."

The man called Luke spoke up. "I am a physician, dear lady, and I have made it a quest to determine the truth of what Brother Paul has spoken. I can verify he indeed speaks the truth. I have not performed any miracles, but I have been a witness to many miracles I cannot deny. Brother Paul was stoned in one city by idol-makers, thrown out of the city, and left as a dead man. After prayer was made for him, he was healed and able to get up and reenter the city to encourage the believers there."

Paul looked around at the women. "You are all familiar with the Jewish holy day of Passover, are you not?"

They nodded.

"Then you know it is called 'Passover' because through the prophet Moses, God told His people to kill a lamb and spread its blood on the doorposts of their homes in Egypt. God said, 'When I see the blood, the death angel will pass over your homes. The death angel will claim the firstborn in every home in Egypt that does not bear the blood of the lamb.'"

Paul continued. "Is not the lamb roasted on a spit, a vertical skewer thrust through the body and the back legs stretched out behind the animal? Is there not a horizontal skewer where the front legs are stretched out?"

They nodded. Lydia had a picture in her mind of the Passover lamb she had seen many times, roasting on a spit. The skewers formed a cross. The lamb was roasted on a cross. As he saw her eyes open with understanding, Paul smiled. "Jesus was God's Passover lamb."

"The prophet Isaiah you have heard read in the synagogue tells us of the Messiah. What He would go through. That He would be whipped and pierced so we could be healed. He was struck down for the rebellion of my people. We are like sheep that have strayed away. We have left God's paths to follow our own. Yet the Lord laid on Him the sins of us all."

As Paul continued to share prophecies from the Torah and the prophets, Lydia felt her heart quicken.

The truth of Paul's words sank deep in her spirit. She had heard the familiar words from Isaiah through the years in Thyatira, yet did not fully understand them. As she turned toward Delia, Chara, and Jael to see their reaction, she saw they too were listening earnestly to Paul.

Delia turned to Lydia. "We feel God is telling us that the words this man speaks are true, Domina. Perhaps this is why God has brought us to Philippi."

"I, too, sense the truth of his words, Delia." She turned to Paul. "What must we do to know this Jesus?"

"Repent of your trespasses and ask Him to be Lord of your life."

Chara spoke up hesitantly. "Domina, may we pray to know Him also?"

Lydia turned to Paul for confirmation.

"Your servants may indeed, madam, for God is no respecter of persons. Jeshua died to bring salvation to all."

Thoughts rose from her past, bitter thoughts of Plinius and her unhappy marriage. "Must I repent?"

"Only you know the things that stand between you and the Lord. I will pray with you to receive Jesus as Lord, that you might all enter the kingdom of heaven."

The other women looked at each other and each nodded her head, willing to take this step.

Sophia's head was already bowed, silently praying. Lydia glanced at her mother and sighed, recognizing the depth of the bitterness and pain of rejection she carried from her marriage to Plinius. There, by the river, as she confessed those things and laid them at the feet of Jesus, the peace she had sought for so long entered her soul. She confessed her guilt and hurt toward her brother for his treatment of her and her mother. When he saw that they were ready, Paul led them in prayer.

"Lord Jesus, we recognize You as Lord of our lives. We repent of our sins that have separated You from us. We ask You to cover us with Your righteousness that when You see us, You would see the price You paid for our sins. Be Lord of our lives and our Redeemer. From this day we will serve You with all our heart and soul. In the name of Jesus, the Christ, we pray."

When the prayers ended, it was as though the light of the sun had entered Lydia's body. The burden of sorrow and rejection lifted from her shoulders. She shook her head in wonder and looked up to see joy on the faces of Delia, Chara, and Jael. She turned and smiled at Marcia, Avita, Euodia, and Julia, whose faces also radiated the new life they had received. She clasped her hands as laughter bubbled up within her, filling the empty spaces and healing her heart.

"Is it always like this?" she asked in wonder.

Paul smiled at her. "He makes His Presence known, dear lady. I know now with certainty that He sent me here to Philippi to find you. Now that you have received Him, you must be baptized."

The entire group had been listening and each one had to search their hearts. They wished to also be baptized as believers.

Shedding their cloaks and sandals, one by one, the small group of God-fearers, now believers, waded into the water. The water was cold, but it did not seem to matter. Even Sophia was rejoicing as she came up out of the water.

Hektor hesitantly approached his mistress, a question in his eyes. She smiled and nodded assent. With his face alight, Hektor waded into the water to be baptized.

As everyone gathered cloaks and footwear, Lydia saw her mother and the servants into the carriage. They would have to return home quickly to get warm. She then turned to Paul.

"Where are you and your companions staying?"

"We have just arrived and have not as yet found quarters. It is but the ninth hour of the day."

Lydia looked meaningfully at Sophia, who nodded. "If you consider me to be a true believer in the Lord, please come and stay in my home. I wish to know all you can tell us about Jesus." She gazed around at the now glowing faces of her friends. "Marcia, and all of you, let us meet in my home. Paul can teach us. We can meet each week to share what Adonai has done in our lives and learn more about the Lord Jesus."

The women looked at one another and then nodded their heads. Marcia reached out to clasp her hand in thanks. "This is an answer to prayer, Lydia."

Paul hesitated and stroked his beard. "Your husband will not object? We are strangers."

"I am a widow, as is my mother who lives with me. The villa is mine and at my age I do not fear the wagging tongues of strangers. You are men of God and welcome."

Paul barely suppressed a smile at her boldness, but he quickly bowed his head. After a moment of silence, he nodded to his companions. "It is well and we are to go with her. Our work here is not yet finished."

24

*L*ydia felt a gentle hand on her arm as her mother took her aside and murmured, "How are we to get them there? Our cart barely holds all of us."

Paul, aware of their dilemma, raised a hand. "We are used to walking. Do not be concerned. Give us the directions and we will find our way."

Riding home, Delia suddenly spoke up. "Domina, where are we going to put them? All the rooms of the villa are taken."

"That is true," Sophia responded. "Where are they going to sleep?"

Hektor spoke up from the front of the carriage. "Domina, if you will trust me, I believe I have a solution to the problem."

When they reached the villa, Sophia and Delia went into the house to see what they could prepare as an evening meal for their extra guests.

"Hektor." The old servant turned expectantly from the seat of the cart. "What is your solution?"

"There is a small room in the building storing the cart and the animals. It is where I stayed when the villa belonged to the previous owners. I shall move my things back there. Your guests may occupy my room. I'm sure it will accommodate four cots. The previous owners left some here. I shall bring them to the house."

Adonai had an answer. "Thank you, Hektor. I will send Jael and Chara to help you"

The old caretaker hurried to put the carriage away while Lydia entered the villa and paused at the entrance to the dining room. It was large enough. She just needed to add a couple of benches from the atrium.

In a flurry of activity, Hektor, Jael, and Chara set to work. They made sure the cots were clean and found appropriate linens, preparing Hektor's former room for their guests. The four cots fit well, with two lengthwise against each wall. There was even room for Hektor's small table and lamp that remained at his insistence.

Satisfied that the room was ready, Lydia sought out her mother and Delia in the kitchen. They sliced some cheese from the storeroom, placing it on the table along with a bowl of olives that had been preserved in brine. Delia hurried in with a bowl of fresh pears and apples that added color to the table. Sophia suggested they heat the lentil stew. Then Delia sliced bread from the previous day's baking and placed it next to some dipping sauce. Hektor brought up wine from the storeroom and a pitcher of water to dilute it.

Lydia had left Paul and his companions speaking to others at the river and was not surprised when it was nearly an hour and a half before the four men arrived at the villa.

As she stepped forward to greet them, Chara and Jael came to stand near Sophia. As a servant, Delia would not speak, but she glanced at her mistress, her eyes questioning. To talk at the river was one thing, to bring strange men into the home was another.

Lydia stood by her mother's side and greeted her guests. "Welcome to my home," she murmured. "We have prepared a room for you. I regret that we do not have separate rooms for each of you, but you should be comfortable. Hektor will show you the way and where to refresh yourselves."

Paul looked around and smiled, his keen eyes looking warmly at the two servants and the caretaker. "Thank you, Madam. It is far better quarters than some we've had. May the Lord God bless this house and reward you for your hospitality."

The other three men added their thanks as Hektor indicated they should follow him.

When they had left the atrium, Delia shook her head and addressed Sophia. "Domina, do we truly know these men?"

Sophia turned and regarded her for a moment, knowing it took courage for Delia to speak her mind. With a smile, she answered. "Have we not received Jesus as our Lord? There is no reason to fear. These men serve the one true God and have traveled far to tell us of Jesus, who came to earth to show us what God is like. I believe our God led them to the river just for us. Paul will be sharing his thoughts after our evening meal. If you have any more questions, he can explain everything more clearly."

Delia hesitated, but with four more mouths to feed, she had work to do. She followed her mistress to the kitchen.

Jael continued to stand by Lydia. "Domina, his words went deep into my heart. I feel the Savior there. I wish to know more of him."

"As do I, Jael. Today we learned much, but this evening I look forward to more of what Paul can tell us of Jesus."

Jael's eyes held unshed tears. "I believe they are men of God, but I also pray no harm will come to you, Domina. I do not understand all, but I believe and I feel Him here in my heart. I wish to hear more of this man...a God who came to earth...."

"I, too, Jael." She put a gentle hand on Jael's arm.

Jael smiled. "Shall I prepare you for dinner, Domina?"

"Yes, of course." They ascended the stairs together.

While the men ate with restraint, it was obvious they were hungry. Delia made sure there was plenty of food to go around.

After the meal, Lydia rose and led her guests to the main room of the house. Hektor had added extra chairs, and as Sophia and Lydia sat, she glanced at the three faces of their maidservants, alight with the joy of their afternoon baptism at the river. Lydia smiled to herself as she noted their eagerness to hear more about the Savior.

Lydia felt peace settle in her spirit. She had done the right thing by inviting the man Paul and his companions here. She glanced at her mother and received a smile of encouragement in response as Paul began to speak.

"Tell me, Mistress Lydia, how you first came to be a God-fearer, and why you came to the river today."

Lydia sensed stillness in this man that enabled him to be in control of each moment. His dark eyes held her and she knew she could leave nothing out.

She told him how her mother, as a Jewess, had raised her in the synagogue and taught her of the one true God. Yet in her heart she felt that somehow the rituals and the rote prayers left her empty. She felt there had to be more. She told him about her father's death and her brother's decision to send her and her mother from their home when she refused to get rid of the dye business.

"It is difficult for a woman to run such a business. Why did your father leave it to you?"

"When my brother entered the army, he refused to have anything to do with it. At last, when there was no other way to save his business from being sold, my father agreed to teach me the trade."

"Your home was Thyatira. Yet you and your mother live here in Philippi." His statement was more of a question.

Lydia hesitated and looked to her mother. Sophia gave a slight shrug and nodded her head. "My father, realizing what might happen with his death, transferred the ownership of this villa to me. He stayed here when he came to Philippi for the business. It would be a home for my mother and me. When my father died and I would not give up the business, my brother forced us to leave our home. Even though it is far from Thyatira, it was a place for us to go. When the previous factor left, we found a trustworthy man named Nikolas who manages the shop for us."

Paul smiled then. "You have endured a great deal, but God has gone before you and paved the way. It is no coincidence we met at the river." He then shared how he had sought to go into Asia but the Holy Spirit had prevented them, not just once, but twice. "Then God sent a dream to me, of a man from Macedonia who was pleading for us to come and help them. After several stops we ended up in Philippi and, seeking believers, came to the river. When I met you and your mother there, I knew the reason for my journey."

Lydia felt her eyes widen. "You came to Philippi for *us*? Adonai led you here?"

Paul nodded. "I am to build a church in Philippi, and as new believers come into the fold, you will be instrumental in helping me."

"How can I help?"

"Just as we are meeting here. Soon other new believers will begin to gather. If you are willing to welcome them to your home as you have welcomed us, the church will grow."

Lydia thought a moment. Is this why she and her mother came to Philippi? Is this where Adonai was leading her? Even as her mind debated, excitement rose up in her.

"I will do as Adonai leads." Yet, as she said the words, a faint fluttering of doubt entered her mind. What was she agreeing to?

There were voices in the atrium and Lydia recognized that of Nikolas. It was the third time he had come to hear her read the Scriptures in the evening. He held the bag of receipts in his hand as he entered the room and stopped. His eyes narrowed as he took in the bedraggled group of men gathered there.

Lydia rose. "Ah, Nikolas, you are welcome. Come meet my guests." She turned to Paul and his companions. "This is the manager of my shop, Nikolas."

At his puzzled expression, she elaborated. "Paul is a teacher who shares more fully the gospel of Jesus the Christ. He and his companions are staying here at the villa."

Nikolas, who had been contemplating the strangers, nodded his head at the introduction, but when Lydia revealed that the men were staying with her, he turned suddenly to face her.

"Is that wise, madam? When it is known these men staying in your home are traveling preachers, troublemakers, there could be talk which would not be favorable to your reputation."

Lydia drew herself up and with her back to her guests, murmured, "That is for me to decide." Then, she gestured toward a nearby bench. "Come and join us to hear Paul's teaching."

His jaw set, Nikolas put the bag of receipts on the bench. "I have work to do." He nodded to Sophia and Lydia, and with a last glance at Paul, turned on his heel and strode from the room. The door was not closed quietly.

25

There was a heavy silence in the room. Lydia's face felt warm with embarrassment as conflicting thoughts raced across her mind. Nikolas was her employee. It should not have mattered to him what actions she took. Yet he was concerned for her reputation. No one knew she owned the fabric shop and she knew few people in Philippi. Paul came to stand before her and interrupted her thoughts.

"He has many things on his mind, dear lady. He will return, for he is destined for God's work."

Lydia frowned. *God's work?* Before she could reply, Paul turned to his small audience and continued speaking of the Lord. Lydia quietly entrusted her wayward thoughts to God and sat back down, glancing at Jael, Delia, and Chara, thanking Adonai in her heart that now her entire household were believers. She then gave Paul her own undivided attention.

He looked around at each face for a moment. "My friends, God saved you by His grace when you believed. And you cannot take credit for this; it is a gift from God. Salvation is not a reward for the good things we have done, so none of us can boast about it. We are God's masterpiece. He has created us anew in Christ Jesus, so we can do the good things He planned for us long ago. So now you Gentiles are no longer strangers and foreigners. You are citizens along with all of God's holy people, the Jews. You are all members of God's family. Always be humble and gentle. Be patient with one another, making allowance for each other's faults because of the love of Christ. Do not bring sorrow to God's Holy Spirit by the way you live. Remember, He has identified you as His own, guaranteeing that you will be saved on the day of redemption. Be careful how you live. Make the most of every opportunity for the days are evil. Understand what the Lord wants you to do...."

As Paul began to share the ministry and miracles of Jesus and the message of why He came, she sat mesmerized by his words. He was not a great orator, but the fervency with which he spoke and the message he brought burned in her soul. Philippi held her destiny. Deep within, Adonai was drawing her to something beyond herself.

The words poured over and around her. The holy Son of God loved her so much He left the heights of heaven to die for her. Because He was willing to endure that terrible death to reconcile her to Himself, to become a sacrifice for her sins, one day she would have the privilege of entering heaven. It was an enormous concept, yet she knew beyond the shadow of a doubt that the words Paul spoke were life and truth.

She caught Sophia's eye, and Lydia sensed her mother knew the same.

The hour grew late and Paul's message drew to a close. Silas, Timothy, and Luke had remained quietly in the background. Lydia sensed they had heard Paul's message many times and yet they listened as though they were hearing it for the first time. Would this story of love and redemption ever become old? The disciples of Jesus had been commanded to go into the entire world and preach the gospel. She marveled that Paul, who had persecuted the fledgling church in his misplaced zeal for the Lord, had been redeemed in such a way. She had not seen a bright light or heard the audible voice of the Lord, yet in the darkest times of her life, had she not heard in her spirit the whispered words of love and comfort? She had known Adonai from childhood because of her mother's faith, yet her heart had longed for more, something to fill the emptiness within. Whatever she was seeking had eluded her until now. She became sure that the meeting by the river had not been chance, but a step toward the destiny God had for her.

Paul thanked her for her hospitality and the fine dinner. He went around to each new believer, encouraging them, then he excused himself and, followed by Timothy and Silas, went to retire for the night. Luke, the physician, lingered behind. She looked at his strong face, the high cheekbones and the neatly trimmed beard. His dark eyes were kind.

"Dear lady, do not be concerned about your manager. He wrestles with emotions he does not understand. God is calling him and has a path for him to follow." The wise eyes twinkled. "Trust the Lord to deal with Nikolas."

She sensed there was something that he was not saying, but he then merely inclined his head and left the room.

She turned to Sophia and, embracing her, murmured, "Let us take our rest. We have much to think about."

When Jael and Chara approached, ready to attend to their mistresses, Lydia studied their faces. "You have heard the teacher. I rejoice that you have joined my mother and me in our faith."

Sophia glanced around. "Did you see Hektor? I thought he was listening to Paul also, but he has gone."

"We will speak to him in the morning, Ima."

The four women ascended the stairs and parted as Sophia and Lydia entered their respective rooms. Jael brushed Lydia's hair and helped her put on a light linen sleeping garment.

With the familiarity of the years they had spent together, the atmosphere changed when Jael and Lydia were alone. In public they were mistress and slave, but alone, they were friends.

"Never have I heard such words, Domina. It was as though they were spoken just to me. I knew that this man Paul spoke the truth."

"He has an amazing story, does he not, Jael? He has suffered much, perhaps for what he has done, but one cannot help but see and feel the joy that fills him."

They spoke for a short while and then Jael, always attuned to her mistress's needs, helped her into her bed and, leaving a small candle burning in the corner of the room, quietly left. Lydia lay in the semi-darkness, contemplating the events of the evening and found herself thinking once again of the words and actions of Nikolas. She should fire him for his insolence. Yet she knew she could not run the business without a manager and would be hard-pressed to find a replacement. She had no choice but to keep him in spite of it all. Perhaps she could persuade him to come again to hear Paul. Then she wondered why this was important to her. Just the thought of those piercing eyes troubled her. She turned on her side. Why did the man upset her so? Giving her tumbling thoughts over to her Lord, she closed her eyes and let weariness lull her into sleep.

26

While Lydia waited, struggling with irritation, Nikolas continued working, his back to her. He knew she was standing in the doorway. He could not have missed the sound of the small cart when she arrived.

"Nikolas!"

He turned slowly but there was no apology in his look when he faced her.

She took a deep breath, swallowing the angry words she was tempted to speak. "I was hoping you would stay to hear Paul's message. You indicated you wanted to know more about the Jewish God."

"The Jewish God, yes, not some ragged preacher spouting about miracles."

"He has come to share with us about Jesus of Nazareth, the Son of God and promised Messiah, who died to redeem us."

"A Jewish rabbi? How could a rabbi redeem us?" His stance became a little less combative and Lydia was emboldened.

"Would you judge a man before hearing him out? Come this evening and ask Paul all the questions that are on your heart. When you have heard what he has to say, then form your judgment."

"Are you not concerned for your reputation? Four men staying in your villa, and you a widow?"

"Nikolas, God sent this man to answer the desire of my heart that I have held all these years. I know he speaks the truth, and Jesus has become my Lord and Savior. How can I not offer them shelter from their travels in exchange for this great gift?"

He studied her face, and she knew he could not help but see the joy that rose like warm wine in her heart when she spoke of her Savior. His frown changed to a look of puzzlement. He took a step toward her, but stopped, and she sensed suddenly there was more than the divide of employer and employee between them. Why did she react so when he was near? Did she want him to come closer?

"I will come this evening if you wish it, madam. If he is a charlatan, I will know it."

She willed her heart to calm down, and keeping her tone businesslike, nodded. "Thank you, Nikolas. Now shall we discuss the shop? Tell me how the sales are going."

She learned that the shop's reputation continued to grow and another shipment had come in from her son-in-law in Thyatira only the day before. Nikolas pulled out a scroll and handed it to her.

"From your daughter, madam."

Lydia hastily unrolled the missive.

Dear Mater,

I am big with child but all is well. We miss you greatly. I must warn you that Cassius has returned and came to see us. He wanted to know where you and Grandmother were. He left in a rage when he understood where you had gone and of the villa in Philippi. I do not know what he thought you would do or where you would go when he left. He or Lucadius may come to Philippi, but I do not know what he plans. You are in our prayers. May Adonai watch over and protect you and Grandmother.

With love, Marianne and Marcellus

Panic raised its ugly head but Lydia fought it down. What could Cassius do? She legally owned her villa and the business. She looked up and forced herself to smile. "My daughter is well. Soon I will have a grandchild!"

"That is good news, madam." His face softened a little as he regarded her.

Lydia held the scroll to her chest. "If only I were not so far away. I do not wish to return to Thyatira and it will be a long time before they can come to see me, if they can at all." She could not give in to the sadness and fear. For so many years it was just Marianne and herself. Then after the death of her father, and the ultimatum from Cassius, she and her mother were far from the city they had grown up in. Would she ever be able to hold her first grandchild? She sighed and turned to the business at hand.

"Is the ship still in the harbor?"

He nodded. "They take on cargo and leave the day after tomorrow."

"That is well. I will send a letter to my daughter and son-in-law immediately."

She had been looking down again at the scroll as she spoke but when she looked up suddenly, she caught a look on his face. Compassion? He'd resumed his pose of nonchalance but it had been there. Did he pity her? She lifted her chin and turned to go back to the cart. In her bag was the money Marcellus faithfully sent from the shop in Thyatira. She could only thank Adonai for His provision.

"I will come this evening," Nikolas called after her.

She didn't turn around or respond, anxious to gather her writing materials at home. A grandchild coming soon. She sighed. How old would the child be before she saw it, if at all? Then she thought of Cassius. He could be cruel if he wanted revenge for her father's decision. Could he wreak havoc with her business here? He was capable of that. What if he came and found Paul and his companions living in her villa? Once again, panic and fear rose like bile in her throat. She bowed her head and began to pray, trusting the unknown to the Savior who had captured her heart.

∗——∗——∗——∗

As soon as they reached the villa, Lydia went to her small writing desk and pulled out a piece of parchment.

My dearest Marcellus,

What comforting news that Marianne is to bear a child. My heart longs to see her and be with her at the baby's birth. Somehow perhaps I can work it out to travel to Thyatira in the future. In the meantime, tell Marianne that her mother and grandmother send their love. The business is going well thanks to the regular shipments of the fabrics. Thank you for your faithfulness in handling the business in Thyatira. Nikolas is a reliable manager here and well-liked by our customers.

I regret that Cassius caused you any concern. I doubt he or my uncle will come to Philippi, but Cassius can be unpredictable. I will meet that challenge when it arises. We have met a traveling man of God called Paul. He has shared with us the life of Jesus, a healer and worker of many miracles. Your grandmother is convinced He is the Messiah the Jews have looked for all this time and I believe this also. Tell me what you have heard of Him.

Blessings and love from both of us,
Ima

Lydia studied the letter. Should she mention Jesus? Would this upset her daughter and son-in-law if they have not heard of him? Would they mention this to Cassius? After a moment she swallowed her anxiety and sealed the scroll. With a heartfelt prayer, she went to find Hektor to send him to the ship with her letter.

———◆———◆———◆———

Lydia shared her anxiety over Marianne's news with her mother as they walked in the small orchard.

"Ima, do you think Cassius or Lucadius will come here?"

Sophia sighed. "It is hard to know just what Cassius will do, or Lucadius for that matter. We can only pray and trust our God to watch over us."

"He could make trouble for me, especially if he finds Paul and his companions living here."

"You have been a virtuous woman, daughter. You are welcome to receive guests in your own home." Sophia paused. "You are sure all is legally sealed?"

"Yes, I made sure everything was in order after we arrived. I spoke with the man my father arranged it all with and examined the documents. Cassius cannot do anything."

"I fear he will find a way to make trouble for you, Lydia. From the time he was a boy, he sought retaliation whenever he felt threatened."

Lydia reached for her mother's hand. "We must pray, Ima, for I am uneasy in my spirit. Something is coming, and I don't know what it is."

After their heartfelt prayers, Lydia felt more peace than she had for the last few days.

"Let us join our guests for the evening meal. Paul tells me others will be joining us tonight."

Sophia raised an eyebrow and studied her daughter's face. "And will Nikolas be one of them?"

Lydia didn't want to talk about Nikolas. She merely shrugged and began to walk more quickly toward the villa.

When Lydia and her staff later gathered after the evening meal to hear Paul, she took pleasure in the fact that she was able to welcome two more believers, a man and a woman, into her home.

Paul had spent more time by the river talking to those gathered there and she had a feeling these two were only the first of the converts that he would send to her. As each one hesitantly settled themselves on cushions and benches, Paul seemed jubilant.

"Your home will be the first church in Philippi, dear lady."

Just as Paul began to preach, there was a firm knock at the door and Hektor admitted Nikolas. Barely glancing at Lydia, Nikolas settled on a nearby chair, his arms folded in silent disapproval.

"Dear friends and fellow believers," Paul began, and shared once again how he had met Jesus on the road to Damascus. He did not speak as a great orator, but there was no mistaking the fervor behind his words.

"Everyone has heard of the great lawgiver, Moses. Through him the law was given to my people, but with the law came the knowledge of sin. How do I know that my actions are sinful to a holy God, but that the law tells me so? We are human and to my dismay, the things I want to do that are right, I don't do. The things I don't want to do, I do. It is the sin nature that is in every man. The blood of bulls and goats cannot redeem us, though my people faithfully followed the law to sacrifice them. Adonai teaches that without the shedding of blood, there is no remission for sin. The Passover lamb only remitted our sins for the year, and had to be sacrificed year after year for the sins of the people.

"Adonai, who had promised a Savior through the centuries, finally redeemed us Himself. Jesus, God's lamb, birthed through a virgin, became the perfect sacrifice, for He carried holy blood not tainted with the sin of Adam. Consider the Passover lamb. Skewered on two rods, one vertical and one horizontal. Was not the Lamb of God also spread on a cross? Jesus grew in wisdom and stature with men and God and walked the earth, healing His people and showing us what God is like. Finally, as ordained by the Father, the holy blood of Jesus was shed once and for all so that whosoever believed in Him would not perish, but have everlasting life."

Lydia covertly watched the face of Nikolas as Paul went on speaking, quoting the Law and the Prophets about the Messiah to come that Jesus had fulfilled while on earth.

"According to the Book of the Law, every year my people are required to slaughter a Passover lamb to atone for the sins of the people. Yet Christ came as God's lamb, sacrificed for us, once and for all. It is His blood, shed for us, that provides redemption for those who believe.

"One of the great prophets, Isaiah, tells us that 'We all, like sheep, went astray; we turned each one, to his own way, yet Adonai laid on him, Jesus, the guilt of all of us.'"

Nikolas interrupted. "This Jesus you speak of comes from Nazareth. I am told by a Jewish friend that, according to Scripture, Messiah comes out of Bethlehem, near Efrat. How can you explain that?"

"In the days of Caesar Augustus, the emperor called for a census. This is a historical fact and has been documented. Each family was required to return to the house of their clan to register or face serious consequences. Joseph, the earthly father of Jesus, was of the house and lineage of David. He was required to travel to the city of Bethlehem, the city of David, to register. His wife, Mary, great with the child of Adonai, was required to travel with him. There, in Bethlehem, the child was born. The Son of God, the Messiah. As they were instructed by Adonai, they named Him Jesus, salvation."

Paul went on quoting Scripture after Scripture from the Book of the Law concerning Jesus. Nikolas listened intently, gradually unfolding his arms and leaning forward. Lydia thought he might interrupt Paul again, but he seemed mesmerized by what was shared.

176 Diana Wallis Taylor

The other believers, including her staff, listened with rapt attention. When Paul finally finished what he had to say, Lydia realized he had been speaking for over two hours, but no one appeared restless or inattentive, including Nikolas.

As the other guests thanked Lydia for her hospitality and began to take their leave, she wondered if Nikolas would also slip out without speaking to her. To her amazement, he and Paul were speaking quietly in a corner of the room. She would have to wait to learn what was said. To her relief, there was no anger on the face of Nikolas.

Sophia bade her goodnight and with her handmaid, Chara, ascended the stairs to retire. Sophia seemed more weary than usual and Lydia decided to speak to Luke, the physician, in the morning. She had noted his eyes focused on Sophia with a look of concern.

Lydia waited in the atrium until Nikolas finished speaking with Paul. To her surprise Paul clapped him on the shoulder and nodded. Her mind roiled with questions but she kept her face bland as Nikolas approached her.

"Thank you for coming. Was Paul able to answer your questions?"

A slight smile played about his lips as if he knew what she was truly asking. "Yes, he was able to answer my questions. You must forgive me, madam, for my misgivings about Paul. He truly appears to be a man of God. I will hear him again another evening."

Lydia breathed a sigh of relief. Why was it so important to her that Nikolas believe? She watched him stride away from the house and found herself smiling.

27

The next evening, before Paul was to speak, Lydia and her mother sat in the inner garden after the evening meal. Lydia sensed that her mother had something on her mind and waited for her to speak.

"Lydia, you know that in our home your father would not let us take part in any of the Jewish holy days. Now that there are just the two of us, that barrier is gone. Since it is nearing the date of Passover, I would very much like to celebrate with a Seder. Paul has talked about it but the new believers have not really experienced it. Do you think Paul might lead us in a Passover Seder?"

"Ima, that is a wonderful idea. How better to remind all of us how Passover speaks of the Messiah? I will speak to Paul this evening."

When Paul entered the living room where chairs and cushions had been put out for the believers, Lydia approached him.

"Paul, my mother and I have a request." She shared her mother's idea.

His face lit up with a large smile. "Praise be to our God. That would be a blessing to all of us. I have prayed as to how we could celebrate Passover." He thought a moment. "Most of our believers are Gentiles. Perhaps it would be best to have an overview along with the Passover meal."

Lydia was delighted. "Then let us plan on it. You can verify the foods and other things we need for the evening and we will invite the other believers to celebrate with us. We can do this in place of our usual *cena*."

Sophia listened, and then after sending Delia for a scroll, began to write down the ingredients they would need for the celebratory meal.

Later, Lydia looked around at the assembled group and smiled. "We have a most wonderful opportunity coming up. The Jewish Passover is in three days. Paul has agreed to lead us through the Seder meal. We will start in the early evening in place of our own evening meals so come prepared to be blessed by our teacher."

Heads nodded all around and from the pleased look on their faces, they were all looking forward to the event.

The next day, Delia went to the marketplace with Hektor and obtained as many of the ingredients as she could find, including a lamb shank that had been prepared for roasting. She readied the different ingredients according to Paul's instructions.

Timothy showed her, Jael, and Chara how to set the proper table. There was a bowl of salted water and a sprig of parsley and near them a plate with a ground horseradish, a roasted egg, a lamb shank, a radish, some *haroset*, which was a sweet mixture of chopped apples, nuts, and cinnamon mixed with wine, and a few bitter herbs.

When all were gathered around the table, some of the men reclined and the others sat on benches or chairs. Luke, Timothy, and Silas joined them as Paul took his place at the head of the table, while Euodia, the youngest, sat at his right side. Sophia was seated at his left as the guest of honor, being the oldest member there.

"The plate you see in the middle has certain ingredients," Paul explained. "The *haroset* represents the red-brown clay and mortar used by Israel in making the bricks for Pharaoh's pyramids. The sweetness is a reminder of God's redemption from slavery, not only by man, but by the lives we used to live.

"The lamb shank is a reminder of the Passover lamb sacrificed every year by the High Priest for the sins of the people. As Adonai's lamb, the sacrifice Jesus paid for our sins was for all time." He went on to explain that the roasted egg symbolized a peace offering and the Israelites were to eat the bitter herbs as a reminder of the springtime during which Passover occurs. The horseradish represented the bitterness which the Israelites suffered as slaves in Egypt.

He then nodded to Sophia.

Sophia's face was lit with joy at participating in the Passover. She stood, and with her head covered, placed her hands over her eyes and recited the ancient Hebrew blessing before passing her hands over the candles in front of her.

Blessed art Thou, O Lord our God, King of the Universe, Who has set us apart by His Word, and in whose Name we light the festival lights.

Paul lifted the first glass of wine and asked those assembled to rise as he lifted up the cup toward heaven and recited the *kiddush*, or prayer of sanctification. "We have four cups of wine, to reflect on the fourfold joy of the Lord's redemption."

He then led them through the second ceremony, which was the washing of hands. Each guest was brought a bowl and towel and water was poured ceremonially over their hands. After, they ate the parsley dipped into the bowl of saltwater, "as a reminder of the tears of pain and suffering shed by the Jewish people in slavery," Paul told them. Lydia glanced toward her own slaves and wondered what they were thinking.

Paul then explained that the unleavened bread was broken in half, part wrapped in a napkin, and part hidden somewhere in the house. Just so, the body of Jesus was broken for us and buried, or hidden away, in the tomb.

Paul told them there were four questions the youngest child in the house would ask. He explained that John was the youngest disciple and was the one who asked those questions at that last Passover supper with Jesus.

Paul lifted the second cup of wine and then recited the Passover story, beginning with Abraham, called out of the land of Ur; then God's promises to the patriarchs; the story of Joseph and his brothers; the enslavement of the Jewish nation, the deliverance at the hand of Moses; and the giving of the law at Sinai.

As the ten plagues were described, Paul poured a small amount of wine for each one, then, before they joined him in sipping from their wine, he explained that this is when the *Hallel*, Psalms 113–118, would be sung. Since most of those gathered were not familiar with them, he went on to the next segment. Hands were washed again and the upper portion of the unleavened bread and the middle portion was broken into pieces and distributed. A filling of horseradish was spread between two pieces of the unleavened bread. The sharp horseradish brought tears to their eyes to signify the sorrow of the Jews who were slaves in Egypt.

They then ate the Passover meal that Delia, Chara, and Jael had prepared: roasted lamb with bitter herbs, glazed chicken with nut stuffing, honeyed carrots, stewed fruit, and a sponge cake. Delia could not find what she needed for Timothy's description of the gefilte fish or matzah ball soup. She made a vegetable soup instead.

After they had feasted and conversed, Paul then poured the third cup of wine. "This is called the *cup of redemption*. It is with this cup that our Lord began the ceremony of communion, reminding His disciples of His coming death, when He would be sacrificed for their redemption. Each family sends a child to the door to look for Elijah." He pointed to the cup of wine in the center of the table. "This is Elijah's cup. They are hoping that Elijah will step through the doorway, drink his cup of wine, and announce the coming of the Messiah." He smiled benevolently around the table. "Of course we know He has already come."

He continued, "Just before our Lord was betrayed and went to the cross, as they left the upper room for the garden of Gethsemane, they sang the prophetic words of Psalm 118. Those of you who might be familiar with it may join me."

Timothy, Silas, and Luke joined Paul in singing the words, and Sophia and Lydia chimed in.

The stone which the builders rejected
Has become the chief cornerstone.
This was the LORD's doing.
It is marvelous in our eyes.
This is the day the LORD has made;
We will rejoice and be glad in it.
Save now, I pray, O LORD;
O LORD, I pray, send now prosperity.
Blessed is he who comes in the name of the LORD!

Then Paul poured the fourth cup of wine. "This is called the *cup of acceptance* or *praise*. It represents the cup that Jesus said He would not drink until He drank it with His disciples in the kingdom."

At the end of the meal, Luke produced a scroll and read another portion of Psalm 118. As he read, Lydia listened to the verses and felt a quickening in her spirit. What God had done for her in all that she had been through was truly a miracle. She realized how Adonai had led her step by step.

Open to me the gates of righteousness;
I will go through them,
And I will praise the LORD.
This is the gate of the LORD,
Through which the righteous shall enter.
I will praise You,
For You have answered me,

And have become my salvation.

As Paul closed with a prayer, Lydia looked back and saw how Adonai had given her victory over her marriage to Plinius, given her a daughter that was the joy of her heart, given her an occupation that would support her and her mother, and brought them here for His purposes to begin a church that would love and serve Messiah, the Lord Jesus.

No matter what happened with Cassius or any other difficulty, Adonai was with her and she could trust Him with her future.

Some of the believers lingered after dinner, talking and praising God for sending Paul to them to teach them about the Messiah. But later, when Lydia lay in the silence contemplating the evening, a question came: *What would they do when Paul was gone?*

28

*L*uke spoke with Sophia the next morning, asking gentle but probing questions. Her mother agreed to let the physician examine her but insisted that her tiredness was just due to her age. As Chara helped Sophia dress, Lydia followed Luke down to the atrium to hear his opinion in private.

"It is her heart, my lady. She is not strong. The loss of her husband, the treatment by her son as you shared with me, and the move here have taken their toll."

"What can I do for her?" Anxiety at the thought of losing her mother rose, tightening her chest.

"See that she does not overtax herself and gets plenty of rest." Perhaps sensing her panic, he added, "Nothing is imminent, my lady. She could have many more years if she takes care of herself."

Their conversation was interrupted by the sound of hoofbeats. She was not expecting anyone. *Soldiers?* Lydia stiffened. *Why would they be coming here?*

Sophia hurried down the stairs, her hand over her chest. "Lydia! It is Cassius and your uncle Lucadius! I saw them from the window."

Was this the reason for the apprehension she'd sensed for days? Cassius had come at last. The fact that he'd brought her uncle caused even greater alarm. She reached for her mother's hand and they offered a quick prayer for protection and courage, then waited as Hektor opened the door to their visitors.

"Is there no one to take our horses?" Cassius was already loosening his cloak and pulling off his helmet.

Hektor took their traveling cloaks and other items and, placing them in an alcove nearby, hurried down the steps to lead the two horses into their small stable.

Sophia stepped forward, summoning a gracious smile. "Welcome, my son. It has been a long time. And Lucadius, to what do we owe the pleasure of your company?"

Cassius looked around the atrium, then moved closer to Sophia and inclined his head. "You are looking well, Mater. The change of scenery seems to be good for you." Then he turned and focused on Lydia. "You also seem to be doing well, dear sister. It seems the shop Pater started here is thriving."

"We are managing. Welcome to my villa, Cassius, Uncle." Lydia could not help but emphasize the word *my*. "It is good to see you. Will you join us for the evening meal?"

Cassius smiled again, but it did not reach his eyes. He nodded. "We will do that. We also need accommodations for the night." He glanced up to see Jael and Chara standing at the foot of the stairs. "Tell your servants to prepare rooms for us."

Lydia took a deep breath. "Unfortunately I cannot do that. We have few rooms and I already have guests."

Cassius turned to their uncle. "It would seem we are not welcome."

The fear that gripped her seemed to dissipate with her silent prayer, and she saw her brother for the bully he was.

"You are welcome, Cassius, and you, too, Uncle, but as I said, I have guests already in our one guest room."

The face of her uncle became hard as he spoke. "We stopped at the shop before we came here. Your so-called guests are a group of itinerant preachers. Traveling from town to town to prey on foolish women who listen to their drivel."

Cassius's eyes narrowed. "We met the man who manages the shop. No doubt the two of you work closely together. Do you have room for him here?" His insinuating words shocked Lydia. Was he accusing her of impropriety with Nikolas?

"Nikolas is an employee, Cassius, no more than that. I am fortunate he knows the business well."

Cassius rolled his eyes. "Of course." She wanted to throw something at his smirking face.

Her brother unbuckled his sword and handed it to Hektor as the servant stepped through the door. As Hektor put it with the other items in the alcove, Cassius shrugged. "Perhaps it would be best if you tell your *guests* to find other quarters, dear sister. You have legitimate family here now."

Sophia looked at Lydia and gave a slight shake of her head, but remained silent.

Surprised at the calmness with which she spoke, Lydia drew herself up and faced her brother and uncle.

"Cassius, as I said, we have guests and the villa is small. You are welcome to join us for *cena*, but you and uncle will have to find lodging in the town. There is an inn not far away that will accommodate you."

Her brother's eyes glittered with anger as he rubbed his chin with his hands. While Lydia knew she was within her rights and there was nothing Cassius could do, she had learned in the past the repercussions of his temper.

Cassius suddenly smiled. "You are right, Lydia. We have come at an inopportune time, have we not, Uncle? Let us enjoy a meal with family...my dear mother and sister. Perhaps we will have an opportunity to meet your other...guests."

186 Diana Wallis Taylor

Cassius had something in mind, Lydia was sure, but perhaps if she got her brother to talk about his travels in the army, he would be more agreeable.

Turning to his mother, Cassius smiled again. "You have fared well under Lydia's care, Mater."

"Lydia has done all she could under the circumstances." She sighed. "I have missed you, though our last parting was not amiable."

He took her arm as they followed Lydia to the dining room. "I thought you would persuade Lydia to give up the dye business rather than leave your home."

"Had you anticipated how we would live after you returned to the army?"

"It was only to cause Lydia to come to her senses. I anticipated you would go to Marianne. I did return before the two months were up, Mater…and found you already gone."

Sophia stopped and faced him. "And if we were still there?"

Cassius made a magnanimous gesture with one hand. "Of course I would not have put you out of our home. I would have just insisted that Lydia give up the dye business. You would have then been under my protection."

Sophia continued to look steadily at her son and Cassius could not meet her gaze. "I thought so," she murmured finally. She gave him her sweet smile. "No matter, my son, it is good to see that you are well and thriving in the army. I see you have reached the rank of centurion. We are most interested to hear of your military exploits." Lydia saw that she and her mother had the same idea.

Cassius accepted the change of subject only too readily and, as they seated themselves around the table on couches, he helped himself to some cheese and fruit. He never seemed unwilling to talk about himself.

"I am commander of the Fourth Century of the Cohort and command one hundred men. I am confident that in five years I shall make First Century, the highest rank of centurion."

He was expanding on his latest skirmish when suddenly the door to the villa opened. Paul, Silas, Luke, and Timothy entered the atrium. Lydia rose quickly to greet them and spoke in low tones.

"I have unexpected guests. My brother and uncle have arrived from Thyatira."

Paul considered her words a moment, knowing something of her background.

"Would it be better for us to leave, dear lady? We do not wish to cause you any undue hardship."

"I wish you all to stay, Paul. The believers will be coming this evening as usual to hear you teach. My brother and uncle have already been told I have guests and that they need to find other accommodations in the town."

He nodded, and his eyes searched her face. "I surmise that it was not received well."

She sighed and shook her head slightly. Then with determination, "Come."

Lydia led her guests into the dining room and as they seated themselves around the table, Cassius watched with ill-hidden disgust.

"So my sister welcomes beggars into her home?"

Paul eyed him calmly. "We are not beggars, sir. We are teachers and we travel to share the gospel."

"And what is this gospel?" said Lucadius.

"That the Savior, the Messiah we Jews have been looking for through the centuries, has come. He is the Son of God who redeems those who believe in Him."

Lucadius turned to Cassius. "I have heard of this so-called Messiah, a wandering rabbi by the name of Jesus. Supposedly while He was on earth He performed miracles and proclaimed Himself to be the Son of God. The Jewish leaders wisely crucified Him and put a stop to the movement...called The Way, I believe."

"Ah yes, Uncle. I, too, have heard of Him. One of my fellow centurions was at the crucifixion. He tried to talk to me about the man but I dismissed it. He was never the same after that. Finally retired from the army and went about telling people this Jesus was who He said He was."

Lucadius chuckled. "Probably mad."

Lydia fumed that they would discuss her Lord in such an offhand way, and in front of her guests who under dangerous circumstances nonetheless traveled proclaiming their message to all who would listen.

Cassius turned to Lydia. "You believe this insanity?" He smiled maliciously. "Perhaps you and Mater have gone mad with all you have been through. Perhaps I should declare you both incompetent. I would then need to take over the villa and, of course, the dye business."

Doctor Luke spoke up, his words sharp and clear with anger. "As a doctor I can declare them quite competent, sir."

"You are a physician?"

"Yes. And well-known in patrician circles."

Lucadius put down the bread he had just dipped. "If you are an educated man, why do you travel with the likes of these?"

"Because after careful research and speaking with those whose lives have been changed by the Master, I also am a believer."

Lucadius glanced at Cassius and rolled his eyes. "It is obvious that my niece has been taken in by these charlatans. We were right to come here."

He turned to Lydia. "Who owns this villa? Would he be pleased with the use of it?"

Lydia felt a calmness steal over her and the presence of Adonai reassure her. "I own the villa, Uncle, thanks to my father's provision."

Cassius's eyes flashed with anger. "So Pater made plans for you behind my back. How fortunate for you both."

"It was you that forced us to leave our home, Cassius. Pater knew what you might do and made arrangements for us."

Cassius sneered. "And the dye business. How insightful of him."

Sophia spoke up. "You do not care about your father's trade, my son, your life is the army where you are doing well. What difference could this mean to you?"

He leaned on the table, his eye boring into hers. "I am *paterfamilias*, head of our house. You should be under my protection… and authority."

Paul had been watching and spoke quietly to Silas next to him before facing Cassius.

"I am well-instructed in the law, sir. Your sister is legal owner of both this villa and her business."

Cassius stood suddenly and glared at Paul. "You, a Jew, dare to tell me of the law? You are a nobody, a charlatan who sows his lies wherever he goes."

Paul looked him in the eye. "I am a Pharisee, sir. Thoroughly educated in the Law under Gamaliel, but in this time, called by the Master to share the gospel. Whether I am in need or in abundance, that is my life's work."

Lucadius spread his hand to include Silas, Luke, and Timothy. "And you support yourselves by taking advantage of weak women like my niece and sister-in-law?"

Cassius turned flashing eyes on Lydia. "Either these men leave your villa and you return to your senses or you will rue the day you defied me." He jerked his head in the direction of his uncle who also rose.

Hektor, who had obviously been listening, was waiting in the atrium with Cassius's cape, sword, and helmet.

Cassius yanked the items from Hektor's hands and glared at Lydia and Sophia who had quickly risen and followed them.

He turned to Hektor and snarled, "Bring our horses!"

Sophia clasped her hands in anguish and faced her son. "You are busy with the army, Cassius. Why should it matter to you if we are happy and content here?"

His face softened for a brief moment. "I would not deny you happiness, Mater, but under these circumstances I cannot condone this situation." He turned to Lydia, his upper lip lifting in disgust. "Tell your friends to beware. I have powerful friends in this city. They do not care for strangers who stir up trouble."

"We shall return, niece," added Lucadius. "Perhaps we will find you've come to your senses in the meantime."

When their horses had been brought to the front of the villa, her brother and uncle quickly mounted and, tugging the reins, rode out toward the city without a backward glance.

Lydia turned toward the dining room. Paul and his companions were conferring with one another in low tones. The tension had brought tears near the surface, but she fought them down and regarded her guests. "My apologies for the behavior of my brother and uncle."

The men were thoughtful, but Lydia detected a slight appearance of fear in Timothy.

"Do not pay them any mind, Paul. They can bluster but they cannot hurt me. I am within my legal rights as a Roman citizen."

"Silas and I are also Roman citizens, dear lady, yet I feel in my spirit that trouble will find us as it has in other cities. Your brother's words are not idle threats."

Sophia' eyes widened. "Have you had any trouble in Philippi?"

Silas shrugged. "So far only a slave girl who will not leave us alone. She follows us everywhere. We learned that she tells fortunes for the profit of her masters. She screams for all to hear, 'These men are servants of the Most High God. They are telling you how to be saved!'"

Paul nodded. "Sooner or later I will have to deal with her."

Lydia understood. "That could be a problem for you."

"Yes." The word hung in the stillness.

29

As the servants cleared the table and began to prepare for the gathering that evening, Sophia turned to Lydia, her face troubled. "I fear for us, Lydia. I know your brother well. He does not like to be told what to do and he was so angry. He will seek revenge in one way or another."

"You are right. We just do not know what he will do. We can only pray and ask Adonai to watch over us and protect us." She forced a smile and took Sophia's arm. "Let us go in and hear more from Paul. The others should be here soon."

Hektor admitted the group of believers that evening and there were new faces among them. In a matter of days Paul had gathered a small congregation, eager to hear his teaching on Jesus, the Messiah.

When Nikolas arrived, putting his traveling bag on a bench in the entry, Lydia let out a sigh of relief. She needed to speak with him and inclined her head toward the door to the garden.

As they stepped outside, Nikolas murmured, "You are troubled by your brother and uncle's visit?"

She glanced toward the road in front of the house as if expecting Cassius and her uncle to ride up to the house again.

"Yes. He told me they were at the shop. Did they cause any trouble for you?"

194 Diana Wallis Taylor

"It was only inferred. Cassius fingered the fabrics and I didn't like the look on his face. He is planning something. He asked a few questions about the business and I merely told him we covered expenses. He didn't ask to see the books."

Her eyes widened. "Would you have shown him our accounts?"

"No, they were not his to see. I would have been in my rights to keep them from him. As a precaution, I brought the books with me tonight. I also took, ah, other measures."

"Other measures?"

"Just to protect your interests. As I said, he is planning something and I do not know what it is. I thought it best to be careful."

As his eyes met hers, Lydia felt a jolt in her chest, suddenly very much aware of the strength of this man. At least there was one man on their side.

"I thank you, Nikolas, for your loyalty and understanding. As you say, this matter is not done and Cassius will be back."

Nikolas looked toward the house. "Shall we join the others? "

They returned to the room where the believers had gathered. For the sake of the newcomers, Paul shared again his experience on the road to Damascus. Then, he spoke of the Passover.

"Each year, at Passover, the High Priest lays hands on a sacrificial lamb that is then slain, sacrificed for the sins of the people. But Adonai, seeing our need, sent His Son, Jesus, the Lamb of God. Jesus laid aside His deity and came down to His people, taking the form of a man. He became our Redeemer. Those who believe in Him shall no longer perish but have everlasting life. For God laid on Him the iniquity of us all. Christ is God's Passover Lamb; God's sacrifice for all time. And Adonai has sent us to you with the admonition: 'I have set you as a light for the Gentiles, to be for deliverance to the ends of the earth.' How gracious is Adonai who does not wish that any man or woman, Jew or Gentile, perish."

Paul himself was not an imposing figure, Lydia thought. One would not pick him out on the street, yet when he spoke there was power and authority in his words and his audience was intent on listening, nodding their heads at his life-changing message.

Lydia pushed the anxious thoughts of her brother and uncle aside and opened her mind to receive the precious word that Paul was sharing with them.

As the believers filed out one by one, some speaking with Paul or Silas, some speaking for a moment to Luke, Nikolas waited patiently. When they had all gone, he picked up his traveling bag and handed Lydia the scrolls with their accounting figures.

"The books, for your safe-keeping, my lady. I felt it unwise to leave them in the shop tonight."

"Thank you, Nikolas. It gives me courage to know that you are looking out for my interests."

He smiled. "I am glad to be of service. After all," and his smile widened, "I am most grateful for employment."

He turned and went quickly out the door before she could respond.

She watched him mount his mule and start the ride back to town. She was suddenly thankful that he slept so close to their valuable fabric—although she could hardly believe Cassius would ever stoop to sabotage.

Jael sensed her mood as she helped Lydia undress for bed.

"Domina, you are worried?"

"For what little good it does, Jael."

"Adonai will protect you, will he not?"

Lydia gave her a rueful smile. "Yes, He will. I must trust Him with my worries." She moved to the cushioned chair so Jael could brush her hair.

"Your brother had much anger. He needs the Messiah, Domina."

"Yes, that he does, Jael. It is not knowing what he will do that concerns me."

"We pray for you, Domina. I fear there is trouble coming."

Lydia sighed, remembering her brother's words. "Knowing Cassius, it would seem very likely."

Jael put a hand on Lydia's shoulder. "We will be strong. All of your household, Domina, we will believe together."

Lydia reached up and covered the hand with her own. "Yes, Jael. We will believe together."

When her handmaid had gone, Lydia lay quietly in bed, considering the events of the evening. She thought of Jael's words and her heart lifted. Her entire household, such as it was, were now believers. Then she thought of Cassius, and began to pray; for her brother, for her uncle, and for Paul and his friends. What would the morning hold?

30

The day dawned warm and sunny, a good day to go into Philippi for the baths. As Jael and Chara prepared clothing and necessary items for their mistresses, Lydia made sure her guests had breakfast. Paul and his companions would go by the river to look for other people with whom they could share the gospel.

She stood by the door. "May Adonai go with you and lead you to those who are open to your message."

Paul smiled. "The church in your home is growing. There are others who hunger for more than the law can give them. Adonai will lead us to them."

As she watched the four men start down the road, she had a strange sense of foreboding. Was Cassius still in Philippi with her uncle? Would they continue to make trouble for her? Would he try to damage the shop? She could not rest until she learned he had returned to his duties with the army, far from Philippi.

Hektor brought the small carriage to the front of the villa and the women stepped in.

"I must admit I am looking forward to the baths." Sophia settled herself with an air of expectation.

Doctor Luke had been keeping a watch on Sophia during their stay. His concern caused Lydia to be vigilant over her mother's

198 Diana Wallis Taylor

activities as well. She felt sure the baths would relax Sophia and make her feel better. Lydia turned to Hektor when they were ready and nodded.

They spent a leisurely morning at the baths and, when they were dressed, prepared to go to the agora to do some shopping. As they approached the marketplace, they heard a commotion. Two men were standing in the middle of the street and a young slave girl was screaming something at them.

"It's Paul and Silas!" Lydia exclaimed as Hektor pulled to a stop.

"These men are servants of the Most High God! They are telling you how to be saved!" the girl screamed over and over. Paul suddenly pointed at the girl and said, "In the name of Jesus the Messiah, I order you to come out of her!"

The girl screamed again and fell in a heap on the street. There was silence and then the crowd began to murmur among themselves. Paul helped the girl up and she looked around, her face bewildered.

Two men suddenly stepped out of the crowd and one grabbed the girl by her arm. He looked at her face and then turned to Paul. "What have you done?"

"I cast out the snake spirit that was in her. She is healed." Paul answered calmly.

The man who held the girl struck her forcefully across the face and flung her down to the ground where she lay in a heap, sobbing. "You are no use to us any longer. May you die in the streets!" He turned to Paul, almost snarling. "You have destroyed our profit!" He leaped on Paul and Silas and two others came to his aid. They began dragging them toward the main square where the judges sat.

Sophia gasped. "We must help them." She turned to Lydia. "What can we do?"

Lydia started to climb out of the carriage. "I can vouch for them." But before her feet could touch the ground, she felt a restraining hand on her arm. It was Luke.

"Madam, you cannot get involved. The crowd is out of control. They sense blood. Think of your mother. Return to the villa. We will return as soon as possible and let you know what happened. Please, leave now."

"But…Paul and Silas…."

"We have experienced this before. Our God is in control. Just gather the other believers and pray."

Lydia glanced at her mother's blanched face and the fear on the face of their maidservants.

Another voice came from the other side of the carriage. It was Nikolas.

"I heard the commotion. What is happening?"

"They have arrested Paul and Silas and dragged them before the magistrates," Luke answered. "I suggested that the women return to the villa."

Nikolas turned to Lydia. "He is right. When a mob becomes angry like this there is no telling what they will do."

"I could vouch for him," Lydia urged, still unconvinced.

Nikolas's face was clouded with concern. "If you try to speak up for Paul and Silas, you could be in harm's way. Please, Lydia, return to the villa. I know the jailer, Clement. When I find out what is going to happen to Paul and Silas, one of us will let you know."

Lydia sat back down in the carriage. They were right. As a woman, there was little she could do. "Thank you, Nikolas. We will be praying. Just bring us word as soon as you can."

He nodded and the carriage began to move. She watched the three men move cautiously toward the outskirts of the crowd where they could see what was happening. Then with a sigh, she leaned back in the carriage.

Suddenly Sophia put a hand on her arm. "Lydia, the slave girl. Her masters have abandoned her in the street."

Lydia looked where her mother was pointing and saw the slave girl on her knees in the street, holding her arm. Her face was streaked with tears and she appeared dazed.

"Hektor, stop." Lydia turned to Chara and Jael. "Bring the girl to me."

The two women left the carriage and, glancing apprehensively toward the mob, spoke to the girl. She shrank back from them, but Jael took one arm. When Chara took the other, the girl cried out in pain. Chara put an arm around the girl's waist instead and they brought her to the carriage.

Sophia reached out. "Quick, help her in. She is injured. We'll take her to the villa. When Doctor Luke returns he can look at her arm. I fear it is broken."

The slave girl stared at them and whimpered. "Dominas, I have done nothing wrong. Please, let me go. Do not take me to the authorities."

Sophia put a hand on the girl's face. "We are taking you to our home to help you. Your masters have disowned you, but the God we serve will not."

The shouting of the angry mob grew faint as Hektor drove the carriage as fast as he dared away from the city.

As they neared the villa, Lydia suddenly remembered. Nikolas had called her by her first name.

31

After making the girl as comfortable as they could, Lydia gathered her staff and they began to pray earnestly for the safety of Paul and Silas. They beseeched Adonai to protect the men and let them come to no harm. As she waited for news, the shadows grew long over the garden wall and the sun went down.

She looked out toward the road as her apprehension grew. Would Luke and Timothy be arrested also? Delia came to her side, also peering for any sign of the men.

"You have extra work with our guests here, Delia, but you have managed well."

"Thank you, Domina." She hesitated, then said, "I have liked listening to Paul."

"His words are truth."

"Yes, Domina. My heart tells me his words are true and I rejoice with you that we have come to know Jesus as the Messiah."

Joy rose in Lydia's heart. Her whole household. How good Adonai was to surround her now with believers.

When the servants returned inside, Sophia and Lydia sat on a bench under one of the olive trees. Sophia confessed she had prayed earnestly for a solution to the problem of Cassius. They could only wait, hoping he and Lucadius would return to Thyatira and leave them alone.

As the chill of the evening crept through the garden, they were just considering returning to the house when the sound of a commotion reached them. Jael ran to the garden. "Dominas, there is trouble. Master Timothy has run all the way from the city with news. Master Luke is not far behind him. Come."

As they hurried into the villa, Timothy was sitting on a chair, gulping air in between swallowing the water that Delia had brought him. Luke entered the villa along with Hektor who had hurried in from the stable.

Lydia put a hand to her chest, her heart pounding. "Timothy, Luke, what has happened?"

Timothy spoke between breaths. "My lady, the shop...a couple of men tried to set fire to it. Nikolas chased them away with a sword...and was able to put out the fire. I don't think they knew anyone was in the shop. There was some damage and Nikolas told me to tell you not to worry. He can repair it, but the shop would be closed for a few days."

Sophia moved closer. "What about the fabrics? Were any of them ruined by the fire?"

Timothy shook his head. "There is a store room a short distance behind the shop. Nikolas moved all the fabrics into it after the shop closed. He suspected something might happen." His face became somber. "At least it happened while he was in the back room, or the whole shop would have burned."

Lydia almost ground her teeth. Cassius was behind this. If he couldn't get her to give up the shop he would destroy it for her. She silently thanked Adonai for Nikolas's quick thinking.

"Tell me of Paul and Silas. What has happened?"

Luke hesitated. "Dear lady, the magistrate ordered them arrested."

There was a gasp from Sophia. "Arrested? On what charges?"

"It was over the slave girl Paul was concerned about. The one who was following them around proclaiming them to be servants of the Most High God. Her owners were furious and accused Paul and Silas of causing trouble in the city and advocating customs that are against Roman law. When they were arrested and dragged to the market square, the judges listened to the mob and had them stripped and flogged."

Lydia gasped. *Flogged?* Her mind raced, considering what she could do. "Where are they now?"

"They are in the town jail, in chains. I would have been there with them if Timothy and I had not come from another street where we were buying supplies."

Lydia called her servant. "Jael, get my cloak. I must see what I can do to help them."

Timothy glanced at Luke and then back at Lydia. His face was drawn. "Something you must know, my lady. Your brother and uncle were part of the mob. Since he was a Roman officer, it was actually your brother who whipped Paul. He could have called a lower-ranking soldier, but he did not."

Lydia felt like a sword had pierced her heart. So this was his revenge. She steeled herself and resolved to do whatever it took to free Paul and Silas.

"How can I help them?" She looked from Luke to Timothy.

Luke shook his head. "I would not get your hopes up, madam. If your brother, a centurion, is involved in this and the judge is persuaded they have broken Roman law, you will not be able to help them."

"Oh, Luke, I must try. Adonai will help me."

"The hand of the Lord moves as He chooses, madam. Always seek His plan first. There is nothing you can do this evening. They will come before the magistrate in the morning. They could be released if they promise to leave town and not cause any more trouble. It has happened before."

Sophia approached Luke. "Doctor Luke, the slave girl who was healed is here in the villa. We found her in the street. I believe her left arm is broken."

Luke's brows raised in question. "You brought her here?"

"Her owners threw her down in the street telling her she could die there. She was of no more value to them."

"I will tend to her. Show me where she is. Be aware, though, that her owners have the right to change their mind and retrieve her again."

Sophia nodded. "We will come to that matter if it arises. Until then, she is safe here."

Lydia watched them leave the atrium. A sense of guilt washed over her. She had forgotten about the girl in her anxiety about Paul and Silas.

At the sound of hoofbeats, Chara rushed in. "Domina, it is your brother and uncle. They are returning."

Lydia sent up a quick prayer for courage. "Warn Doctor Luke and hide the girl. No one must know she is here."

"Yes, Domina." Chara hurried away toward the back of the villa where Luke was tending to their young charge.

As Hektor opened the door, Cassius swaggered in. His face was smug and his eyes glittered. He and Lucadius handed their things to Hektor and stood before her. The face of her uncle was guarded, but Lydia faced them with more calm than she felt.

"Cassius! What are you doing here? Have you not caused enough distress?"

A sneer spread across his handsome face. "I expected you to come into the city to try to free your 'guests,' Lydia. Your efforts will come to naught. They are not going to be free for a long time."

"Why are you doing this, Cassius? Why should what I do with my life at this point matter to you? We had no idea you would be returning to the villa in Thyatira to reverse your decision. We did what we thought we had to do after your harsh dictum. We endured difficulty, and now we are happy here. You know I've been a God-fearer all my life. We are only briefly providing a place for Paul to teach before they move on to the next city."

He reached out and took her arm, his fingers pressing painfully into the flesh. Timothy stepped forward, but she warned him off with a glance.

"I do not like to have my plans thwarted, Lydia," he snarled. "I wanted to sell the business. It would have given me a nice profit. Of course, you and Mater would have been well-taken care of in our own home."

"Under your protection and patronage."

"Of course. You are still reasonably attractive. I'm sure I can find a suitable alliance for you."

She jerked her arm away. "An alliance? Not marriage?"

He waved a hand. "Come now, Lydia. You are past the child-bearing age. Why would marriage be necessary?"

She could only stare at him, barely hiding her disgust. So that's what he wanted for her, to be some wealthy Roman's companion. Hidden in a villa away from his wife. She shook off the thought and brought the conversation away from herself.

"Let those men go, Cassius. They have done no harm and they will leave the city. They are godly men, not criminals."

"That is for the magistrate to decide. Of course, as a Roman centurion, I'm sure I could manage to persuade the judge to release them, but on one condition. You turn the business over to me and return to Thyatira."

The man was mad! How could such a monster be related to her? She drew herself up and gathered her courage. "If we cannot free our friends, Adonai will find a way. I will not give in to your demands."

He stepped back, his eyes glittering with anger. "You shall regret your decision, my sister. And your so-called friends shall pay the price." His eyes lingered on Timothy for a moment.

"Two of your *guests*," he almost sneered at the word, "will trouble you no longer. It's a shame the other two weren't with the ones I had arrested or you would be rid of all of them once and for all."

"So you had them beaten and thrown into prison. How clever of you, Cassius." Then a remark Paul had made one day came to mind, and she knew it was from Adonai.

"You of course questioned them carefully and made sure they had a hearing as Roman citizens."

Cassius blanched. "Roman citizens?" He knew the penalty for falsely arresting Roman citizens without a fair hearing and a lawyer.

"How could I know they were Roman citizens?" Cassius waved a hand but she saw the fear in his eyes.

"Perhaps because you were so intent on your revenge you could not hear them tell you above the roar of the crowd." Luke had returned to the atrium and spoke confidently.

Surprisingly, Lydia felt pity for her brother. "Perhaps it is time for you to return to Thyatira. If the prefect here in Philippi finds out what you have done, it could go hard with you."

Luke spoke again. "I know the law. You could lose your rank and even your property, if the authorities choose."

Lucadius, who had listened with growing alarm at the exchange, turned to his nephew. "Cassius, they are right. Perhaps no one knew the name of the centurion who whipped them. If we leave Philippi before someone recognizes you, it might be best."

Indecision marred his handsome face as Cassius debated his uncle's words. Finally, he nodded. "Let us seek passage on the nearest boat leaving Philippi. I will disguise myself so no one sees I am a Roman officer."

He looked at Lydia, and although calculating, his face showed a hint of pleading. "You will not tell the authorities?"

Cassius asking a favor of her? This was a first. Lydia nodded. "And Cassius, on the matter for which you came, actually, I have been considering what to do with the dye business. I will let you know what I decide."

His brows raised, but he just nodded. Almost grabbing his helmet, sword, and cloak from Hektor, he and Lucadius rushed out into the night and rode away as quickly as they had come.

Lydia listened to the hoofbeats fade away. In spite of all the grief her brother had caused her and her mother, and the situation with Paul and Silas, he was her brother. She found herself half-wanting him to make the ship.

She turned to Luke. "How is the girl?"

"I straightened her arm. It was merely out of the socket, not broken. She is resting. Poor child, she has been through a great deal."

Lydia followed him back to the room where her servants slept.

"Jael, since she has your bed, you may sleep on the couch in my room."

"Thank you, Domina."

Sophia was sitting in a chair by the girl's bed, keeping watch. When their young guest opened her eyes, Lydia spoke kindly to her. "What is your name?"

She looked fearfully at those gathered around her. "It...is Karam. You are kind to help me, Domina, but they will just find me again."

Lydia sat down on the edge of the cot. "Who will find you?"

Karam sighed. "My masters. It is not the first time they have thrown me out in anger. Usually when they are drunk. They always find me and make me tell fortunes for them. It brings them money."

Timothy, who had been standing in the corner of the room, spoke up. "You will not be able to do that anymore, Karam. Paul has healed you."

Sophia put a gentle hand on the girl's arm. "If you are no longer a profit to your masters, perhaps they will not seek you."

Luke nodded. "I did hear one curse you and tell you to die in the streets. I believe Mistress Sophia is right. They may not look for you."

"No one knows you are here, child," added Sophia. "You are safe. We will not tell the authorities."

Large tears slipped down the girl's cheeks. "I will work hard to repay you for your kindness."

Lydia studied the girl, "How old are you, Karam?"

"Sixteen, Domina. I was taken from my parents when I was eight. Even then I could see into the future. When my new masters saw my gift, they began to force me to tell the fortunes of their friends, for money."

"So you have been doing this for eight years? Where are you from?"

"Syria."

"Are your parents alive?"

She shrugged. "I do not know. I was in the fields when the raiders took me. It was a small band. Perhaps they did not enter the village."

Lydia glanced at her mother, and Sophia nodded. They were thinking the same thing. If they could find out her village, perhaps they could return Karam to her people.

The girl was tired and her eyes began to droop. Lydia shooed Timothy and Luke toward the door. Sophia glanced back at the sleeping girl a moment, and then followed Lydia and the others out of the room.

Sophia retired for the night, obviously exhausted from the day's events. Lydia watched her mother ascend the stairs slowly. The dark circles under Sophia's eyes did not bode well for her mother's health.

Returning to the main room of the house, Lydia found some of the other believers had quietly entered and were gathered in small groups, praying.

Avita, one of the first women she and her mother met at the river, came up to her. "We heard about Paul and Silas and gathered as many of the group as we could to pray for them."

The group knelt and prayed earnestly for Paul and Silas, beseeching God to have mercy on them.

The door opened again and Nikolas came in. "I have encouraging news, if you want to call it encouraging."

Everyone hushed to hear what he had to share.

"Paul and Silas are still in the prison. They will not see the magistrate until morning." He almost chuckled. "The jailer, whom I know, told me I could not see them and that although they are securely locked in the chains, they are singing hymns at the top of their lungs."

"Hymns?" Lydia was astounded. "They are in chains, beaten and bleeding, and they are singing *hymns?*"

Nikolas nodded. "The other prisoners, including the jailer, have been listening to them for the past several hours."

There were murmurs of disbelief in the group.

"In the morning we must do something." Lydia hated the pleading note in her voice.

Nikolas glanced at Timothy and the rest of them. "Have you not prayed? Is not the God you serve and Paul advocates able to save him? Would you rush in and create a greater problem?"

The other believers nodded. They would return home and continue to pray for Paul and Silas. Thanking them for coming, Lydia waited until the last one had gone before turning to Nikolas. She had to relieve the burden weighing on her heart.

"It was my own brother, Cassius, who whipped Paul. It was his retaliation. I cannot stand by and do nothing."

He sighed heavily. "May I again point out the obvious fact that you are a woman, madam, and cannot go charging into the jail to free Paul and his companion. They have to appear before a magistrate and answer to the charges. And you, Luke and Timothy, are part of their group. You could end up in prison with them, and make matters worse."

Lydia almost wrung her hands in frustration. "But Nikolas, the charges are false. If the judge didn't listen to them before, why would he listen now? They could remain in prison."

"Lydia," he began, "let me go and inquire in the morning. You may be able to be in the background at the trial, but you would be wise to remain silent."

She started, realizing he had called her by her first name again. "You would do that?"

"If it will save my benefactress some embarrassment, yes."

She looked at Timothy. He shrugged. "Perhaps he is right, dear lady. At least you might be able to see what is happening."

"Very well. I believe you and Luke should remain here at the villa for safety. I will see my father's lawyer-agent, Magnus Titelius, and see if there is something he can do to help them."

"Until morning."

After he left, she stood looking at the door for a long time.

32

*L*ydia was up long before the sun rose. She had tossed and turned most of the night. Jael remained asleep, her soft snores the only sound in the room.

She stared out the window into the first light of the coming dawn. What if she couldn't help Paul and Silas today? Her thoughts turned over and over in her mind. What if the lawyer could not help them either? Were they doomed to remain in prison?

"Jael, wake up. Help me dress."

Her maidservant rubbed her eyes and jumped up quickly. "I did not know you were awake, Domina. Forgive me." Jael turned to see that it was still dark outside. Only the crowing of their one rooster told them dawn was near. She glanced at her mistress, a question in her eyes, but began to draw clothing out of the cupboard.

When Lydia was dressed, she went downstairs quickly for a cup of warm mustum. Delia was already up, preparing breakfast.

"Just some cheese and bread, Delia. I need to go into town as soon as it is light."

Delia shook her head, but did as she was told.

After Lydia had eaten, she felt the food sit heavily on her stomach. Perhaps it was not a good morning to eat after all.

She waited impatiently for Hektor to bring the small carriage. Luke and Timothy joined her.

"Dear lady, why not let Timothy go with you. He would not be recognized so readily and you should not go alone. It would bode well to have a male chaperone."

Lydia weighed Luke's words. "If you are sure he would not be recognized as being with the rest of you?"

Luke smiled. "Young Timothy has always known how to fade into the background. People will just think him one of your slaves."

Timothy coughed into his cup of wine.

"Very well, but I need to leave now."

As Timothy joined her in the carriage, Lydia glanced back at Luke. "Look in on my mother, Luke. I am worried about her."

"I planned on doing that. I pray you bring us good news."

On the way into Philippi, Timothy and Lydia spoke little, each occupied with their own thoughts. Lydia wondered what Luke and Timothy would do if she could not free their companions?

Adonai, we need Your help. Show me what to do. Give me favor with the magistrates. Give Paul and Silas favor with the magistrates. I do not know what to do. Grant me Your wisdom.

The response was clear in her mind as she prayed, and it startled her. *Trust Me.*

She debated whether to go to the shop first and seek the help of Nikolas since he seemed to know the jailer, or go to the lawyer's office. Since it was early, she reasoned that the lawyer may not be there as yet. She would go to the shop.

Nikolas was already arranging bolts of cloth and as he turned to see who had entered, his eyes widened.

"You are up early, madam."

Keeping her tone businesslike, she tried to be calm in the face of those dark eyes.

"We must do something about Paul and Silas. We cannot let them just languish in prison at the whim of those men who owned the slave girl."

His lips pressed together and he took a deep breath. She suddenly realized he was trying to control his temper.

As he spoke, his words were measured for emphasis. "Were my words yesterday not enough? You cannot go to the jail, however good your intentions are, madam. The jailer would not listen to you because he is following the orders of the magistrates. You cannot go to the magistrates, as they must convene the court to hear the case against Paul and Silas. Then it would be a question as to why you, a Roman matron, is concerned with their case. You would make their situation worse and begin a flow of gossip I don't think you want to start. You have come all this way, at this early hour, for nothing." He emphasized the final word.

Lydia was not given to tears, but the extent of her frustration brought them close to the surface this time. She sat down suddenly on a padded bench. "I am certain there must be something I can do."

Timothy, who had been standing quietly in the doorway, came and sat down next to Lydia. "It is no comfort to you, dear lady, but Paul has been through many things in his quest to share the gospel. He has been beaten before, stoned, shipwrecked, and endured many other hardships. Adonai guides him, and he has always come through. There is a purpose here we cannot see. Only our God knows. We must trust that Adonai will bring good out of this."

Nikolas appeared thoughtful. "If it would make you feel better, I will go to the jail and speak with Clement again. He can tell me when Paul and Silas will appear before the magistrates. Timothy, if we have any customers, charm them until I get back." With a half-smile in Timothy's direction, Nikolas left the shop.

The slave of one of the Roman families came into the shop. Timothy jumped up to greet him. The slave was in charge of goods for the household and studied the many fabrics with a discerning eye. "Where is the manager of the shop?"

"He was called away on a business matter. He will be back shortly. Would you care to wait as we are, or come back this afternoon?" Lydia listened to the exchange with interest. Many households had a slave that ran their home and purchased goods. It was best not to offend them. To her relief, Timothy was the soul of courtesy.

The slave, dignified in his demeanor, debated a moment. "I will return in the afternoon." Timothy nodded graciously to him and the man left. To Lydia's relief, no other customers came while they waited.

Almost an hour went by and both Lydia and Timothy cast anxious glances toward the entrance.

Just when Lydia's anxiety seemed unbearable, they heard voices coming down the street toward the shop. Timothy listened and then joy flooded his face as he stood up and rushed to the door to greet not only Nikolas, but Paul and Silas as well. They walked stiffly, but their faces were full of joy.

Lydia caught her breath and rose also. *Paul and Silas here? What in heaven?*

As Paul entered he took Lydia's hand. "We thank you for your prayers and your concern, dear lady. As you can see, our God has set us free."

Nikolas was shaking his head. "If I had not seen the evidence I would not have believed it."

Lydia looked from one to the other. "What happened? How is it you are here, free?"

Paul glanced at Silas and motioned for him to sit. As Timothy and Nikolas also sat, he began his miraculous tale.

"It was midnight, and Silas and I were rejoicing that we had been allowed to suffer for the name of our Lord. Suddenly an earthquake struck the jail. The prison doors flew open and the chains fell from our ankles and wrists. Evidently the other prisoners were also freed. When the jailer saw we had all been freed, he assumed we would escape and drew his sword to take his own life. He knew the penalty for allowing prisoners to escape!"

As Paul paused, Nikolas added, "I saw the prison. It was in shambles."

Silas smiled and shook his head. "The jailer's family lived next door and his wife brought a lantern to see if her husband was all right. Fortunately, the earthquake was confined to the jail and the other prisoners were so astonished they remained where they were, watching Paul and me."

Paul nodded, and continued. "We didn't want the man to lose his life because of us and called out to let him know we were all still there. No one had escaped. When his wife appeared with the lantern, he saw indeed that we were still all there."

Silas took up the story. "He fell down at Paul's feet wanting to know how he could be saved. The jailer's family was not harmed and they followed their mother to the jail to be sure Clement was alive. When Paul shared the gospel with them and told them that if they believed in Jesus as Lord, they would be saved…all of them responded."

Paul smiled. "After they washed our wounds in a pool in the jail that was fed by rainwater, we baptized not only Clement but also his whole family. The jailer called another guard and left the other prisoners in his keeping. The new guard was so overcome with what he saw, he could only nod. Clement not only took us to his own quarters, but set food in front of us, for we had not eaten since leaving your villa. He also brought our clothes which had been put aside when we were beaten."

"But how are you here? What about the magistrate, the court?" She looked from one to the other in bewilderment.

Paul stroked his beard. "Ah, that too was in the hands of Adonai. It seems the Roman centurion who beat us neglected to ask if we were Roman citizens." He looked meaningfully at Lydia, and her face reddened with embarrassment. They both knew who the centurion was. "We tried to tell him but he paid no mind. This morning, when the magistrates decided to let us go, they sent an officer to tell the jailer to release us with a warning. He told us we were free to go in peace."

Silas chuckled. "Paul faced them and said, 'After flogging us in public when we hadn't been convicted of a crime and are Roman citizens, they threw us into prison. Now they want to get rid of us secretly? No! Let them come and escort us out themselves.'"

Lydia hesitated. "The Roman centurion who beat you. Did the magistrate know who he was? Did he press any charges?"

Silas glanced at Paul. "He seems to have disappeared. No one could find him."

"Paul, he is on a ship back to Thyatira." She searched his face, wondering if he would tell the authorities who the centurion was.

Paul considered this a moment. "It is just as well."

Nikolas spoke up. "Tell them the rest of the story, Paul."

"Ah yes. Well, the magistrates, when they heard we were Roman citizens, evidently became frightened. They of all people know the law about persecuting a Roman citizen in this way without a proper trial. They rushed to the jail and apologized profusely. Then they escorted us out of the jail and asked us to please leave the city. We agreed."

Lydia shook her head. Adonai worked in wondrous ways. Why did she doubt that the Lord had a plan? "Come back to the villa to refresh yourselves. I'm sure Luke will be most glad to see you."

Paul nodded. "We need to prepare for our journey. We agreed to leave Philippi but we would like to say farewell to all those who have come to know Jesus and meet in your home. I have an added gift I would like to leave with you."

Lydia's heart was so full of what Adonai had done, she didn't think to ask what the gift might be.

Lydia looked at the carriage and realized that not all of them could ride. As she turned to Paul, he waved a hand. "We are used to walking, dear lady. We will see you at the villa in due time."

"I'll walk with Paul and Silas," Timothy said.

Hektor, waiting with the carriage, had seen Paul and Silas coming, and knowing they were freed, bore a wide smile on his face.

She turned to Nikolas. "Will you come also?"

He appeared to consider the question for a moment, then nodded his head. "I will come." A smile played around his lips. "I must mind the shop for my employer, but I will be there this evening."

"Join us for *cena* then."

"With pleasure, madam."

She wondered why she suddenly felt shy around him. She shook off the strange feeling, nodded, and entered her carriage. How happy her mother and the others would be with the news of the miraculous release of Paul and Silas.

33

*A*s the carriage pulled up in front of the villa, Lydia was startled to see Luke waiting, and the expression on his face was grim.

"Luke, what is wrong?"

"It is your mother, madam. She has had an incident of some kind. Her heart. She is very weak."

Lydia rushed up the stairs to her mother's room with Luke right behind her.

"Ima, are you all right?"

Her mother's face was pale as she lay on her bed. Chara put a cool cloth on her mistress's forehead, her eyes filled with concern.

"Lydia, I'm so glad you are here. This heart of mine seems to have a life of its own. I'm sure I'll feel better after a day or two of rest." She looked at Lydia and gripped her hand. "You are home. What did you find out about Paul and Silas?"

Lydia covered her mother's hand with her other hand. "They are safe. I will let you hear the story from Paul's lips. We serve a wonderful God."

"Then Paul will be teaching tonight?"

"Yes, one last time and will say goodbye to all of us. He and Silas must leave the city."

Sophia sank back against the pillows. "He must leave? So soon? What will we do when he is gone? Who will guide our small church?"

"Adonai knows our need. Perhaps I will continue as leader."

Sophia's eyes closed.

"We need to let her rest." Luke motioned toward the door and Lydia reluctantly rose to follow him.

"I will stay, Domina." Chara remained by the side of her mistress.

Lydia, thankful for the servant's devotion to her mother, nodded.

When Paul, Silas, and Timothy reached the villa, it was obvious that they were exhausted from their ordeal. Luke immediately saw to their wounds. Putting a healing salve on the cuts, he murmured. "The magistrates assume you left the city when they saw you walking down the road. They do not know where you are. It would be good to rest and recoup your strength before we begin another long journey."

Paul saw the wisdom of the physician's words and agreed. "We will stay a few more days longer, then we must go. The Lord has other fields for us to work in and other towns to visit."

Lydia, listening to this exchange, was relieved. They had Paul's wisdom and teaching for a little while longer, at least.

With her mother resting and Paul and Silas quietly planning the next journey, Lydia went out to their small orchard and sat on a bench. Their fledgling church was heavy on her mind. Without a strong leader, they might go their separate ways again. She was not a teacher herself and knew they should name another leader. But who? The voice she trusted came to her on the soft breeze blowing through the trees.

Trust Me.

Before long, Luke joined her. He was carrying a parchment, which he unrolled and studied.

"You are writing something, Luke?"

"A journal. I have been documenting events as they occur and stories that others have told us about the miracles of Jesus. People who were there and experienced them firsthand."

"Is this your only scroll?"

"No, I have many more in my traveling bag. I've gathered much information on our travels. The stories encourage new believers."

"How did you, a physician, happen to join with Paul and Silas on their travels?"

"It was instigated by the questions of a friend. I promised him I would look into this Jesus and learn the truth of the rabbi's ministry. I came to know Jesus as my Lord and now I wish to record all I can about His life."

"That is a noble effort, Luke. Will you record the incident with the jailer and your time here in Philippi?"

He smiled. "I already have."

"May I ask for your wisdom, Luke?" Lydia began. "What am I to do about Karam? I would wish for her to be restored to her family, but have no idea how."

The doctor thought on it for a moment.

"Your factor in the shop, Nikolas, has many connections. Also, much information is shared among the slaves. If Nikolas cannot help, perhaps Hektor knows of someone who can."

"Thank you, Luke, I will do that. She seems recovered from her ordeal, but I am afraid her masters will try to find her and she cannot be found here."

They sat quietly, listening to the bulbul birds calling to one another in the treetops. A sense of melancholy stole over Lydia. Her father was gone, she probably would never see her brother again, Paul and his friends were leaving. If her mother passed away one day, she would be alone. Suddenly the business did not seem that important. Should she marry again, and to whom? She had done well with the business this last year, but had it become more of a burden?

She would be wealthy, but die a lonely old woman.

As if sensing her thoughts, Luke turned to her. "How is your daughter?"

Lydia brightened. "She is well. I have a grandchild in Thyatira. I know not even whether it be a boy or girl, but I long to hold the child."

"Had you given any thought to traveling home for a short visit? You could see your daughter and her child. I am thinking the trip would not be a hardship on you."

She knew he was referring to her financial status. Excitement began to fill her. She and her mother could return to Thyatira for a while. They could stay with Marianne and Marcellus. And she could see her grandchild. Then she thought of the shop. Could she rely on Nikolas to maintain everything if she were gone? She knew him, and yet she didn't know him. Would he feel abandoned?

"Of course, I must be sure my mother is up to taking another sea journey."

"That is why I mention it. I feel it would be good for her. She has missed her friends in Thyatira."

"She told you this?"

"She lived there all her life. She has come because she wanted to support you in your decision. I think she's been lonely."

The thought had not occurred to Lydia. She had been wrapped up in the shop and making sure the villa was working out for them. Then with Paul and his friends. She recalled seeing her mother looking out the window one day, a wistful look on her face. Lydia chided herself for neglecting to see how she had uprooted her mother from all she knew to come here. Sophia had never complained.

Delia came and called them to the evening meal. Sophia was determined to join them and came downstairs with Chara's help.

Delia outdid herself. With five men to feed as well as the usual household, she was in her element. The young slave girl, Karam, made herself useful even with but one strong arm, and Delia was grateful for the help.

The two women served millet with saffron, raisins, and walnuts, then lentil salad with watercress, onion, garlic, and boiled and crumbled eggs, followed by a chicken, leek, and garbanzo bean stew with bread for dipping. For dessert, there was a bowl of fruit in the center of the table and some slices of cheese. Paul and his companions smelled the various aromas and in no time were reclined on the dining benches.

There was a knock at the door, and Nikolas was admitted. He too caught a whiff of the meal and smiled appreciatively.

Paul and Silas ate heartily in spite of their ordeal. Lydia was glad to see that over the time spent with her, Timothy had filled out considerably. It made her wonder what they ate when they were on the road. She would make sure they took as much food as she could provide when it came time to leave. She stole a glance at Nikolas and started when she saw him already looking at her. There was a strange expression on his face, almost tender. But he quickly turned to Luke and engaged him in conversation.

34

That evening the believers, having heard the news, returned eagerly to welcome Paul and Silas. They marveled at Paul's story and the miraculous provision of the Lord.

Paul paused and looked around at their eager faces. "You have believed and been baptized with water. Now I want to share with you about a gift."

There was a small murmur as the believers looked at each other with raised eyebrows. What was this? They turned and looked at Paul expectantly as he began.

"On the day that the Lord rose from the dead, He appeared in the upper room to his disciples. They were discouraged, fearing the Romans, and not knowing what direction to go. He came and taught them for forty days, as He spoke to them about the kingdom of God. The Scriptures told about His rising from the dead. The disciples had heard Him, but like many of us when we are told something, they didn't really understand. Then, on the fortieth day, He led them out to the Mount of Olives and told them to wait for the promise of the Father. He said, 'John baptized you in water, but in a few days you will be immersed in the Holy Spirit.' Then He was taken up in a cloud and disappeared from their sight. As they strained for one last glimpse of Him, two white-robed men appeared before them, saying, 'Men of Galilee, why are you standing there staring into heaven? Jesus has been taken from you into heaven, but someday He will return from heaven the same way you saw Him go.'

"The disciples returned to Jerusalem to the upper room. Those present were the eleven remaining disciples as well as Mary, the mother of Jesus, several other women, and the brothers of Jesus. In time others gathered until there were nearly one hundred and twenty believers. At that time, since the disciple Judas had betrayed Jesus, as I shared with you earlier, they drew lots and Matthias was named to become an apostle with the other eleven.

"When the day of Pentecost arrived, the believers were still meeting together and waiting for the promise of being endued with power from on high. Suddenly there was a sound from heaven like the roaring of a mighty windstorm, and it filled the house. Then, what looked like flames of fire appeared above the heads of every believer. They were all filled with the Holy Spirit and began speaking in other languages as the Holy Spirit gave them this ability."

He waited a moment for them to process this and then continued. "At that time, since it was Pentecost, there were devout Jews from every nation staying in Jerusalem. When they heard the noise, everyone came running and the believers spilled out of the house, praising God in the languages they were given. The people were amazed to hear these unlearned disciples praising God in every language present in the crowd."

Paul smiled, "The disciples were accused of being drunk, but it was only nine o'clock in the morning. When I visited the disciples years later after I'd become a believer and was called by the Lord Jesus to be an apostle, the Holy Spirit was still moving in the church. This is the gift I wish to give you from Adonai, for strength and for power to know who you are in Jesus the Christ. It is for every believer, should you choose to receive it."

There was a murmuring among the group, but then all eyes were upon Paul. Lydia glanced quickly at her mother, who nodded and then at Nikolas, who also nodded his head. The others added their assent.

Nikolas spoke. "I believe we are all in agreement. Whatever Adonai has for us, we wish to receive."

Paul began with Lydia and moved around the room laying his hands on each of their heads and saying, "Receive the gift of the Holy Spirit, in the name of Jesus of Nazareth."

One by one the believers began praising God, each in the language given them. Lydia felt joy rise up in her heart and fill her as she praised her God with a fervor she had never known. She felt she could pray all night. The maidservants and Hektor joined them, evidence once again that slave or free, they were all equal in the sight of God.

As the group gradually grew quiet, they again looked to Paul, joyful tears streaming down the faces of many.

His smile was benevolent. "My children, born to me through the Holy Spirit, I must leave you, but I leave you fully equipped to continue the church, to share the gospel, to face any hardships you may experience for your faith. Remember Silas and me and how our God moved in a mighty way to release us from jail. We are not finished with our work and thus He set us free to move on to other towns to share the good news of Jesus, their Savior and Redeemer. Remember what you have seen and heard and stay strong."

After he led them in a closing prayer, the group began to disperse; those who lived in Philippi to their homes and Chara ascended the stairs with Sophia, as Jael and Delia began to put away the few refreshments and secure the kitchen for the night. Timothy, Silas, and Luke returned to their room. At Paul's indication, Nikolas waited in the atrium after the others had gone for a private conversation with Paul.

Lydia stood alone in the room, her mind turning with many thoughts, and most of them concerning Nikolas. She was drawn to him in a way that caused her both anxiety and exhilaration. What was she to do? Then, Paul motioned for her to join Nikolas.

"Dear lady, you have opened your heart and home and Adonai has rewarded you with a group of believers. God has shown me that Nikolas is to lead you. I have felt that from the first time he came to the villa." His eyes twinkled. "There are great things ahead for both of you as you submit to His will. Trust Adonai to show you the path ahead."

What was Paul saying? Nikolas was to lead in Paul's place? She started to question this decision, but realized how much she had seen Nikolas grow from the first time he listened to Paul's teaching. She remembered Luke mentioning that the two of them had gone over the scrolls Luke had written, Nikolas absorbing all the information he could. Paul had chosen well, but once again, a man would be in authority over her, and her employee at that. Part of her spirit rebelled.

When Paul retired to join his friends, Lydia turned to Jael who waited patiently for her to retire. "I will be up in a moment, Jael. Wait for me in my room."

She watched Jael go up the stairs, then turned and faced Nikolas. "I will not dispute Paul's choice, but I…." She didn't know how to say what she felt.

Nikolas smiled down at her, and, to her surprise, his voice was tender. "There are many things Adonai has shown me, but you are not ready to hear them. Just remember this, dear lady, in the eyes of our God, all men and women are equal. I work for you, but there is something between us. I know you have felt it."

She looked up at his face, and felt herself sway toward him. She had been strong for so long, with no one to lean on. She caught herself and stepped back, her eyes wide with the conflicting emotions that coursed through her. He did not touch her, but his eyes searched her face.

"I need to go. Goodnight. Sleep well." He turned and in a moment was gone. As she listened to the hoofbeats grow fainter, she put her hand on her heart and, remembering what she had seen in his eyes, fled up the stairs.

35

*P*aul looked around at the joy-filled faces of the small group of believers. It was time for him and his friends to move on.

Nikolas stepped forward and sought Paul's attention. "We, all of us, wish to present you with a gift. You need support for your ministry. Each of us have contributed according to our ability and we wish to give you this." He handed Paul the leather pouch, heavy with coins. Lydia was glad Marcia had told her the day before what they were going to do so she and Sophia could also contribute.

Paul held the pouch in his hand and his eyes moistened. "Thank you all for your most generous gift. It will be used most gladly for the kingdom of God." He turned to Lydia. "Dear lady, it has been a joy to be with you." He glanced at Nikolas. "The Lord has shown me that you will bear much fruit in Philippi for the kingdom."

Nikolas moved to Lydia's side. "I will do my best, but you leave large sandals to fill, Paul."

He turned to Sophia. "You have work to do also, dear lady. It may not be here in Philippi, but trust God to lead you."

Sophia gave him a puzzled look, but then smiled. "You have blessed my daughter and her household beyond measure. May Adonai go with you and protect you."

After moving back so the others could say their goodbyes, Lydia turned to Luke. "Will you remain with Paul?"

"I will continue with him a little longer, yes, recording what I see and hear."

Timothy spoke up. "We all thank you for your gracious hospitality." Then he added with a grin, "We hate to leave Delia's good food."

There was a ripple of laughter among the group and then they moved back and watched as the men gathered their traveling bags and strode purposefully down the road, headed for the cities of Amphipolis and Apollonia in Thessalonica. The group watched almost in silence until the figures rounded the bend and were out of sight.

The rest of the believers returned to Philippi, but Nikolas remained. He watched Sophia go into the villa and furrowed his brows a moment, then turned to Lydia.

"It is my understanding that your mother longs to visit your family and friends in Thyatira. If you have deemed me worthy of your trust, then go with her to see your grandchild. With your permission, I will keep the believers together."

Lydia sighed. "Yes, my mother does want to return, and we have the main business in Thyatira. I also long to see my daughter and grandchild." She looked into his face that was filled with concern. "You would have to handle the business alone." She thought a moment. "You will continue to leave the funds with father's lawyer-agent, Magnus Titelius. He received the funds from the previous factor when my father was not here."

He smiled. "I am honored that I have your trust. That would work well for me if he is still agreeable to the arrangement."

"I'm sure he will be."

"Would I and the believers have your permission to continue to meet here at your villa?"

She had not considered that. "Yes, that will be easier than finding another place while I am gone. Hektor will be here to care for the house and I believe we will leave Delia. My daughter and son-in-law have servants running their villa. My mother and I will need only our own maidservants, Jael and Chara."

"How long do you plan to be gone?"

"I don't know, Nikolas. I must pray about this and seek God's leading."

Once again, the warmth in his eyes flooded over her. For a moment she could think of nothing else.

"Then I pray Adonai will lead you back to Philippi," he murmured, "and soon."

She must keep this on a business level, the urge to press into his arms was too strong. She took a step back. "It would be best if you meet me at the office of Magnus Titelius tomorrow. He needs to be aware of my travels and our arrangements."

As he started to leave, she remembered her conversation with Luke. "I have another matter that I am concerned about."

He raised his eyebrows and waited.

"The slave girl Paul healed. She cannot remain here if I am gone. Her owners could find her and make trouble for Delia and Hektor. I want to return her to her home in Syria but I do not know how to go about it."

He frowned. "That is indeed a problem. You are right in that she should not remain here. She must get out of Philippi. Give me a day to ask some discreet questions and I shall report what I find."

"Thank you, Nikolas. Until tomorrow."

A slight smile seemed to play about his mouth as he inclined his head. "Until tomorrow."

When Nikolas was gone, Lydia rebuked herself. That man was disturbing her peace. Becoming flustered at her years was unbecoming. A few weeks away in Thyatira would be a good thing. She hurried into the villa to talk to her servants and her mother.

36

The next day, Hektor drove Lydia and Jael into Philippi to the offices of her lawyer. She had sent word ahead to prepare for her visit. When she arrived, she found Nikolas standing outside the building, waiting for her. After a brief greeting, she told Jael to remain with the carriage and led Nikolas to the lawyer's office. They sat down on a bench to wait to be summoned. Lydia could not help but remember the last time she was here, and how much her situation had changed since. This time, she felt confidence.

"Domina," the young slave held a scroll in his hand and searched her face. "You are Lydia of Thyatira?"

"Yes."

"My master requests that, for the moment, you see him alone."

Lydia's brows furrowed, but she rose and followed the slave into the lawyer's office. His large desk was once again covered with scrolls. He rose and inclined his head. "You have come, perhaps earlier than the year, but nevertheless, I have documents that you must be aware of."

"Documents?"

He leaned his bulk against the massive desk. "Your father made additional provision for you, should you not make a success of the fabric business...."

"Should I not...."

"And also a provision for you if you *were* to make a success of the business."

"I don't understand."

"Madam, your father was a wealthy man and shrewd in business. Although his son retains the villa as *paterfamilias* and has been given a substantial sum to care for it, his life is the army. You have done admirably well, beyond anything we expected, and have made a successful life here in Philippi. Should you show yourself resourceful in business, he felt it worthy to entrust additional funds to make up for the matter of uprooting your life and depriving you and your mother of your home."

It was a long speech, but Lydia was still puzzled. She opened her mouth to ask a question, but the lawyer continued.

"Here are his instructions and the sum of money that has been held in trust for you."

She took the scroll and began to unroll it. As she read, she felt her eyes widen and her heart beat a little faster. The sum named in the scroll was beyond her imagination. She didn't really have to depend on the business any longer to live comfortably in her villa.

"Sir, how am I to handle such a sum?"

"It has been deposited with the bankers. When needed, you may withdraw any sum you wish."

She was now a wealthy woman, independent and successful. What more could she have asked for? Then she thought of Nikolas, and after telling the lawyer what she needed him to do, he nodded assent and motioned to his young slave, "Bring in the man Nikolas."

Magnus considered her manager with shrewd eyes, his hand cupping his chin as Nikolas entered. Lydia held her breath, but then sensed approval in the lawyer's demeanor as he indicated to Nikolas to be seated.

"You have done well handling the shop. The other merchants speak well of you and madam's fabrics are reputed to be the finest in Philippi. Your reputation is good. There is no word of you in the brothels."

Before Nikolas could protest, the lawyer held up a hand. "It is in my client's best interests that I see who she has entrusted her business to."

"I have handled the monies from her shop with honor. She has had no call to distrust me."

"True. But your predecessor was not trustworthy, hence you come under greater scrutiny."

"Then you approve his handling the business while I am gone?" Lydia looked up at the lawyer who was again stroking his chin.

"Yes, he may bring me the funds on a weekly basis as the previous manager did...that is, until he decided to leave the city." Then, Magnus actually smiled. "Yes, but, madam, I suggest you do return to the city as soon as it is possible."

Lydia fought down a flash of irritation, keeping her face bland. She would be gone as long as she needed to be.

With their business concluded, Magnus waved a hand of dismissal and returned to his mass of scrolls as before.

Once outside, Nikolas stopped her. "You are not pleased with the arrangement?" He had noticed the change in her demeanor, no matter how carefully she covered it up.

"It is not you, Nikolas, it is men telling me what they think I should or should not do. I am not a young girl anymore, subject to a man's authority."

His burst of laughter goaded her further.

"That is amusing?" she asked frigidly.

"Madam," he murmured between chuckles. "No one would take you for anything but a strong, independent woman."

She frowned, puzzled. *What did he mean?* She turned away. "I have to see to my household. We will travel to Neapolis as soon as we can book passage on a ship traveling to Thyatira. As agreed, you may continue to meet with the believers in my home until I return."

"I will seek news of a ship for you. When you are ready, I will bring a wagon to transport you and your baggage to Neapolis."

"Thank you, Nikolas." He helped her into the carriage and stood back. Their eyes met briefly, but she purposely looked away, head high.

37

*A*s dawn sent its light to flood the villa and the grounds, Hektor and Nikolas carried the last of the women's traveling cases and placed them in the wagon. Delia followed him with a large basket filled with as much food as she could pack for the first part of their journey: dried fruit, nuts, cheeses, fresh bread, and bottles of wine and water. After two weeks of waiting, Nikolas had informed her of a ship arriving in Neapolis that would be returning to Thyatira.

Nikolas waited until Lydia came down the steps of the villa, followed by Sophia, Jael, and Chara. "The ship leaves three days after its arrival. It is the same one you sailed on. The captain will be notified that there will be four passengers arriving for passage."

"How did you…" she began.

"I sent word back with the men who brought the shipment last week on another ship. They informed the dock master. It was expedient, since you have decided to return home…for a time."

As he added the last few words, she felt him searching her face. Did he believe she would stay in Thyatira? She turned away and gave Hektor some last minute instructions on the house, then addressed Delia who was unhappy about being left behind.

"It is best that you remain to care for the villa along with Hektor," she assured her. "The believers will still be coming and

Paul has asked Nikolas to lead them. They will need refreshments, and Nikolas will make arrangements for any funds you need for supplies."

Delia glanced toward Sophia. "I wish I were going with you, Domina."

Lydia put a gentle hand on her arm. "I know, but it will be enough that my family must make room for the four of us. They have their own servants and a cook."

Delia sniffed and nodded. There was nothing more to say.

When the four women were settled on the wagon, Nikolas flicked the reins and they began the ten-mile journey to Neapolis.

*　　　*　　　*

For Lydia, the journey back to Neapolis seemed shorter than when they had come. This time, as the wagon moved swiftly toward their destination, she was very aware of the quiet strength of the man she sat next to.

When they were underway, Nikolas spoke in a low voice, for her ears alone. "The person you were concerned about. I have friends traveling to Syria who are to be trusted. They will take Karam with them, disguised as their daughter. They also have a young son so they should not attract attention. No one will be looking at a family for the girl. My friends shall come by the villa tonight. Karam has been told of this and to be ready."

Lydia's heart lifted. She nodded her understanding in silence. She and Sophia would pray that the couple would be able to locate Karam's village and her people.

Nikolas stopped halfway on their journey to let the women tend to their needs and eat something. Jael and Chara commented on the scenery and talked quietly between themselves. Lydia glanced at her mother from time to time but Sophia seemed lost in thought. Lydia puzzled over this. Was Sophia concerned about their welcome in Thyatira? It was not Marianne nor her household, for she and her mother would be welcomed gladly. Was it the prospect of seeing her home again, a villa Sophia was no longer able to be mistress of? Or was her mother concerned as she was of another confrontation with Cassius? Her mind turned with possibilities.

"You are far away, madam." Nikolas interrupted her thoughts.

"It has been less than a year, but I feel we have been gone longer."

"You miss your home in Thyatira?"

"Only my daughter, and of course her family. I look forward to meeting my small grandbaby."

"It may be they may persuade you to stay?"

She glanced up at him but his eyes were on the road ahead. Was he concerned for his job at the shop? If she did not return, what then? She had enough money now to live without the shop, but she enjoyed being a businesswoman, though she could not proclaim it publicly.

"My future is in the hands of Adonai. He will show me His will."

This time his eyes met hers. "He sent Paul to Philippi. You have a group of believers meeting in your home. Perhaps He has already shown you His will."

She was startled by his frankness and started to respond but clamped her lips closed instead. Nikolas said no more and they rode in silence.

Sophia put a hand on her arm. "It will be good to visit our city again. I am anxious to see Marianne. Imagine, a great-grandchild. It seems like such a short time ago she was a child, and now she is a young woman with a family."

"It will be good for both of us, Ima."

With only one more short stop to stretch, they soon neared the city and Lydia looked up to see the shore birds dipping and diving over the port. A large commercial ship sat rocking at anchor and Nikolas pointed to it. "Your ship, madam."

Their baggage was unloaded on the dock while Nikolas went to get the captain

"Greetings, Madam. I am honored you are once again passengers on my ship. You may find the voyage more pleasant than the last time. The weather should be agreeable."

Sophia smiled at him. "That is good to know, Captain Stamos."

He raised his bushy eyebrows in question and turned to Lydia. "You have not been in Philippi long. Did you not find the city to your liking, madam?"

"Philippi is a fine city, and much to our liking. We are returning to visit family. My daughter and a new grandchild."

He beamed. "Ah, that is good. Welcome aboard my ship. You will have our one cabin as before, perhaps a bit more comfortable since I see you are one less in your group."

As the captain motioned to a sailor to help with their baggage, Nikolas had been standing aside quietly but now he gave a nod of his head to the captain as if to confirm something. Lydia wondered a moment, but turned to send Jael and Chara ahead with her mother to arrange the cabin.

"Perhaps you can rest awhile before we set sail, Ima."

Sophia nodded. Her face looked drawn. It had been a long day for all of them.

Lydia turned to Nikolas who was standing by the gangplank. "Thank you, Nikolas, for bringing us here and arranging our passage. Captain Stamos was kind to us on the earlier voyage and it will be good to be under his protection again," she said properly.

Nikolas looked down at her, appearing to want to say something, but evidently thought better of it. His eyes looked into hers and once again she felt drawn into them. What was happening between them? She had to gain control of her emotions. This would not do. She was of the upper class and his employer. It was not seemly. She took a step back and gave him a perfunctory smile.

"Farewell, until we return."

"Until you return."

She turned and quickly made her way to the cabin. She did not look back.

───────── ◆ ─────────

They were indeed fortunate enough to have fair weather for the trip. Lydia and her mother were able to spend some time at the rail, this time to look out over the vast expanse of the Aegean Sea.

Lydia observed the billows that rolled beneath the ship and felt as though her emotions rolled through her in the same way. She was excited about seeing Marianne and her grandchild, yet at the same time felt she was being pulled away from something. Could she make a life again in Thyatira? Did she want to? Her mind was muddled over concern for Sophia. Her mother was not well. It was more than fatigue. Perhaps, as Doctor Luke mentioned, her heart was just weak. She thought of her father's death, something to do with his heart, and the pain with which he died. She felt panic rise as she considered her mother dying the same way. Was this trip to Philippi too hard on her? On and on the thoughts trampled their way through her mind. She said nothing to Sophia about this, not wishing to cause her more alarm. Chara was also aware of the health of her mistress and watched over her carefully on the trip.

They would be landing in Troas and Lydia wondered who would be waiting to welcome them. They would have to travel overland again to Thyatira. Lydia hoped they had mentioned that there were going to be four of them.

"Domina?" Jael had come up behind her and was holding her cloak. "Do you not wish for this? There is a chill in the air this morning."

She let Jael put the cloak around her shoulders. "Thank you, it is cool. How are my mother and Chara faring?"

"Your mother is still resting and Chara is feeling better." Jael smiled. "The sickness of being at sea is not so great this time."

Lydia raised her eyebrows. "That is good news."

Captain Stamos kept an eye on the four women during the voyage and often came to the rail to speak with her.

"Will someone be meeting you in Troas, madam?"

"I'm not sure my son-in-law will have gotten word of our arrival in time. We may have to secure a wagon."

"This was a sudden decision, then?" He stroked his beard and contemplated her.

"I'm afraid it was. My mother's health has not been good. It seemed like the right thing to do."

"If you find there is no one to meet you, perhaps I can help. I have contacts in Troas. Let me know if I can be of service."

She breathed a sigh of relief. Adonai was looking out for them. The captain bowed briefly and turned to begin instructing his first mate for their arrival in Troas.

As they entered the harbor, Lydia's heart beat with excitement, and Sophia must have felt the same way, for she came to join her at the rail. The two maidservants stood behind them enjoying the sights and sounds of a ship coming into port. The first mate was shouting orders to the crew who were manning ropes, bringing down sails, and beginning to move cargo up on deck. The seagulls dipped and soared over the ship, crying out to one another as their keen eyes sought any morsel of food the ship might cast into the water. Men at the docks waited for the ropes to be flung to them to secure the ship. In due time, the gangplank was lowered and Captain Stamos made sure the ladies were escorted carefully down to the landing. Their baggage was brought from the ship and stacked at the back of the landing. Sophia and the maidservants sat on them and looked up at Lydia. What were they to do next?

She scanned the landing and surrounding areas for any sign of Marcellus or Sergio. She didn't expect Marianne to come with a baby to tend. Just when she was ready to turn back to the ship and speak with Captain Stamos, she saw a familiar sight. The large *carpentum* they had originally traveled to Troas in, and sitting in the driver's seat, grinning, was Sergio's trusted slave, Macedon.

38

In no time at all Macedon had their baggage stowed and had helped them up into the carriage. He bowed to Lydia and Sophia.

"My master received news of your arrival, Domina, and determined when the ship would come in. He has charged me with your safekeeping to Thyatira."

"We are most grateful for your care, Macedon." Lydia replied. "How is the family?"

"They are most happy with the arrival of the young master, Alexander, Domina. He is a worthy child."

Sophia beamed. "A boy. Alexander. A fine name."

The movement of the carriage suggested that Macedon had been admonished to bring them to Thyatira with haste. When they did stop to rest and partake of some food in one of the small towns, Lydia suggested that they would arrive in better spirits if they were not jostled so much. She said it kindly, and the big slave was torn for a moment weighing his master's admonishment against her request. As she did her best to look imperious, he nodded. "I shall drive with less vigor, Domina."

It had not been so long that they forgot the inns they had stayed in; one very poor and one of good repute. They avoided the former and found another inn that was better suited. Sophia longed to stop at the baths again, but, knowing it would distress their driver, said nothing.

Lydia also would have liked the baths after the long voyage, but assured her mother, "Let us arrive at the home of Marianne and Marcellus with haste. There will be plenty of time then to rest and refresh ourselves."

Macedon slept with the carriage and fortunately there were no incidents on the way. Jael, remembering her frightening event with the two men on the previous journey, stayed close to her mistress.

When they finally approached the city of Thyatira, Lydia looked out toward the sea where she knew the dye works were found. She wanted to stop at the shop and greet Sargon to thank him for sending Nikolas to help her and for handling the sales of the fabrics so well. She knew he served Sergio and Marcellus now in her stead, and fortunately there had been no word of any defection such as what she dealt with in Philippi. But she was even more anxious to see Marianne and her grandson. She also knew that Macedon would fulfill his master's wishes and not take kindly to a detour.

As the carriage at last stopped in front of the villa of Marianne and Marcellus, Sophia looked out. "I had forgotten how large it was. Marianne is indeed fortunate to have such a dwelling."

Lydia agreed. "At least they should have ample room for us."

The door opened and, to Lydia and Sophia's delight, Marianne hurried out, holding her son.

"Ima! Savta! You are here at last." She embraced her mother and they wept with joy as Marianne put Alexander into Lydia's waiting arms. At six months old, he looked up at his grandmother with surprising calmness and curiosity. She kissed him on the top of his head.

"Such a handsome child. You are so fortunate to have given your husband a son, Marianne."

"Adonai has favored us, Ima."

Sophia moved forward to embrace her granddaughter and exclaim over Alexander. He held his arms out to her and with delight she held him close to her heart.

"Oh Savta, I have missed you so much. Did you believe you would have a great-grandson so soon?"

"I am the most fortunate of women, child. He is a beautiful boy."

Marianne then led them into the villa where Marcellus was just entering the atrium. He embraced Lydia and then Sophia after she had handed Alexander back to his mother

"I thank Adonai that you have all arrived safely." He turned to a young woman who stood nearby. "Please show them to the rooms they will occupy while they are here."

The servant nodded her head and indicated that they were to follow her. Lydia had only been in the villa once. She and Sophia passed through spacious colonnaded hallways and Lydia, glimpsing the inner garden, vowed to spend some time there. The flowers and shrubbery were prolific.

At one of the rooms, the slave opened the door and indicated that they enter. She spread her arm toward the room. "It is to your satisfaction, Domina?"

"Yes, it is quite acceptable."

They left Chara and her mother to get settled and moved to the next room. It was as large and spacious as her mother's. When a male slave deposited her baggage in the room, Jael set to work unpacking Lydia's things.

"When you and the mistress are settled, Domina, your maids will be shown to their place in the servant's quarters."

Lydia debated a moment about asking for a cot for Jael to share her room, but thought better of it. What she did in Philippi would perhaps not be looked on with favor here.

An hour later, the same servant appeared to lead Lydia and Sophia to the dining room to join the family for the evening meal.

When she saw the table and the food spread out, Lydia realized how hungry she was. The meals on their trip from Troas to Thyatira had been uninviting to say the least.

The table was laden with a goat cheese and melon appetizer with chopped olives, a dish of saffroned millet mixed with raisins and walnuts, lamb and lentil stew flavored with coriander, and a platter of grilled quail. Another platter held fig cakes, and for dessert there were dried apricots and pomegranate seeds in honey syrup. It was a feast fit for Caesar!

A servant appeared with a bowl of warm water to wash their hands and another removed their sandals.

As they ate, Lydia shared the success of the shop in Philippi, with thanks to the adept management of Marcellus and his father, sending the fabrics and overseeing the dye works.

Marcellus smiled ruefully. "It is good that Kebu is adept at managing the dye works. I try not to interfere any more than necessary."

Lydia understood. He preferred not to be around the odious part of the business any more than he needed to. "The process is fascinating," she responded. "But a little hard on the senses."

Marianne spoke up. "How is the manager in your shop? I understand the one who served Sabra fled with some of the funds."

"Nikolas has proved to be honest in his handling of the shop. I have trusted him to take care of things while I am gone."

Sophia had been quietly listening and turned to Marianne. "Did your mother write to you about Paul and the men that came to Philippi?"

Marcellus and Marianne glanced at each other and Marianne spoke tentatively, "We did receive your letter, Ima, and were wondering about these men. What is it they were teaching? As God-fearers we have believed in the Jewish God, Adonai. Like the Jews we believe in a Messiah coming, but according to these men, He has already come. Can you tell us about this Jesus?"

Lydia put down the date cake she had been holding and sent a silent prayer to her God to give her the right words. She began to relate the story of Jesus as Paul had presented Him. She shared how Paul had first persecuted the believers who followed what they called "The Way," and how Jesus had appeared to him and radically changed his life and direction. She told them of Doctor Luke and how he was traveling with Paul, keeping an account of people they talked to who had witnessed the miracles Jesus performed.

Marcellus interrupted. "We understand that this Jesus also died, and it is said He rose from the dead after three days."

"That is true, Marcellus. Jesus fulfilled every Scripture in the Torah that spoke of the Messiah, even to where he was born. Not in Nazareth, where he was raised, but in Bethlehem, the City of David, due to a census ordered by Caesar Augustus. The census forced his parents, Mary and Joseph, to travel to Bethlehem when she was great with child."

"There is a change in you, Ima, that we can see. Also in Savta. We, Marcellus and I, would like to know more about this Jesus."

"I will share what I know."

Sophia thought for a moment. "I believe your mother should tell you about Paul and Silas and what happened with the jail."

Marcellus frowned. "These men were in jail? What crime did they commit?"

"None," answered Lydia. "Paul healed a slave girl who was telling fortunes. He commanded the demon that possessed her to leave. When her owners saw that she would bring them no more money, they had Paul and Silas arrested, beaten, and thrown into prison. Paul tried to tell them he was a Roman citizen but no one heard him above the noise of the crowd."

She sighed. "Your uncle, Cassius, was in the midst of it all, and that is another story. He was the one who wielded the whip."

"My uncle was there? Then they did seek you and Savta out in Philippi!"

"Yes. He and Uncle Lucadius."

Marcellus shook his head. "I knew when he did not find you here he would somehow learn where you were. I suspected at the time he had no good intentions."

Marianne turned to Sophia. "Go on with your story, Savta."

Sophia continued, "At midnight, Paul and Silas were rejoicing to suffer for their Lord and were singing hymns. Suddenly, there was an earthquake and all the cells were opened and the chains on each prisoner were broken off. It was an act of our God." She went on to relate how the jailer and his family had received Jesus as their Savior and been baptized. The next day the leaders, learning they were Roman citizens, condemned without a proper trial, hurried to release them."

"What about Cassius? He is a Roman centurion. Surely this was a bad omen for him? He could lose his rank." Marcellus looked from Sophia to Lydia. "What happened to him?"

Lydia sighed. "He came to my villa, swaggering with the deed he had done. When I informed him that both Paul and Silas were Roman citizens, he knew he was in trouble. I believe he hoped the officials did not know or remember his name. He and Uncle Lucadius left the villa in a hurry, intending to leave the city on the next ship!"

Marianne hid a smile behind her hand and Marcellus chuckled. Lydia knew Marianne was tender-hearted, not wishing something to happen to a member of the family, but as she told the story she realized how foolish Cassius's actions appeared.

Lydia then related the news of the small group of believers who met in her villa and that Nikolas was leading the group in her absence, since Paul and his companions had gone on their way to other destinations.

At this moment, Sophia suddenly sat back in her chair. Her face was gray. She put a hand to her chest and turned toward Lydia but couldn't speak.

"Ima, what is wrong?" Lydia was on her feet and Chara appeared instantly. She had evidently been standing behind one of the porticos, watching her mistress.

Marcellus and Chara together helped Sophia up and Marcellus scooped her up in his arms and headed briskly toward Sophia's room. "Summon the physician," he called over his shoulder.

They laid Sophia on her bed and Chara loosed Sophia's clothing as Marcellus turned his back to give them privacy.

When she was settled in her bed, Marcellus brought a cushioned seat and Lydia sank down by her mother's side. "Where do you hurt, Ima? Is it your heart?"

Sophia could only nod. Lydia held her mother's hand and they all began to pray. As their heartfelt words filled the room, Sophia began to breathe more easily and some color returned to her face.

They prayed until one of the servants announced the arrival of the physician. Marcellus excused himself, murmuring that he would return later.

The physician asked some pointed questions and Lydia quickly admitted that this had happened before. She also related what Doctor Luke had told her.

The doctor listened carefully and after examining her mother, rubbed his chin with one hand. When he learned they had just arrived from Philippi, he shook his head.

"It is my opinion that the journey was harder on your mother than you believed. Her heart is not strong. She needs a great deal of rest and I would suggest no more long journeys!" He mixed a packet of powder with water and Sophia was helped to drink it.

"It will help her sleep." The doctor had not insisted in bleeding her mother, which was a relief. He then bade them farewell and promised to return in a day or two to see how her mother was doing. "Call me if there is an immediate need."

No more long journeys, Lydia thought. Did that mean her mother could not return with her to Philippi? What would she do?

Marianne, ever intuitive, grasped how that news would affect her mother. "Ima, my grandmother is welcome to stay with us as long as she wishes. If the journey is not a good thing for her, let her remain with us at such time as you must return."

Return alone? She rose and, glancing down at her mother who was now sleeping, managed a wan smile. "I must pray about this, Marianne." She could not impose on her daughter and son-in-law indefinitely and she had nowhere in Thyatira to go. Her mother had been her confidante and companion since her father died. She could only hope that perhaps after several weeks of rest, Sophia would be strong enough to return with her. With a last look at her sleeping parent, Lydia put a hand on Chara's shoulder. Sophia's faithful servant would watch over her mistress.

Lydia reluctantly bid Marianne and Marcellus good night. She returned to her room to seek the strength of the God who was always with her.

Jael was waiting for her. "Your mother, she is better, Domina?"

"She is sleeping."

"You are sad, Domina, but surely she will recover as she did before."

Lydia was thoughtful as Jael helped her prepare for to retire for the night. "I'm sure she will be better with lots of rest."

"But there is more that troubles you?"

"The doctor said no more long journeys."

Jael was brushing Lydia's hair and her hand stopped in mid-air. "Does that mean she cannot return with us?"

Lydia nodded, and both were silent for a time.

"Rest, Domina, and in the morning perhaps things will be clearer for you."

"I must pray, Jael. Adonai must show me what to do."

"I will pray for you. Our God will show us the way."

Her servant lifted the covers and Lydia slipped in. The bed was comfortable and she was indeed weary. She closed her eyes and listened as Jael put clothes away in the cupboard, picked up the small flickering lamp, and departed for her quarters, closing the door softly.

When she had gone, Lydia lay in the silence, listening to a fountain somewhere outside her room. It was a pleasant, soothing sound. After some time, unable to sleep, she got up and slipped to her knees beside the bed.

"Oh God who sees me, my heart is heavy. If my mother cannot return with me, I must go alone. I may never see her again. Not until I see her in Your kingdom. I do not want to face this. Please help me."

She remained on her knees, crying out to God with all the sorrow she carried.

My daughter, I am here. You have a destiny. Can you not trust Me for this? I will strengthen you for what lies ahead. Rest in Me.

"Yes, Lord. I trust You." She bowed her head and relinquished her cares to Him. "Whatever Your plan for me, Your will be done."

She remained on her knees a long time, communing with her God and feeling the warmth of His presence. Paul had said the Lord would never leave her nor forsake her. When peace finally reigned in her spirit, she slowly climbed back into bed, and fell into a deep sleep.

"Come and help us," the voices called. "We are lost and cannot find our way. Show us the way." Faces were all around her and their arms were reaching out to her. "What can I do?" she cried. "I am only one person." Someone reached out a hand to her. It was a strong hand and the arm extended was muscular. She could not make out the face, and just as she grasped the hand—

Lydia sat straight up in bed. It was a dream. What did it mean? The room was still dark and the song of a bird sounded melancholy in the stillness. She lay back down, closed her eyes, and slept again. This time she woke to sunlight streaming in the window and Jael's quiet footsteps on the marble floor as she opened the cupboard and gathered clothes for her mistress for the day.

"My mother?"

"She is awake, Domina, and feeling better."

"Oh, I am relieved to hear that. Help me get dressed quickly. I must go to her."

When Lydia arrived, Marianne looked up with a smile. She was sitting by her grandmother's side and Chara was feeding Sophia a soft gruel.

"Ima, I am heartened to see you are better this morning."

Sophia looked up, her voice weak, "I am better. I'm sure I will get stronger with rest."

Marianne caught Lydia's eye and gave a slight shake of her head. Her eyes were full of concern.

Lydia's heart beat a little faster. She could only keep her face calm and smile down at her mother with what confidence she could muster.

Sophia wanted to see Alexander and a servant brought him in. He smiled and made sounds at them. Sophia was delighted and murmured softly, "I'm so glad I came to see him. It was my dearest wish." She reached up and touched his cheek. "Bah, bah, bah," he chortled, and she smiled at him, her eyes alight with love.

When her mother had again drifted off to sleep, Lydia slipped from the room and sought out Marcellus. She wanted to visit the dye works and the shop. He was agreeable and had his slave bring the carriage around. It was smaller, like the one Lydia used in Philippi, and not as cumbersome as the *carpentum*.

They visited the dye works and Kebu was pleased to see her. She could see that he and Marcellus had a good rapport between them.

"All is well, Domina." He beamed. He showed them the dye vats and the slaves dipping in the fleeces to determine the correct color. Never had she seen a more beautiful purple than the color that was finally produced. It gave her a sense of pride to be able to carry on the business as her father would have wished.

She praised Kebu for his fine work and then they left to visit Sargon. A Roman matron was in the shop and once again she was privy to Sargon's talents in persuasion and making each customers feel like they were the most important person in all of Thyatira. She and Marcellus stood unobtrusively on the side of the shop, pretending to examine the bolts of purple cloth themselves. When the customer had at last made her purchase and strode from the shop, Lydia greeted Sargon.

"Domina, it is good to see you!" He smiled, then became serious. "I hear that your mother is not well."

The slaves have a news line all their own, she thought. How quickly word spread.

"She is better, Sargon. How is the shop doing?"

"Ah," and he grinned at Marcellus. "The young master is most adept at your accounts, Domina. He has done well."

Marcellus cleared his throat and stroked his chin self-consciously.

"I like the business," he said modestly.

Lydia strolled around the shop, admiring the bolts of beautiful purple fabric. She thought of her days hiding behind a curtain to watch Sargon deal with the household slaves and matrons who came to the shop. So long ago it seemed, and yet it wasn't.

A new customer came into the shop and having been satisfied that all was under control with her business, she and Marcellus returned to the villa.

When she entered Sophia's room, she was surprised to see Iola and Yorgos standing at the foot of the bed. Evidently they had spoken to Sophia, but she was now sleeping again. Their old age was more evident than Lydia remembered. She wondered how much longer they could take care of the villa in the absence of Cassius.

"We came to see the mistress," Iola offered.

Marianne smiled. "They came to the door and asked to see her. They worked for her so long I couldn't tell them no."

"It is good to see you both. How are things at the villa?"

Yorgos bobbed his head. "The garden thrives, Domina, as it did when you were there."

Iola glanced at him. "It is lonely, Domina. The master is seldom home. He is away most of the time with the army. He was here a few weeks ago, but perhaps not himself. We stayed out of his way as much as possible. He and your uncle conferred one evening over dinner and then they were gone the next day."

And came to Philippi, Lydia thought to herself.

"We will let my mother rest. Come, let us go to the garden. I would speak with you both."

Puzzled, they obediently followed her to the large inner garden. Yorgos looked around with pleasure at the fountains, the rose bushes, the profusion of marigolds, hyacinths, narcissi, and herbs—saffron, cassia, and thyme. There were two mulberry trees and several dwarf fruit trees.

"This is a good garden, Domina. It is cared for well," he pronounced.

Lydia asked them to be seated and they gingerly lowered themselves onto a stone bench.

"Marianne must speak to my brother Cassius. Taking care of a large villa is getting hard for you both. I can see that. She will make arrangements to care for you and I can only hope that in time my brother will release you. Do you have any family?"

Iola considered. "I have a sister. She became a slave when I did, but has since been freed by her master. She would welcome me."

"And Yorgos?"

"I have no one, Domina."

"Then if my daughter can persuade Cassius to release you, you may come here to live out your days. She has told me as much."

Tears came to Iola's eyes. "You are a kind mistress and generous. Let us hope it will be as you have said."

Yorgos nodded his thanks. "We will pray it will be so, and that the master will release us."

At the mention of the word *pray*, Lydia was reminded of her own faith. She shared with them what she and her mother had found in Philippi and their eyes grew large.

"Surely this is a greater God who has done these things," Iola murmured. "I would like to know this God."

Lydia prayed with them the words that Paul had taught them and saw the peace settle on both their faces.

"Thank you, Domina, for telling us about Jesus. I feel Him here in my heart." Yorgos touched his chest.

Lydia's heart sang. A miracle that the first people she was able to lead to the Lord were two old servants who were dear to her.

When Iola and Yorgos finally took their leave, it was with great hope that Cassius would free them. They had to wait until his next visit home when hopefully Marianne or Marcellus could speak with him.

Lydia remained in the garden, savoring the warmth and watching butterflies flit from plant to plant. Some sparrows called to each other in the mulberry tree in good cheer. But as storm clouds threatened to gather and the breeze changed to a wind, Lydia drew her cloak about her and went back inside.

There was little for Lydia to busy herself with in Thyatira except checking the accounts and being astonished at the sum deposited in her name with the bankers for investment. Added to what her father had set aside for her in Philippi, she began to wonder what Adonai would have her do with her profits. She committed her question to her God and waited patiently for an answer.

During the visit with her daughter, son-in-law, and grandson, she and Sophia were also able to renew their acquaintance with Sergio, the father of Marcellus. He was pleased with what his son had accomplished and, along with Sophia and Lydia, doted on the grandbaby.

At dinner one evening, when Sophia felt strong enough to join them, Sergio turned to Lydia. "Shall you be returning to Philippi, madam?"

She nodded slowly. "I only wait for my mother to regain her strength to accompany me."

There was a silence at the table and Lydia caught a look between her daughter and her father-in-law. Sergio considered her words for a moment. "And if your mother is not strong in the coming weeks? Then what will you do?"

Lydia did not want to consider that. She looked across the table and for a moment watched Sophia pick at her food. *What if she is not strong enough?* The unwelcome question echoed in her head.

Marianne spoke up. "What will become of the believers meeting in your home, Ima? Will they disband if you do not return?"

Lydia considered Delia, who had reluctantly been left behind. Lydia could not leave her there. And the believers. Then there was the shop…and as she thought of the shop, Nikolas's face came to mind. She realized with a shock that she had never once seriously considered *not* returning to Philippi. In her heart, it was her home.

But she only smiled at Sergio and Marianne. "It appears I have much to pray about."

Sergio studied her face beneath knit brows but remained silent.

After dinner, the nurse brought Alexander and, with his smiling eyes and baby sounds, he entertained them all.

Lydia rose. "I would walk in the garden a while."

"I will come with you," Sophia rose, unsteady for a moment, but then moved toward Lydia, and taking her arm, they went out to the garden together.

After strolling slowly, admiring the flowers, and listening to an owl, calling to his mate,

the two women sat down on a stone bench by the fountain. They had spoken of the garden and the various herbs that Sophia recognized, but neither spoke of the subject foremost on Lydia's mind. Philippi.

"Ima…" Lydia began, "how are you really feeling?"

It was a time for honesty, and Sophia turned to her. "I am weary, child. My body no longer does what I want it to do. The shadows come and I feel our God is calling my name."

Lydia let out a small sob. "I cannot bear it when you speak that way. I do not want you to leave me. I don't want to return to Philippi alone."

"You will not be alone, Daughter. Our God goes with you and His Spirit walks with you. Whatever the path ahead, He has chosen it for you."

There was a pause. Then Sophia spoke again, more gently. "You do not speak of him, my daughter, but I see what I see when you are with Nikolas."

"But Ima, he works for me. I am of the patrician class. There can be nothing between us."

"You are above him, then? Is that what you think? Did not Paul emphasize that there is no bond and free? That we are servants ourselves, of the living God? I see the way he looks at you when you are not looking. He loves you, child. He is a good man, honest, and a servant now of Christ. Have you ever thought that Adonai has a plan for both of you? Think of how God sent Paul to our city, to the riverside where we were meeting. Think of the church that has begun in your home. Do you think this is all happenstance?"

Lydia's felt her eyes widen in astonishment. She stared at Sophia. Never had she considered Nikolas's feelings, only her own. Never had she thought that the two of them may be part of a larger plan.

"Are you sure of his feelings? Perhaps you misinterpreted him."

Sophia laughed softly. "Not only am I sure of *his* feelings, but I know *you* are in love with him as well."

In love, with Nikolas? Lydia searched her heart for the truth of her mother's words.

Sophia put a hand on her arm. "As much as I would like to, Adonai has told me I shall not return with you. My time here is growing shorter. Now that I know our Savior, I do not fear death. As Paul told us, 'to be absent from the body is to be present with our Lord.'"

A tear rolled down Lydia's cheek. She could not speak. It was too painful to think about.

Sophia looked out over the garden. "One wish, promise me you will do this. When I am gone—I have promised Chara her freedom."

"I will do that, Ima. I spoke with Yorgos and Iola here in the garden a few days ago. They both accepted the Savior. I pray that Marianne will speak to Cassius about setting them free. They are getting too old to tend the villa. Marianne will allow them to remain with her for the rest of their lives if he does that."

Sophia smiled and her eyes shone. "What good news. You are indeed being used by Adonai." Then she sighed. "You know your brother. If he deems this something that you desire, more than likely he will not set them free, just to be difficult."

"That is why I wish Marianne to speak with him after I leave. Hopefully, he has no quarrel with her and he can see for himself how feeble they are getting."

"You said, 'after I leave.' When will that be?"

Lydia started. She *had* said that. And at that moment, she knew she and Jael would be traveling to Philippi alone, and soon.

40

*E*ach evening, Lydia had shared the words of Paul with her daughter and son-in-law. When Marianne heard of the decision of Yorgos and Iola to follow the Messiah, she was amazed, and finally, one evening, she reached out and grasped the hand of her husband.

"We have prayed to Adonai, and we have the assurance in our hearts that the words you have spoken are life and truth. Marcellus and I wish to also follow the Lord Jesus our Savior and Redeemer."

Joy unspeakable filled Lydia's heart. "If you are sure, then let us pray the prayer that Paul taught us and that each of the new believers have prayed."

Lydia explained that they must leave any sin on the altar of their hearts and confess them to Adonai. After a moment of silence while Marianne and Marcellus searched their hearts, they finally raised their heads. "We are ready, Ima."

Her daughter and son-in-law bowed their heads, and Lydia led them in the prayer of salvation.

Marianne looked up at her mother and grandmother. "I have seen the change on your faces, and now I feel His presence here in my heart."

"I too," murmured Marcellus, and the glow on both their faces left no doubt of their words.

They went to the pool in the garden, and after removing their sandals, Marianne and Marcellus were baptized in the name of the Father, the Son, and the Holy Spirit.

Sophia was so full of joy, she could hardly speak. She embraced her granddaughter and Marcellus, speaking words of encouragement. Finally, she allowed Chara to lead her gently to her quarters for the night.

Lydia, Marianne, and Marcellus stayed up half the night, so eager were they to know more about Jesus. Finally, Lydia said, "When you go to the synagogue, listen carefully to the words of the Torah, Daughter. They are the words that Adonai has spoken in the past. They will strengthen you. Adonai will teach you as your heart seeks His wisdom. You will find wisdom also in the psalms and the proverbs. Procure what scrolls you can to read." And with that, she retired for the night.

<hr />

Seeing her mother's frail condition, Lydia could not bring herself to set a date to leave, though she sensed Adonai telling her she was to return as soon as possible. She lingered, torn between the call Adonai had put on her life and the love she had for her mother. Adonai took the decision out of her hands, for a few days later, Sophia quietly left them in her sleep. Chara came to bring her breakfast and found her lying still in death, a peaceful expression on her face. At the maid's cries, the household came running and Lydia sank by her mother's side, weeping; the heaviness of grief like a stone in her chest. Marianne knelt by Lydia, her arm around her mother's shoulders, and they wept together.

Sorrow hung over the household as Marcellus made the arrangements for her mother's cremation and burial. The vase with Sophia's ashes would occupy a niche in the garden of Marianna's home.

Lydia kept her word to her mother and gave Chara her document of freedom. She embraced her mother's faithful maidservant and arranged passage for her with a group traveling to Ephesus where Chara had distant relatives.

There had been no word of Cassius, and Lydia felt the need to be gone from Thyatira should he return. Marianne promised to speak to him about Iola and Yorgos, if Adonai provided an apt occasion. Marcellus went to the waterfront and secured passage for Lydia and Jael on a ship that was leaving in a week from Troas and Macedon.

Lydia spent as much time as possible with Alexander. The child was the joy of her heart and she knew that when she left, she might not see Marianne or her grandson for a long time.

"When Alexander is old enough, perhaps you and Marcellus can bring him to Philippi to visit me."

Marianne held her tightly and they wept again. Lydia touched Alexander on his soft baby cheek. "Goodbye my little one. I will miss you greatly."

"Bye bye," chortled Alexander.

Amazed he knew the words, the family laughed together. Then, after embracing Marcellus and thanking him for all he was doing, Lydia entered the *carpentum* followed by Jael whose tear-streaked face spoke volumes.

Lydia and Jael waved until they rounded a bend and the family was out of sight. She and Jael looked at each other and with a sigh, they rode in silence for a long time, listening to the steady clopping of the mules along the road.

When they reached to docks at Troas, Lydia looked for the name of the ship that Marcellus had booked their passage on. To her chagrin, it was not Captain Stamos's ship. It would be an unknown captain.

As Macedon set their luggage on the dock, Lydia asked a sailor to call for the captain of the ship. A large, burly man strode to the railing and glanced down at them. He looked them over and, seeing her well-dressed as a woman of the upper class, he marched down the gangplank.

"I am Captain Julius. What is it you wish, madam?"

"My son-in-law, Marcellus Marcorius, booked passage for myself and my servant to Philippi on your ship. What accommodations can you provide for us?"

The captain frowned. "I do not usually carry women. My passengers are men and soldiers who sleep on the deck. I have only my own cabin and the quarters for my crew."

Lydia knew he had been paid well for their passage and stood quietly regarding him.

He cleared his throat. "However I will see what I can do to make room." He continued to eye them. "What is your business in Philippi?"

It was a blunt question, and truly none of his concern, but Lydia did not wish to offend the man. She drew herself up and replied. "I am returning home after the burial of my mother in Thyatira. I have a villa in Philippi and our family business."

Somewhat mollified, and realizing he had angered her, he stroked his beard, and once again seemed to appraise her and Jael. "As I said, I will see what I can do."

After thanking Macedon for once again taking them on their journey and wishing him a safe trip back to Thyatira, they sat on one of their trunks while they waited for the captain to make arrangements for them. While they waited, a Roman officer who stood nearby with his tribune approached her. She looked up and for a moment thought he was Cassius, but no, he was an older man.

"Forgive me, madam, but can we be of service to you? Are you and your servant traveling alone?"

His tone was kind, not disrespectful. "Yes. My mother recently died in Thyatira. I am returning to my home in Philippi after some absence."

"I am surprised, madam, that your husband allows you to travel alone. It is not safe these days."

"I am a widow, sir, my son-in-law booked the passage for us." She thought of something else she could add, which might be beneficial in the officer's eyes. "My brother, a centurion in the Roman army, is away and also unable to accompany us."

At the mention of her brother's rank, the officer raised his eyebrows and turned to his subordinate. Then he turned back to her. "We would be most honored if you would allow us to offer our protection in the place of your brother, madam. It is the least we can do for a fellow soldier. Is that not so, Gaius?"

The younger officer nodded. "We will be happy to watch over you on the voyage, madam."

The older officer rubbed his chin. "We have traveled on this ship before. Usually we sleep on deck. It is an unruly crew. I'm sure your son-in-law was unfamiliar with this ship."

Inwardly alarmed at his description, Lydia silently thanked her God for sending these men to offer their protection. "Thank you, sir. We are most greatly in your debt."

The senior officer introduced himself as Flavidius Hadrianus. He turned out to be an Imperial Legate, and, as Lydia knew from Cassius who aspired to a higher rank, the man commanded two or more legions—an important officer indeed. That he would take notice of her and offer to watch over two strange women was a miracle in itself. Only Adonai could have sent him. She had heard stories of women traveling alone, even of upper class families, who had not made their destination but disappeared.

As Lydia and Jael were escorted on board by the two officers, she noted the wary looks of the crew. The legate let the captain know that they would be responsible for the woman and her servant in place of a relative in the Roman army. When the captain noted that the two Roman officers had taken Lydia and Jael under their protection, there was a marked deference in his attitude. He

270 Diana Wallis Taylor

grudgingly moved two of his men out of their quarters and ordered them to sleep on the deck. One of those sailors was then ordered to lead the ladies to their cabin. He muttered angrily to himself as he led the way through narrow passages that smelled of perspiration and other unknown odors. Nevertheless, Lydia thanked the man and surveyed the tight quarters. There were two bunks and two hooks for clothing on the cabin wall. The cabin was obviously in the midst of the seamen's quarters and there was no lock on the door. Lydia took comfort that her valuables were concealed on her person. They certainly could not safely leave anything in the cabin. There was no room for their baggage, and hardly room to turn around, let alone change. Their baggage would have to remain on deck.

Lydia had the horrifying thought that they would have to wear the same clothes the entire five days to Neapolis. If the ship stopped long enough in Samothrace, she and Jael might be able to visit the baths. She sighed. She didn't hold out a great deal of hope for that. At least Jael had the basket with food they had purchased before Macedon took them to the dock. She had no illusions as to the food served on board the ship.

The toilet was located in the bow of the ship, just under the figurehead, and was little more than a hole in a wooden bench. Nearby, a bucket of seawater with a tin cup encouraged the user to pour water into the hole where a wooden trough carried the refuse out a small porthole to the sea. The area was cold and the odor was not much better than the passageway to their small quarters. Lydia and Jael took turns guarding the door for each other since there was no bolt on that door either. Only desperation caused either woman to venture that way.

The Roman soldiers were cordial and Officer Hadrianus revealed he was going to visit his family in Philippi before leaving for his final posting with the army. He was retiring in a year. Lydia was not surprised, for the Roman colony of Philippi was made up mostly of retirees from the Roman army.

"Are you anxious to be out of the army?" she asked.

"I have served in several campaigns, having entered the army when I was eighteen. I worked my way up over the years, but I am not as vigorous as I used to be. And I look forward to spending time with my family."

"You have children?"

He beamed. "I have six. The youngest is ten and the oldest is twenty-four." He glanced briefly toward the young tribune who was looking out to sea on the other side of the ship "My son travels with me to visit his mother. We had word she has been ill of late."

"Gaius is your son?"

He nodded.

"He has done well."

"Yes, he has. You have a brother in the army, but you also mentioned you are a widow. Was your husband in the army also?"

For a moment Lydia's heart pounded. If she mentioned his name, would he know who Plinius was? Would he know how he had died? "Yes, he was. He died in battle." She hoped he would ask no more questions, and she realized he had noted her hesitancy and drew quiet.

Lydia and Jael did not sleep well on the ship. Twice they heard men's voices whispering outside the crude door of their cramped quarters. The first time nothing happened, but the second time, it went on for so long, she started looking around for a weapon of some kind. Her heart beat erratically and she wondered if her benefactors would be able to hear them if she and Jael cried out. To her relief, she'd heard another man whisper loudly, "Fools, get back to your quarters. Do you wish to bring trouble for the captain with the Roman soldiers? The women are not worth a flogging."

Mumbling, the men dispersed and all was quiet, but Lydia could not trust herself to sleep the rest of the night.

Otherwise, the voyage to Samothrace was an uneventful one. The seas were calm and Lydia and Jael were able to spend time on deck. They were happy to share their food with the soldiers. It was a small thing in exchange for their protection. When Lydia and Jael bowed their heads to pray before eating, the legate and his son watched thoughtfully.

The ship was not carrying a large cargo, so their time in Samothrace was only a matter of a few hours. Lydia had the feeling that if she and Jael left the ship for any length of time the ship would leave without them, and take their baggage with it.

"It appears we do not get a bath, Jael," she murmured.

"I am sorry, Domina. I know you were hoping."

Lydia looked down at her tunic, which was showing signs of wear. "I may have to burn this when we reach the villa."

Jael smiled.

They were allowed to leave the ship to walk on the dock and the two soldiers walked with them. The young tribune was kind enough to carry on a conversation with Jael and accompany her to the local marketplace to purchase more food. Lydia walked and talked with the legate.

"The dry bread and gruel served on this ship is abominable, and we are grateful for your generosity." He rubbed his chin and then paused in his steps. "We have noted that you and your maidservant pray over the food. What is your religion?"

They had over an hour to talk and after sending a silent prayer to her God for wisdom, she answered, "I was raised by a Jewish mother and a Roman father. He gave my mother leave to take us to the synagogue. I learned the Scriptures and came to believe in the Jewish God. Now, thanks to a traveling preacher by the name of Paul of Tarsus, I am a believer in the Lord Jesus, the Messiah."

He had raised his eyebrows at the mention of the Jewish God, but the legate nodded at the mention of Jesus.

"I have heard of the man called Jesus. He traveled all over the country, healing and teaching people about His God."

"He is a God for all people, sir. He did indeed heal all who came to Him, and His message was that the kingdom of heaven is near."

"Yes, but He stirred up a rebellion, proclaiming himself the Son of God and a king."

She paused and looked at him earnestly. "He sought no overthrow of the government. His kingdom was a heavenly one. His mission was to turn the people back to the one true God."

"That may be, madam, but it is common knowledge throughout the Legion that the Governor of Judea, Pontius Pilate, put him to death…as a criminal. How is it that men are still speaking of him as if he were alive?"

"Because He is, captain. He died and was buried in the tomb of one of the members of the Sanhedrin who believed in Him. On the third day, He was no longer in the tomb. God had resurrected Him from the dead. People who had been buried in the tombs also rose from the dead and appeared in the city of Jerusalem. Hundreds saw them. His disciples, who had deserted Him when He was arrested, were waiting in an upper room trying to decide what to do when He appeared to them and told them to see His pierced hands and feet and the wound in His side."

He frowned. "It is common knowledge that his disciples came in the night and stole the body away, claiming he'd risen from the dead."

She smiled. "Sir, you are a Roman officer. Governor Pilate sent a 'watch' to guard the tomb. What is the penalty for soldiers to sleep in the line of duty?"

"It is death," he answered firmly.

"Then would the soldiers be sleeping so soundly that the disciples could come and roll the huge gravestone away? His burial clothes were still in the tomb. Would a group of frightened disciples take time to unwrap the body before making away with it?"

He rubbed his chin again. "You have made a valid point, madam. But this is a difficult story to believe. How do you know these things? This all happened years ago, when I was a tribune myself."

"The man, Paul, told us." She then related the story of Paul's encounter with Jesus on the road to Damascus.

"So he was persecuting the believers and then became one himself?"

"Yes. He came to Philippi with three other believers: Silas, Timothy, and a Greek physician by the name of Luke. Luke was traveling with Paul to document the life of Jesus and speak personally to those who had been touched by him."

The ship's bell rang, calling them back to board the ship. As they neared the gangplank, the legate murmured, "This is a strange tale, but you do not seem a woman to be taken in by foolish stories. I will think on your words. Perhaps we shall speak of this again."

She inclined her head and silently thanked Adonai for the opportunity to speak of His Son.

41

*L*ydia stood at the rail, looking across the sea in the direction of Neapolis, remembering her mother and her mother's last conversation with her. Were her mother's words true? Did Nikolas care for her? That was ridiculous. She was seeing something that just wasn't there. Nikolas was handsome and charmed their customers, but if he became aware of the reaction she had to him, he would probably be amused. They were of different classes and she was his employer. How else could he treat her?

Her reverie was broken by the presence of the legate who had come to join her.

"Madam?"

She turned from the rail. "Good morning, sir. We will be in Neapolis soon."

"Yes. I trust you and your maidservant have had a good voyage?"

"To some extent, thanks to you and your son watching over us." She lowered her voice. "I will be most happy to leave this ship. I do not believe the captain likes having women on board."

He chuckled. "You are correct, madam. He does not usually carry female passengers."

"You have been on this ship before?"

"Yes, two or three times over the years. It is not my favorite, but then, a soldier sometimes has few choices."

She nodded and looked back out to sea.

After a pause, he cleared his throat. "I have been thinking on the words you shared with me in Samothrace. All my life I have been devoted to the gods of Rome. Yet I have not found satisfaction in that pursuit. Instead, I wondered how a statue made of stone could hear the prayers of my heart. You seem to have found something in your God that sets you apart. You are sure of what you believe."

"Sir, no statue of wood or stone can answer our prayers. The statues are made with human hands, and how can humans answer their own prayers?"

"You said this Paul had a living encounter with Jesus and it changed his life in every way."

"That is true. Jesus came to earth to show us what the living God was like. To show us how much God loves us. We cannot make ourselves right with a holy God just by doing good deeds, or living a good life, or putting offerings at His feet. God cannot receive us on the basis of what we have done on our own. When we receive Jesus, the Christ, we are covered with His righteousness, and that is what Adonai sees when we come before Him. He sees what Christ has done and not our frail, human selves."

"I have lived long and the army has been my life. It has taken me far from my family much of the time. I have missed the years when my children were small, and many other occasions. I have done things I would like to forget, and yet in the back of my mind, I cannot. Can this Jesus give me the peace I have witnessed on your countenance?"

It was a long speech for him, and Lydia was touched that this hardened soldier had bared his heart. She was suddenly very sure that their voyage on this ship was no coincidence. In a few hours they would be docking in Neapolis, and this man and his son would go their way, perhaps never to meet her again. She drew a quiet breath and turned to him.

"It is not difficult. First you examine your life, and any sins you feel you have committed, however small. You renounce them and ask the forgiveness of Adonai for the things you have said and done. When you do that to the best of your ability, you are forgiven then and there. He does not hold those things against you ever again. Then you ask Jesus to come into your life and be your Redeemer and Lord. You commit your life and future to Him."

He glanced back at his son who was speaking to one of the deckhands on the other side of the ship, and then said quietly, "I would like to do that. Peace is what I have sought for a long time."

She did not touch him, for it would be unseemly, but she murmured that when he had asked forgiveness for the things in his life that had offended God, and was ready, she would speak the words with him.

He closed his eyes and she knew he was laying his sin at the foot of Adonai. Then he opened his eyes and glanced at her, raising his eyebrows. "Now?"

She smiled and indicated he should repeat the words after her.

"Lord Jesus, I lay my sins and offenses at Your feet. I ask You to enter my life as my Lord and Savior. Forgive me and cover me with Your robe of righteousness. I pledge to serve You with my whole heart and soul from this time forward."

She watched his face soften as the Lord took over the life of a new believer. He was an old soldier, toughened by his years of battles, but now his eyes shone with a new light.

"You know Him," she smiled.

"Yes. Never have I felt this peace, this lightness in my spirit."

Lydia thought her heart would burst out of her chest. She would never understand how this change came about, time after time. In her family, her household, she had seen Jesus change lives in this way. Sometimes the change was subtle, and grew as the

Spirit worked in the life of a new believer, and sometimes it was powerfully evident immediately.

Ever aware of protocol, the legate remained quietly at her side but did not take her hand as she felt he wanted to.

"Thank you, madam, for a most precious gift. One I hope to share with my son and family." His eyes were moist as he turned to look out to sea to gain control.

"This time, sir, was ordained by Adonai. He put us on this ship to give me the privilege and pleasure of sharing Him with you. You are not the same man who boarded this ship a few days ago."

"No, and I shall forever be in your debt, madam. For your courage and kindness."

"Not in my debt," she assured him. "But in the Lord's."

At that moment, land was sighted and the activity on the ship suddenly changed as each sailor turned to the tasks that prepared them to enter the port at Neapolis.

Young Gaius strode to his father's side and seeing his father's face, turned a questioning gaze at Lydia.

She gave him a direct look and smiled. "I wish you a safe and pleasant journey home, Gaius. May you find your mother's health much improved. Jael and I have been praying for her."

The young tribune frowned. "You and your maidservant pray together?" He turned to observe Jael, who had been sitting on one of their chests, watching the seabirds soar overhead.

"Yes, though she is my servant, she is also a sister in Christ. Paul taught us that there are no barriers."

"She has told me of some changes in her life. I have found it hard to believe."

The legate put a hand on his son's shoulder. "We have much to talk about after we leave this ship."

A slight smile lifted the corners of the tribune's mouth. "It would seem we do."

Lydia and Jael did their best to stay out of the way of the crew that scurried about the deck. Once before the captain had yelled at her when she and Jael did not move fast enough and a sailor nearly ran into them. Since then, she had been careful to keep both of them as inconspicuous as possible.

"Do you have a way to Philippi? We have someone meeting us with horses or I would offer to transport you."

"Adonai will meet our need, sir. One way or another."

"You are truly a woman of faith. However, we shall stay nearby until we are sure you have made arrangements."

"Thank you. I don't know what we would have done if you had not come aboard this ship."

"It has been our pleasure."

When the gangplank had been lowered, the crew began carrying some of the cargo off that had been brought up from the hold. The legate finally spoke to the captain and two sailors were assigned to take the women's baggage off the ship. Lydia thanked the captain for making a way for her to return home, receiving a curt nod in return. She and Jael left the ship, followed by the legate and his son.

As she looked around trying to determine where she might find a wagon to transport the two of them to Philippi, she caught her breath.

Jael suddenly exclaimed, "Look, Domina!"

"I see, I see!" Lydia responded, trying to keep her composure as her eyes met those of a driver patiently waiting at the dock.

It was Nikolas.

42

He climbed down from the wagon looking like a school-boy who had been caught in a bit of mischief.

"Nikolas, how did you know when to meet us?"

"I learned the schedule of the sailing ships and when they were coming into port from Troas. Your son-in-law, Marcellus, sent word with the last shipment that you were returning home and he was arranging passage for you." He grinned. "This is the third ship I have come to meet."

"Oh Nikolas, I am so grateful for your foresight." She turned to the two officers behind her. "Sir, this is Nikolas, the manager who takes care of the fabric shop in Philippi. Nikolas, this is Legate Hadrianus, and his son, Gaius. They have been most kind to watch over us on our voyage."

Nikolas inclined his head. "I am thankful for your care of my employer. I was concerned about them traveling alone. Even more when I learned the ship they were on."

The legate chuckled. "It has been a most interesting voyage. Your employer is a very unusual woman."

Nikolas frowned, unsure of the meaning of the legate's words, and Lydia saw something in his eyes. Was it jealousy?

Gaius looked across the landing and inclined his head. A young man of eleven or twelve was approaching, leading two horses.

"Ah, we must depart, madam, but it appears you are in good hands. Once again, may I extend our condolences on the death of your mother."

She thanked him again, and after a nod to Nikolas, the legate and his son took their leave and went to mount their horses. In a moment they were riding away from the landing.

Nikolas loaded their baggage in the back of the wagon, and helped Lydia up onto the seat as Jael climbed up to sit beside her mistress.

He paused and turned to her. "Sophia was a kind and generous woman. I will miss her insight and counsel."

Lydia thought back to the beginning of the voyage. She had rested on the small bunk on the ship the first night, silent tears streaming down her cheeks. She felt like a little girl again, missing her mother so much. Sophia had been her friend and companion, lending her strength through Lydia's difficult years. It was hard to believe she was gone. Only the comfort of seeing her again one day in heaven helped her manage her grief. Jael had prayed with her, more as a friend than a slave, and Lydia had been grateful that they shared the love of Adonai.

Now, with Nikolas's words, the grief came back, filling her heart with heaviness and causing tears to rise and threaten to spill down her cheeks.

"Thank you, Nikolas," she managed.

He flicked the reins and the mule started forward, plodding steadily toward Philippi.

She composed herself and asked, "How have the believers been while I have been gone?"

"We are a slightly larger group than when you left, madam. The number of believers has almost doubled. They will be glad to see you. I must confess, I felt unworthy to take Paul's place leading the group, but Adonai has been faithful and we have learned much together."

"That is good news, Nikolas. Paul knew you could do it. He chose you."

"I have done my best."

"And how are Delia and Hektor?"

"Delia has missed you sorely. Hektor has been invaluable." A slight smile tugged at the corners of his mouth. "They have found common ground."

Lydia searched his face. "Common ground?"

He looked straight ahead. "It would seem that a freeman and a slave can overcome barriers."

What was he saying? Was there something between her cook and the manager of her villa? She would get to the bottom of that when they arrived home. Then the import of his words came like a dart into her chest. Nikolas was not a slave, but she was certainly of another class. Was he making a statement about *their* situation?

As they rounded the drive and the villa came in sight, Lydia had a sense of truly coming home. Delia was on the portico, waiting anxiously for them, and Hektor hurried out from the stable, beaming. "It is good to see you home, Domina." He began to help Nikolas unload their baggage from the wagon."

"Welcome, Domina." Delia's eyes filled with tears. "I am glad for your return, but I miss your mother. I am so sorry to hear of her death." She looked around. "Chara did not return with you?"

Lydia put a hand on the shoulder of her faithful servant. "Thank you for your kind words, Delia. No, Chara did not return. It was my mother's wish that Chara be given her freedom. Chara has returned to family."

Delia stared at her in silence and then took a breath. "Then she is most fortunate, Domina." She glanced at Jael who had been standing by, listening. "It is good that she has family to return to."

"Do you have family somewhere, Delia?"

The cook faced her mistress with wide eyes. "I have no one, Domina. I do not wish to leave you."

Lydia merely smiled and inclined her head as they entered the villa. She paused, seeing again the beautiful tile floors and the birds and flowers on the walls and realized how much she loved this villa. What a gift her father had given her. It was home and no one could ask her to leave.

Delia remained nearby, her face indicating she awaited further words from her mistress. Lydia was weary and so many thoughts vied for attention in her mind.

"We will speak of many things, Delia. Perhaps this evening after I have rested."

Delia sniffed, still fighting back tears. "Yes, Domina." She turned and went back to the kitchen.

Nikolas had listened to the exchange with the cook, his face thoughtful. Glancing at Lydia, he placed a small chest on the floor and returned to the wagon to carry another chest into the house.

The two men carried the heavier things up the stairs and placed them in Lydia's room at Jael's direction. Lydia ascended the stairs and paused for a moment at her mother's room. The door was open and all was in order, for a mistress who would no longer occupy it.

She entered the room and looked around, touching the pillow on her mother's bed. She had the urge to fling herself down and give vent to the grief that threatened to overwhelm her, but she fought back tears and drew herself up. Now was not the time. She had responsibilities to take care of. A deep voice rose from the atrium speaking to Hektor and she turned toward the stairs. Responsibilities and…decisions.

43

*N*ikolas watched her come down the stairs, his expression unreadable as his eyes held hers for a long moment. Then he inclined his head. "I have been gone from the shop more than is good for business. With your permission, madam, I will return to my duties. The believers will be here tomorrow evening. They are anxious to welcome you back…also." She noted the added word.

She kept her voice cordial, not trusting her emotions. "Thank you again for your help, Nikolas. I shall be in the shop tomorrow morning. We have business to discuss."

"I shall be waiting." As he turned toward the door, he added, "There is someone who is anxious to meet the shop owner. I gave him no information, but I'm sure he will return."

Her brows knit together and she wanted to ask about the man, but the door had already closed and Nikolas was gone.

Jael stepped up to her mistress. "This has been a long day, Domina. Let me prepare you for rest until the evening meal."

Rest. Yes, that was what she needed. But now, alone in her room with the villa quiet, sleep would not come. She got up and walked to the window, gazing out at their small orchard. She could hear the chickens scratching and clucking among themselves. Somehow it was a peaceful sound. Her future stretched ahead of her like a blank parchment. What did it hold? She longed for something but what was it? Nikolas, ever hovering on the back of her mind, was a road she was not sure she should follow. She acknowledged his presence, both at the shop and as a believer, and confessed to herself that she didn't know what she would do without him.

Her mind in turmoil, she finally sank to her knees beside the bed and yielded her confusion to her God. As she prayed, earnestly seeking Adonai's will for her life, the peace she sought gathered around her like a soft blanket.

⟡

Later, when Jael came to wake her for *cena*, she looked around in a moment of disorientation. Somehow she must have climbed back on the bed and fallen into a deep slumber.

The servants did not eat with the mistress of the villa, and Lydia realized she was going to be eating alone. How she had enjoyed meals at the home of Marianne and Marcellus. His father, Sergio had come also, and her mother was there smiling...there was conversation and laughter. It was a joy to see Marianne so happy. She thought of the hours she was able to hold her grandson. Now she ate by herself. Is this what her life would be?

Then she remembered the picture Adonai had showed her when she was praying...people, here in Philippi, around her table. Rumors were circulating even before she left Thyatira that Rome was not happy with those following "The Way." Many had already left the city and spread to other cities and lands. Would all the believers there eventually be forced to leave? With a sigh, she pushed the troubling thoughts aside and determined to enjoy her meal.

Delia had made a bitter herb salad, with chopped garlic, fresh mint, dandelion greens, watercress, halved grapes, and walnuts, all tossed in a dressing of wine vinegar, olive oil, honey, and mustard seeds. A grilled tilapia and a small loaf of bread to dip in her wine was added along with a small bunch of grapes. As she ate, Lydia mulled over how she could implement some of the changes Adonai had shown her.

The next morning as Jael helped her dress, she brought up the subject of Sophia's room.

"Jael, my mother's room needs to be emptied of her things. It will be a guest room from now on. I will take what I can use, but everything else must be removed. Do you know of those who might have need of her clothing? I know that among the servants information is shared."

"Ah, Domina, this will be a hard task for you, but I understand. Yes, there are those among the poor who would be most happy to make use of those things."

"Good. We will begin later this afternoon. This morning I am anxious to see the shop."

"Master Nikolas will be there?"

Lydia glanced up quickly but Jael had turned away and was drawing sandals out of the cupboard.

"Yes," she said simply.

Hektor brought the small cart around and Lydia could hardly wait to get to the city. But as the cart moved along she frowned. Was it the shop she was anxious to see, or the man who ran the shop? She was in her thirties, a matron, a widow with no family around her. She was also wealthy, the owner of a prospering business that boasted the finest Tyrolean purple in the industry. With the help of Nikolas…and she paused in her thoughts. None of this would have been possible without Nikolas.

Hektor took them through the marketplace and pulled up in front of the shop. Nikolas was talking to a large, burly man who turned and perused her as she entered. Thinking her to be another customer, he stepped aside, prepared to leave.

Nikolas stopped him, and, addressing Lydia, murmured, "This is Quintas, madam. He leads the Dyers' Guild in this city. He was inquiring as to what happened to your father, Atticus."

The man's heavy brows knit together. "Atticus is your father? We learned he was ill and not able to come to Philippi anymore."

"My father is dead, sir."

"Dead? We had not had that news. Who then owns the business? We understood there was a son, but we haven't seen him. He has not come to the Guild meetings."

"My brother is a centurion in the Roman army. He prefers the military to the dye business."

Quintas looked from one to the other and finally blurted, "Then who owns this shop?"

She drew herself up and with a glance at Nikolas, who had a smile tugging at the corners of his mouth, said with authority, "I am the owner of our dye business, both in Thyatira and here in Philippi."

His mouth opened. "A woman? What do you know about the dye business?"

"Everything my father taught me."

"But the Guild meetings...a woman alone would be uncomfortable attending."

"I would not come alone, sir. My manager here could accompany me."

He still sputtered. "But a woman at the Guild meetings...."

She sighed. "If that upsets you that much, then I shall send Nikolas in my place. Would that be acceptable?"

He wiped his forehead with a cloth he'd pulled from his tunic, and hesitated. "We do not have slaves attending unless their masters attend."

Nikolas spoke up. "I am not a slave, Quintas. I am a freeman, and a Roman citizen."

It was Lydia's turn to stare. She did not know he was a Roman citizen. She turned back to Quintas, who was touching the fabrics. "We have long envied you the color of your purple cloth, but none of us can duplicate it. Your father would never share his secret."

She smiled. "And neither shall I." She continued to look steadily at him.

He shrugged. "We could only ask, madam." He stood for a moment and then took his leave, shaking his head and murmuring, "A woman. I would never have guessed."

Nikolas watched him go and his grin widened. "The secret is out, madam. Soon everyone will know who you are. You can no longer hide in the back room."

"Nor do I intend to. I am a businesswoman and find there are more women who are in my position."

She pretended to examine one of the bolts of cloth, running her fingers over the soft fabric. She marveled at the deep purple achieved at the dye works in Thyatira. Keeping her back to Nikolas, she gathered her courage.

"My mother reminded me that Paul taught there is no slave or free in the kingdom. That all are equal in the sight of Adonai."

"I remember his teaching on that."

"I was born to the upper class. My husband was of a wealthy family in Thyatira."

"And was your marriage a happy one?"

"My father chose my husband; I'd known Plinius since I was a child."

"You didn't answer my question."

With her back still to him, she slowly shook her head. "No. He was a selfish man who did not care for our daughter. He wanted a son and in the ten years we were married, I was unable to give him one. He died in battle, and I did not grieve for him." Surprised at her own candor, she realized what she had said. She had finally admitted the pain.

"And after he died?"

"Since there was no heir to protect my status, I was forced to leave the villa in favor of one of Plinius's brothers and return to the home of my parents."

"Madam, all that is past, is it not? In the knowledge of our Lord, you have begun a new life. Are you able to relinquish the past and be open to what Adonai has for you?"

She turned then and realized he was only a few feet away. She found herself looking into the depths of his eyes and was suddenly afraid of what she saw there. Emotions wrestled in her heart. Love was an emotion she was afraid to consider. The only love she had known was that of family.

"Nikolas, I...."

"This is a battle you must fight with yourself," he said softly. "But when you have won, I shall be here."

Her voice sounded small. "Will you be at the villa this evening? I will be reading from the psalms."

"The believers will be coming also."

"I shall look forward to seeing them all again."

He smiled. "You may be surprised. The group has grown in your absence."

"That is what Paul wanted." Then she felt emboldened. "Will you come for *cena*?"

He seemed amused, but nodded. Just then a matron entered the shop with her attendant. He suddenly became impersonal. "That would be agreeable, madam."

As he turned to greet his customer, Lydia quickly left.

44

*B*ewildered by the strength of her emotions, Lydia turned toward the other shops in the marketplace, with Jael close behind. She stopped to gather her thoughts by a small shop selling togas. She admired several in a variety of colors and then impulsively purchased one of fine, soft linen in a light green shade. She also bought a jade pendant that caught her eye. "I believe I shall wear them this evening, Jael."

"They are beautiful, Domina."

As they walked through the agora, Lydia was aware of the deference of the merchants. People were glancing her way. The merchants always sought to sell their wares, but there was a difference now. They all clamored for her attention. No doubt gossip had already spread concerning her status. Ignoring the merchants waving their wares at her, she handed her parcels to Jael and they quickly returned to the cart. She decided that perhaps it would be better if Delia and Jael did the shopping from now on.

"Hektor, take me to my lawyer's office."

Leaving Jael in Hektor's care, she hurried to the office of Magnus Titelius, who received her, his face grave.

"May I extend my sincere condolences at the death of your mother? I was recently informed of this sad matter."

"Thank you. I shall miss her greatly. It was strange to return home and not have her there."

"I understand." He cleared his throat. "Madam…may I call you Lydia, since we will continue to be in contact over many matters?"

"Only if I may call you Magnus."

He inclined his head. "Of course." He sat down and put his fingertips together. "Allow me to state that there are other matters that concern me. A group meeting in your home?" When she started to speak, he raised his hand. "Many have been seen coming and going. Nikolas leads this group?" He raised his eyebrows in question.

She collected her thoughts and prayed for guidance before speaking. "In my absence, yes. I was a God-fearer in Thyatira. From the time I was young, since my mother was Jewish, we attended the synagogue to learn the words of the ancient Scriptures, which the Jews call the Torah." She waited and he nodded his head for her to continue.

"Some months ago, a man by the name of Paul came to Philippi with three other men. My household had come to the river to pray, seeking others who believed as we did. Paul was there and shared his faith in the Jewish Messiah who had already come. His name was Jesus and He traveled about Judea, healing the sick, working miracles, and teaching. He proclaimed that the kingdom of heaven was at hand, that He was the Messiah the Jews had prayed for through so many centuries. No other man has ever done the things He did: opened blind eyes, caused the lame to walk, and many other miracles, witnessed by thousands. Jesus came to show us what God is like and then to show us how much God loves us. At the appointed time, Jesus went to a Roman cross and died, taking our sins on Himself. He was resurrected on the third day, and was seen by hundreds of believers and non-believers alike. Paul taught that if we believe on Jesus as the Christ, and receive Him as our

Redeemer, our sins are forgiven." She paused, but Magnus was listening intently and did not comment.

"I believed Paul's words, and my entire household believed and was baptized that day. It changed my life in ways I cannot begin to describe. I was a different person. Since that day, I've invited other believers to join me at my home, to share their stories and pray together."

It was a long speech for her and now she waited for his reaction.

He rubbed his chin and sat back in thought. "Paul and his companions were arrested, beaten, and thrown in prison. Something over a slave girl."

She sensed he knew more than he was indicating, but she continued.

"It is because he healed her of the demon that allowed her to tell fortunes. She had been following him and Silas for days. You must also know of the earthquake that released not only Paul and Silas but all of the prisoners, felt only in the jail. That was God's doing."

He cleared his throat. "Yes, a strange phenomenon to be sure." He was beginning to look uncomfortable. "At least they were released and left the city." He knit his brows together again.

"I have heard of this Jesus, but only as an itinerant preacher and teacher. If He was who He said He was, how did He come to die like a criminal on a Roman cross?"

It was the same question the Roman officer had posed. "It was part of God's plan, Magnus. In the Jewish religion, on Passover, the High Priest lays his hands on a sacrificial lamb each year transferring the sins of the people to the lamb. The lamb is then sacrificed, atoning for our sins. This is done every year in Jerusalem. What Paul taught is that Jesus became God's lamb. Sacrificed for our sins once and for all."

Had she said too much? Would he think her a foolish woman listening to stories?

"You are indeed persuasive, madam. I will think on these things. As to the matter I mentioned earlier. I was concerned that people were coming in and out of your home for a different reason. I am glad to lay my concerns to rest. It is just a matter of your religion."

She breathed an inward sigh of relief. This was not a man to antagonize. Better a friend than an enemy.

Suddenly he was back in business mode. "Concerning your shop. You have revealed yourself at last. The entire Dyers' Guild is digesting the news."

She stared at him in puzzlement. "That was but an hour ago! How did you know so soon?"

Magnus chuckled. "I do have my spies, dear lady. It is how I keep abreast of the news in Philippi."

"Meaning the head of the Dyers' Guild?"

He must have gone straight to Magnus, but why?

He didn't answer that. "There have been rumors about the owner of your shop, but no proof. As you know, there are other women such as you who are coming to the fore and handling business matters. It is a time of change."

"At least I no longer have to hide in the back room."

This time he chuckled. "No, I would say there is no longer a need for that. Will you now remain in Philippi?"

"Yes, this is my home now. My business is doing well, my family is handling the dye works, and shipping from Thyatira has gone smoothly."

"You will continue the group in your home?"

"Yes, in the loss of my mother, it comforts me to have around me those who love the Lord Jesus as I do."

"You do not consider marriage, madam?"

She fought down a touch of irritation. That was not his concern.

She merely smiled. "There is no one at this time. I am enjoying, for once, not being under the authority of a man."

He stood and came around the desk. "You are a very unusual woman, Lydia. You have proved yourself in the business of selling the purple cloth. I myself have purchased some of it. It is quality." He stood looking down at her. "You may change your mind on marriage one day."

She rose, sensing it was time to leave, and thanked him for his help and counsel. "You will continue my business interests as before?"

"Yes, madam. It is proving to be a most interesting occupation." She did not wait for him to elaborate.

Back at the villa, Jael took the purchases up to her mistress's room while Lydia went to the kitchen to see what Delia had planned for this evening's *cena*. There would be fresh pears from their orchard with aged cheeses; *garum*, a fish sauce mixed with wine; a medley of cooked vegetables including green beans, cabbage and yellow squash, and fresh bread. For dessert, fruit tarts sweetened with honey.

"A good selection, Delia." She related her experience in the marketplace and as Delia clicked her tongue in sympathy, Lydia smiled. "You may continue to do the shopping, Delia. It was extremely exhausting for me."

When she'd left Delia, Lydia went to the alcove where she kept her scrolls of Scriptures. As she pulled one out for this evening's reading, it was the thirty-seventh psalm.

Don't worry about the wicked or envy those who do wrong.
For like grass, they soon fade away.
Like spring flowers, they soon wither.
Trust in the Lord and do good.
Then you will live safely in the land and prosper.

Take delight in the Lord, and he will give you your heart's desires.

She thought of her brother Cassius. Would she see him again and be able to share with him the love of God that she had found or would leave her alone? Would the church in her home prosper and the believers be safe from persecution here in Philippi? If Marcus knew of their gathering, so did others. She delighted in her Lord, but what were her heart's true desires? Sometimes it seems they remained in the back of her mind, as she kept them at bay. Questions chased themselves around in her mind.

Commit everything you do to the Lord.

Trust him and he will help you.

He will make your innocence radiate like the dawn,

And the justice of your cause will shine like the noonday sun.

She bowed her head and laid her heart before Him. Only He could show her the path she was to take. He had led so far, and she'd learned to trust Him. The face of Nikolas came to mind. What was her path there? He had become indispensable in her life, yet she still held back from considering anything more. Then in her heart she sensed His words: *Are you trusting Me, child?*

Was she totally trusting Him, or was she holding back from giving all of herself to her Lord, no matter how He led?

She read on:

Be still in the presence of the Lord, and wait patiently for him to act.

She put the scroll down and sat quietly. He was her strength. She went out into the orchard and sat on a stone bench under the sycamore tree. As the birds chirped their cheerful melodies around her, she waited for her Lord to speak to her heart, yielding all that she was to Him.

Thy will be done, Lord. Behold your servant. Show me a clear path and I will follow.

As His peace enveloped her, she knew what she must let go of at last.

45

Jael helped her put on the new green toga and the pendant Lydia had bought in the agora. "You look very beautiful, Domina," Jael said with a knowing smile.

Lydia pretended she didn't hear, but she was pleased.

Nikolas came just as she was sure he'd forgotten the evening meal. Watching from her window, she was struck again by how handsome he was, how sure of himself, as he walked toward the villa.

She welcomed him, feeling suddenly shy in his presence. His eyes took in her appearance and she could not miss the admiration she glimpsed there. His greeting, however, was friendly but reserved. Was she disappointed? She turned and led him into the dining room.

He began to relax and, as they ate, told her that their small group of believers had been sharing the love of God and the gospel with others.

"We may have to find a larger building if the group continues to grow. We now have Clement, the jailer, and his family coming, as well as the young guard from the prison who witnessed the earthquake and all that took place. He has been baptized in the small stream outside the Neapolis gate. One of the men from the

School of Medicine who knows Doctor Luke is also coming. He says Luke is coming back soon to teach at the school."

"It will be good to see the doctor again. He was so helpful to my mother."

"Yes, but right now Paul needs him. It would seem that preaching the gospel of Christ has its physical limitations."

"If you mean being beaten and jailed, from what Paul shared, this has happened before."

She paused as she reached for a piece of cheese. "Did you know Luke was keeping a journal of their travels?"

"Yes, he did share that with me on one occasion. He is doing this for a mentor of his by the name of Theophilus."

It suddenly occurred to Lydia that having dinner with Nikolas reminded her of meals with her parents, when they shared the news of the day. It seemed so natural to sit and talk with Nikolas over their food. As she was contemplating the similarity, Nikolas interrupted her reverie.

"I know you wish to read from the psalms, but I must tell you that the format for the meetings has changed a little."

She had been about to take a bite of a pear but put it down. *What was this?* "How have you changed it? Do the believers not wish to hear the psalms?"

"That is not the problem. We have many very new believers, who need to be strengthened in their faith. Some have shared their stories of how they came to knowledge of the Savior and how it has changed their lives and families. They wish to learn more of the Lord. They are like children who have been given milk, but now desire solid food."

"That is a strange comparison." Inside she felt a small flame of anger kindled. Why would he feel free to change things, just because she was not there?

Perhaps sensing her emotions, he added softly, "It was not my wish. They asked for additional Scriptures. They are so hungry for more."

She was somewhat mollified. Before she could offer to seek other scrolls to read, he continued. "I have led the group, but soon we will have men established in the faith we can designate as elders. They will take turns leading. That is how Paul suggested we build the church. In time there will be those who are ready to lead groups like ours."

Again the words came to her mind. *Trust Me.* She had been in charge, yet remembered how Paul shared that he set up elders in each city to take charge of each of the new churches he founded. It was not up to one person to continue to lead. They were all equal in the sight of God. It was time to relinquish control.

She rose. "We had better prepare." She gave him a side glance. "Though tonight I may sit and listen."

His eyebrows went up but he said nothing, only a slight smile playing around his lips.

———————

There were almost fifteen people when the last one had entered the atrium, and some had to sit on pillows on the floor. They greeted Lydia warmly, sympathizing with her over the loss of her mother but glad she was back among them. Nikolas introduced her to the new believers who had joined the group in her absence.

As Lydia looked around the room at the faces of the people gathered there, the joy was evident. The original believers had shared the gift of the Holy Spirit as Paul taught them, and the praise and prayer flowed from full hearts.

Lydia was amazed as she heard stories of persecution in other cities and how their God had protected believers and led them to Philippi and her villa.

Then Nikolas read from the Book of Isaiah:

Have you never heard? Have you never understood?
The Lord is the everlasting God,
The Creator of all the earth.
He never grows weak or weary.
No one can measure the depths of his understanding.
He gives power to the weak and strength to the powerless.
Even youths will become weak and tired,
And young men will fall in exhaustion.
But those who trust in the Lord will find new strength.
They will soar high on wing like eagles,
They will run and not grow weary.
They will walk and not faint.

One by one, members of the group spoke out and shared what the Scripture meant to them, women as well as the men. Lydia realized that though they were a small group for now, God would grow their numbers. They would meet here until there was no more room and then she would help them find a larger building. She had a sense of being part of a great work God was doing in their city.

She had noticed that Delia and Jael were welcomed, not as slaves to be condescended to, but as equal believers. She needed to consider what she wanted to do about that. Hektor was a freeman, but he and Delia seemed to be interested in each other. What would become of them if she freed Delia? Or if she freed Jael as her mother had freed Chara?

She looked up suddenly to see Nikolas watching her. She did not feel agitated by his gaze as she had at other times. This time peace filled her as she quietly acknowledged the bond between them. He studied her face a moment, smiled with a nearly imperceptible nod, then turned to speak with the man next to him.

Delia brought in some small cups of diluted wine and a loaf of bread. Nikolas quietly explained that the bread was to celebrate the body of Christ that had been broken for them and the wine represented the blood of the Lord that was shed for them. It was a sacred time as they prayed and shared together. Lydia was touched. Paul had done that with them before he left, sharing the words of Jesus Himself who asked them to do this in remembrance of Him.

At last, when, one by one, the group filed out the door, and Jael and Delia had returned to their duties, Lydia stood facing Nikolas, alone.

She looked up into his face and saw in his eyes what she had run away from for so long. Her past with its grief and disappointments had passed away. She was a new creature in Christ and all things were new. Now she understood that meant *all* things.

"You have fought your battle, Lydia?"

She nodded. It seemed natural now to hear him call her by her given name. He stepped closer and put a finger under her chin. "I'm glad if I am a part of the victory."

"Oh Nikolas, I've been so full of pride and distrust."

"We cannot understand the mind of God, but we can look back to where we came from and what He has done in our lives. Before he left, Paul understood our destiny, but you were not ready to receive it. You have endured much and have become stronger for it. Paul saw us combining that strength to serve God."

What was he saying? She found the idea sent a flood of joy through her being. "And how do you see us combining that strength, Nikolas?"

"As one."

She had to speak it out in the open: "I am a wealthy woman, Nikolas. Many would see you taking advantage of that, would they not?"

He took a deep breath and let it out slowly. "Yes, you are a wealthy woman, Lydia. You would make a fine match for any man in Philippi. Yet, I do not seek your wealth. I seek the gentle and kind woman I have observed, a woman who loves our God and desires to serve Him."

He took her hands. "And I am not what you think I am, Lydia. I am not a poor man. I am the only son of a wealthy merchant in Athens. I did not seek to deceive you, but had my own battles to fight. I will inherit my father's estate when he is gone...."

She interrupted, confused. "But then why were you in Thyatira and seeking a job in Philippi?"

He sighed. "I was running away from my pain. I lost my wife and son in childbirth and vowed not to marry again, to love again. Everything around me reminded me of my wife and the son I had lost. Not wishing to enter the army, as my father suggested, one day I just left Athens. I traveled and eventually ended up in the purple cloth market in Thyatira. Somehow among strangers I could forget my grief. The man I worked for died, the sons managed to lose all his customers, and I left. I knew Sargon and he sent me here."

"Oh Nikolas, I am sorry for your loss." She looked away. "Perhaps I, too, was running away from the sorrow in my life. My mother came with me here, but it was harder on her than I realized. It was only when I took her back to Thyatira that I understood."

He put his hands on her shoulders and turned her to face him. "Adonai has been speaking to my heart. Before I can serve Him here, I must return to Athens and face my father and my responsibilities. I will come back to you, for there is something between us that must be settled. The church here in your home will grow, Lydia, and there are friends now who will help you. I will find someone to serve you in the fabric shop before I go, but first I *must* know if you wish me to return. Not as an employee, but as someone to share your life and the ministry of the gospel."

She reached up and put a gentle hand on his face. "I first ran from what I considered an impossible match. I was full of pride and felt you were beneath my status. Yet I have seen the man you truly are and that is enough for me. I wish to be more than your employer. If we are to serve our God together—" she paused and bravely lifted her chin, "then let us do it as one."

His eyes were dark with emotion as he took her face in his hands and leaned down to kiss her with a tenderness that overwhelmed her. "So be it," he murmured.

46

As the weeks went by, Lydia found herself looking out the window from time to time, hoping to see Nikolas riding up the road to the villa. Some afternoons, she sat in the garden and unrolled the one letter he had written.

To my beloved Lydia,

I am grateful that in spite of my long absence my father understood and forgave me. It appears that I arrived at the right time. My father's factor was gravely ill and unable to perform his duties handling the imported merchandise. I am acting in that capacity for now. My experience in the dye business and selling the purple cloth has been valuable. I have been sharing the love of Christ with my father, and I feel he is listening, but is reluctant to abandon the gods of Greece. My mother seems more receptive and I pray my life speaks of what I believe to both of them. I think of you every day and the promise of our life together. While I long to return, the Lord has work for me here. You are in my prayers, as I hope I am in yours. Nikolas.

There was no mention of his return.

She looked out at the orchard and watched Hektor pour water around a small seedling he had planted. There was another matter that weighed on her mind. She had observed Delia and Hektor as they went about their work. Their eyes met from time to time and Lydia could not help but see the tender looks they exchanged. Delia was a slave but Hektor was a free man. If she gave Delia her freedom, would they elect to leave? Yet Delia had mentioned she had no family to return to as Chara did. With chagrin, Lydia realized that though she had prayed about the matter, her prayer was but half-hearted, fearing as she did the loss of someone she depended on so much. And in return, the heavens were silent.

In all good conscience Lydia knew she must give her consent. They would have their wedding, but who to perform it? If Paul returned, she would consider him appropriate, but there was no indication of when he would come to Philippi again.

She considered her own wedding ceremony and the Roman rites she had participated in out of respect for her father. Memories of the grief and pain that followed flooded her mind. She needed to let it go, but the years of degradation and anguish still haunted her. Then the face of Nikolas came to mind. Lydia sighed. She found someone who claimed to love her, but he was gone and given her no indication of when he would return.

She watched Hektor work for a while. How he loved the soil and working with growing things. Well, a Roman ceremony was not appropriate. She considered the wedding of Marianne and Marcellus. A Jewish rabbi had married them since they were God-fearers. Yet here, in Philippi, as followers of The Way with the gift of the Holy Spirit, a rabbi no longer seemed appropriate.

Her hand absentmindedly fingered the pearl pendant Nikolas had given her. He would know what to do. Her heart was suddenly filled with longing. She missed his wise counsel. She missed Nikolas. She rose reluctantly and slowly returned to the house for the evening meal.

Another week went by. It had been four months now since Nicolas left to make his peace with his family in Athens. Even if she had to wait there was no reason to make Delia and Hektor wait as well. She had to make a decision. She rose and went to the kitchen where Delia was preparing the evening meal.

"Delia, there is a matter I must speak to you about."

Her servant turned with a puzzled look on her face. "There is a problem, Domina?"

Seeing the woman's anxious face, Lydia smiled. "It concerns you and Hektor."

Delia's eyes widened and her face took on a hopeful look. "Yes, Domina?"

"I've been observing you two. You care for him?"

Her servant lowered her eyes. "Yes, Domina. He is a good man."

"And you wish to marry?"

Delia looked up and nodded. "Yes, Domina. You would object to such a marriage?"

Lydia put her hand on her servant's shoulder. "Yes, he is a good man. I would not object. It is my decision that you marry, but as a free woman."

Delia's eyes widened and tears formed. "You would give me my freedom, Domina?"

"Our Lord has taught us that we are all slaves of Christ." Lydia thought a moment. "The question that puzzles me concerns who would perform the ceremony."

"We have talked about that, Domina." She hesitated, and Lydia realized she and Hektor had probably discussed the matter a great deal.

"We wish to say our vows in front of our group of believers. They would be witnesses of our commitment to each other."

Lydia considered the idea. She and Plinius were married in front of a Roman official who said the expected words over them, and Marianne had been married by a rabbi who had also said the expected words over them; both ceremonies in front of guests who acted as witnesses. If Delia and Hektor recited their vows to each other and the other believers were witnesses, would not God honor their union? She smiled again. After all, who had married Adam and Eve?

"I believe we can do that, Delia. God would witness your vows to each other."

Delia beamed. "Oh, Domina, you have made me a very happy woman. You are kind and generous." She glanced towards the doorway.

Lydia waved a hand. "Go...tell him."

As her servant hurried away to find Hektor and share the news, Lydia sighed deeply. There would be a wedding in the villa, just not the one she hoped for.

The wedding of her two servants was small but joyous. Lydia had given Delia her document of freedom, and both Delia and Hektor had thanked her profusely for her kindness. Although Delia was pleased to be a freewoman, she assured Lydia that she and Hektor wanted to remain in her villa.

Boughs of greenery and flowers decorated the main room of the villa. Jael and Delia had spent hours preparing food: braised cucumbers with olives and goat cheese, date cakes, roast lamb with cumin, pomegranate and poached apricots in honey syrup, and rounds of griddle bread to dip in a garbanzo bean puree. There was also a platter of honey and almond-stuffed dates. Lydia admonished Hektor to make sure they had sufficient wine for the occasion. Jael was moved to the smaller room that had been Hektor's, and Hektor and Delia would now occupy the larger room near the kitchen.

The other believers began to arrive with small gifts, among them a headscarf, a small embroidered bag, two stuffed pillows, and a delicately carved wooden vase. Everyone arranged themselves around the room. Jael led Delia into the room. Delia's face glowed with love as she and Hektor gazed at each other. Delia wore a new toga in a soft blue that seemed to minimize her ample proportions. A wreath of flowers circled her head. Hektor waited with Justus, who had stepped up to take Nikolas's place as leader. The happy couple recited their vows to each other before the small group of believers. Justus then blessed them in the name of the Father, the Son, and the Holy Spirit and tied a small cord around their wrists binding them together.

As the short ceremony came to an end, Lydia felt the Lord's presence and sensed that He was pleased. The group exclaimed over the food and proceeded to eat until they could hold no more. One believer had brought a flute and some of the men who were Jewish grasped hands and danced with abandon. Lydia tapped her foot.

As she watched the happy couple, her own emotions were bittersweet. Would Nikolas return, or would his father demand his presence to help with the business? He did owe his father after all the worry he'd put him through, she reasoned. Her hand went to the pearl pendant. Would his sense of responsibility be stronger than the love they had found? Lydia had written to her daughter on the last ship to bring fabrics from Thyatira, sharing about Nikolas and responding with joy to the news that Marianne and Marcellus were expecting a second child.

Listening to the pleasant conversation a wedding evoked, she watched Jason, the young man who had accepted the Savior but fled from Rome with his family. He'd needed employment and agreed to serve in the shop until Nikolas returned. Lydia had been overseeing the business and teaching him what he needed to know, and Jason had quickly exceeded her expectations and proved himself an excellent manager of the shop.

Just before the wedding, Lydia also gave Jael her document of freedom. Jael looked at the document with tears in her eyes. "Thank you, Domina."

"You may choose what you wish to do now, Jael. You have been a friend when I needed one." Lydia waited. Jael had been with her so long it was hard to consider the possibility of her leaving.

"I am pleased to be a freewoman, Domina, but this is the only family I have known for so many years. Where would I go? I will stay with you."

Impulsively, Lydia reached out to her former slave and the two women, equals in Christ, embraced.

Lydia walked to the window and looked out, enjoying, but not joining in, the music and happy laughter. The sun was going down, painting the trees outside in a golden light. Without Nikolas the future stretched ahead with only the prospect of running her business and the villa and of meeting with the believers. It should have brought her joy, yet it all seemed empty.

Then the music suddenly stopped. There were exclamations of surprise and delight. Puzzled, she turned, and her heart began to pound in her chest. Nikolas was standing in the doorway of the atrium.

They waited until the guests had gone and the bridal couple had retired for the night. Jael put the food away and then withdrew to her own quarters. Nikolas took her hand and led her out to the garden. They stood for a moment, listening to an owl call to its mate and watching as the bird, like a shadow, glided over the trees.

"Your parents," Lydia said softly, "They did not return with you?"

"My mother is not strong. She could not endure a journey at this time. We will travel there after we are married." He grinned. "They are intrigued by a woman who sells purple cloth." Then he tilted his head to one side. "How is the shop? Has Jason proved to be worthy of the task?"

"He has done well." Lydia pictured the intense young man who had proved so capable, not only in the shop, but among the believers. His zeal for the Lord reminded her of Timothy. She smiled to herself. Paul would approve.

Then a thought occurred to her. Nikolas had come back, but how long would he remain in Philippi? Would he want to return to Athens? If they married, what of the believers and the church that had begun here in Philippi? She looked up at him, searching his face. "You speak of traveling to Athens, Nikolas. What of the church that has begun here? How can we leave our small group of believers?"

He shook his head slowly. "My father has understood at last. The son I was when I left and the son that returned to him spoke to his heart. He is willing to hear more about our Lord. And by God's grace, before I left, my mother prayed with me to receive Christ and is now a believer."

"Oh Nikolas, what joyful news!"

He drew her closer and smiled. "I only wish to introduce you to my family, then we will return to Philippi. I promised you we would serve the Lord as one, and we shall. At the time of Paul's visit, he shared with me the vision for the church in Philippi. With God's help, beloved, we will help fulfill that vision."

She leaned against him and the steady beating of his heart comforted her. The empty place within her for so many years was filled with love, and as they stood together, wrapped in each other's arms, she felt the blessing of the Spirit flow over them. Step by step the Lord had guided two separate paths and blended them into one. All she had been through had prepared her for this time, this moment, this vision that stretched far beyond herself. Safe in the arms of her beloved, there was a future to contemplate.

Nikolas lifted her chin and kissed her gently. "We have a wedding to plan, beloved."

She nodded happily, and, arm in arm, they turned to walk back to the villa.

Acknowledgments

$\mathcal{M}$y sincere thanks to Whitaker House for having the faith in me to once again take a little-known biblical character and bring her to life. Lydia, woman of Philippi, was the first Gentile convert in Asia. With the encouragement of the Apostle Paul, she opened her home and started the first church in Philippi. As we can see from Paul's letter to the Philippians, the church grew considerably and established elders—even being one of few churches to send Paul financial help for his ministry. I am grateful for being able to write Lydia's story.

Thank you to my dear friend, Dr. Vicki Hesterman, who taught journalism at Point Loma Nazarene University, for the hours spent combing through the manuscript for errors and necessary changes before it is sent to Whitaker House. To Judith Dinsmore, who once again carefully edited my manuscript for Whitaker House and whose helpful suggestions and encouragement enhanced the final book. To my San Diego Christian Writer's Guild critique group for helping me get past the "forest for the trees" to share their insights and suggestions on difficult chapters: Ann Larson, Mary Kay Moody, Felicia Cameron, Sandi Esch, Linda Crawford, and Jean Mader (our grammar grandma). And finally, always, to my readers, who have encouraged me with their comments through the years. Your kind words have lifted me up at discouraging times. I am grateful for each one of you.

About the Author

Diana Wallis Taylor was first published at the age of twelve, when she sold a poem to a church newsletter. Today, she has an extensive portfolio of published works, including a collection of poetry; an Easter cantata, written with a musical collaborator; contributions to various magazines and compilations; many novels, including *Mary Chosen of God*; *Martha*; *Mary Magdalene*; *Claudia, Wife of Pontius Pilate*; *Ruth, Mother of Kings*; *Shadows on the Mountain*; *House of the Forest*; and *Smoke Before the Wind*, as well as a book on Halloween. Diana lives in San Diego. They have six grown children and nine grandchildren. Readers can learn more by visiting her website, www.dianawallistaylor.com.

Did you enjoy Lydia, Woman of Philippi?
If so, turn the page for more titles from Diana Wallis Taylor.

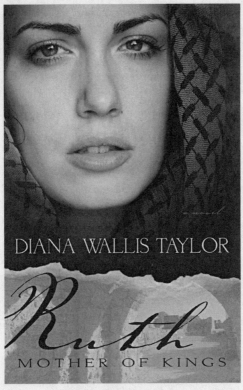

DIANA WALLIS TAYLOR

Ruth

MOTHER OF KINGS

978-1-60374-903-9

The story of Ruth has captivated Christian believers for centuries, not least of all because she is one of only two women with books of the Bible named after them. Now, Diana Wallis Taylor animates this cherished part of the Old Testament, with its unforgettable cast of characters. Experience Ruth's elation as a young bride—and her grief at finding herself a widow far before her time. Witness the unspeakable relief of Naomi upon hearing her daughter-in-law promise never to leave her. And celebrate with Boaz when, after years as a widower, he discovers love again, with a woman he first found gleaning in his field. The story of this remarkable woman to whom Jesus Christ traced His lineage comes to life in the pages of this dramatic retelling.

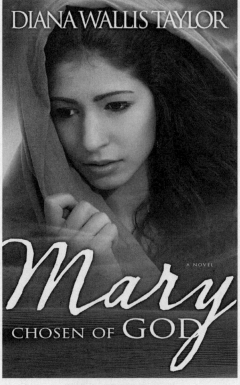

978-1-62911-748-5

Mary is ordinary girl from Nazareth. She helps her mother with household chores, she daydreams about a handsome carpenter's son named Joseph, and at night she lies on the roof and contemplates the stars.

But one evening, a heavenly visitor comes with unexpected news—and her life is changed forever.

Experience the life of the Messiah from the perspective of his mother, who must place her trust and obedience in Adonai, the Most High, as he fulfills centuries of prophecy in the middle of her daily life. Walk with Mary as she witnesses Yeshua grow, mature, minister, and even be crucified—and then raised again, to the kindling of her new faith.

Welcome to Our House!

We Have a Special Gift for You ...

It is our privilege and pleasure to share in your love of Christian fiction by publishing books that enrich your life and encourage your faith.

To show our appreciation, we invite you to sign up to receive a specially selected **Reader Appreciation Gift**, with our compliments. Just go to the Web address at the bottom of this page.

God bless you as you seek a deeper walk with Him!

WE HAVE A GIFT FOR YOU. VISIT:

whpub.me/fictionthx

WHITAKER
HOUSE